THE
LATITUDE
SYNDROME

by

Ravi Sadana

Publishers by Design

Toronto　　　　New Jersey　　　　1999

Copyright © 1997,1998 Ravi Sadana
All rights reserved under International and Pan-American Copyright Conventions. No part of this book may be reproduced, stored in a retrieval system, or transmitted or used in any form or by any means or process of electronic, mechanical, photocopying, recording, graphic or otherwise, without the written permission of the author obtained in advance.

Canadian Cataloguing in Publication Data
Sadana, Ravi, 1949-
The Latitude Syndrome

Includes bibliographical references and index.
ISBN 0-9683989-1-X

1. New Thought. 2. Mind and body. 3. Self-actualization (Psychology)
4. Philosophy, Indic. I. Title.

BF639.S12 1998   158.1   C98-931565-7

Publishers by Design
1001 Bay Street, suite 2614,
Toronto, Ontario
Canada M5S 3A6
(416) 926 1660

Cover design: Johanna Sadana
Also the author of the companion book
The Three Verbs of Being
ISBN 0-9683989-0-1
Presented in drama style for easier reading to convey new ideas through relationships, dialogues and travelogues set in mystical surroundings.

Together they offer a cross-reference resource for an enlightened lifestyle to prepare for the challenges of the new millennium.

In memory of my sister and brother
Devi Vimla
Prem Nath

Dedication

This book and each and every object, entity, thing, idea and concept like 'time' presented herein, are dedicated to:

The Mother Spirit

The essence of the immutable principle of the feminine spiritual primacy and the essence of the cardinal sound constellation, the Gayatri *mantra*.

Acknowledgements

First and foremost to my dear wife Johanna, for being the innocent unperturbed bystander, wondering what was going on, the silent majority shareholder. She helped make it happen by not interfering.

To my daughter Kiren-Maya, who in spite of massive workloads for four years at the University of Toronto, sat up for interminable hours to Haydn, Mozart, Beethoven, Mendelssohn, Schubert and others, night after night, month after month, year after year, listening, marvelling, questioning. Her classic line was, "how did we miss Beethoven's seventh and eighth for so long?"

To Tom Hulce for those raspy moans in the movie Amadeus, while composing the Requiem on his death bed. The indelible scene gave clues to the most poignant insights into one of the many riddles that came up during the six years it took to unravel the mysteries of Mozart's music.

To my brilliant and patient gurus of childhood, of whom there were so many. How they downed foot high glasses of hot milk!

To all the pupils over the years, who took part in the weekly classes, breathing and humming, some clandestinely held in the Board Room at the Clarke Institute of Psychiatry. I learnt more from them than they did from me.

To the volunteers at the Clarke Institute of Psychiatry, who never tired of joining in circles, holding hands, in darkness and in contemplation. How they embraced new concepts was refreshing.

To Fred Wong, my Shiatsu master, for his unsurpassed wizardry.

Declaration

The vast number of ideas, concepts and founding principles inherent in a book with a preponderance of metaphysical thought, as this volume is, are derived and transliterated from sources, rooted in antique empiricism, formal modern research and personal experimentation.

The formulation of the conceptual underpinnings of the three-solitude model of evolution presented in the book, is based on the last condensation of a train of empirical reasoning, rigorously achieved by the author over a period of six years.

Postulations relating to the workings of The Cantilever Effect in the technique of meditative realization of orchestral music were personally cognised by the author after concerted meditation and study spread over forty years.

All other real-time experiential encounters and episodes, chronicled and discussed throughout the length and breadth of the book are based on the author's personal realizations, involvements and knowledge gained by introspective study.

Contents

Foreword i

The living health model 1
   The three components 1
      Physical health 1
      Mental health 3
      Spiritual health 6
   The layered health model 7
      Biogenetic factors 8
      Microbial layer 8
      The lifestyle layer 10
      The nutritional layer 11
      The Latitude Syndrome 11
   Conclusion 11

The Traditional Model 13
   The birth-rebirth cycle 13
   Duality and reflections of duality in nature ... 15
   Discipline and Puritanism 17
   Dharma 22
   Karma 22
      a simple story 28
   Mind over matter 28
   Continuity and Spontaneity 29
   Namaste 31
   Why Om is indispensable to the practice of meditation?
   31
      Commentary 32
   Creativity Consciousness 33
   Mutation 33
   Sound Constellation 34
      Orchestral music 35
   Cantilevers 35
      How cantilevers work? 37
   Interconnectivity (unity) of all entities in universe ... 38
      Good and Evil 39
   Meditation 39
   Prana shakti 40

Time 41
Origin of the swastica symbol 43
    One anecdote 45
    A plausible idea 48
script of the drawing on the cave wall 51

Hybrid Model of Human Evolution 53
   three universal laws 53
   The Three Solitudes 54
      a simpler description 69
   Relationships 69
   Basis of Artistic Creativity 71
      feeling present in the artist 73
      ustad or master Isa Afandi 73
      flux-osmosis 78
   Memory 78
      Lord Buddha 79
      a plausible theory 80
      Seed-ideas - set one 81
      Discussion 81
      Entity one 82
      Entity two 82
      Memory recollection 82
   Intuition 83
   Quantum Physics analogy 83
      Entangled particles 83
      Electron Tunnelling 84
   Some points to ponder 84
   Conclusion 85

Structured Breathing and Sound Constellations 87
   Session one 87
   Session two 91
   Session three 94
   Session four 96
   Session five 98
      The *Gayatri mantra* 98
   Session six 100
   Session seven 104
   Session eight 105

Session nine 109
Session ten 110
  Kundalini shakti 111

Meditative Listening 114
  Introduction 114
  Hypothesis 114
  Memory-joggers 122
  Sound 123
  Object and Implied Object 123
  Conception of Idea 123
  Practice 123
  Orchestral music 124
  Baroque examples for meditative-listening 124
    Antonio Vivaldi 124
    George Phillip Telemann 124
    George Frederic Handel 125
    Johann Sebastian Bach 125
  In conclusion, a note of caution 125
  A practical guide to realizing Classical music 125
    Stream A 125
    Stream AA 126
    Stream B 126
    Stream BB 127
  Path Map 127
    Stream C 128
    Stream D 129
    Stream E 129
  Path Map 130
    Commentary 131
    Telltale signs 131
    Signs to look for 132
  Choice of music for meditative listening 133
    Why Eroica? 133
  The artistic virtues of the Classical era 135
  Musical feeling versus intellect 136
  Music as an internalizing medium 138
  Darshan revisited 140
    Another view 142

Basis of *Surya shakti* - The spiritual sun 143
The physical sun 143
Basis of *Surya Shatki* in man 145
Path leading to self-recognition 146
    four simple principles 146
    four flavors of methodologies 148
Nutrition and culinary lifestyle 149
    Surya shakti seed-idea 150
General Notes on food items 152
    Milk 152
    Grains and legumes 152
    Fluid Temperature 152
    Fibrous bulk
    153
    Preferences 153
The Latitude Syndrome 154
    Basis of the Latitude Syndrome 155
    Balancing for the Latitude Syndrome 156
Table A 157
Diminution factors 157
Recipes and Food Preparation 161
    Suji Halva 161
    Carrot halva 162
    Khir 163
    Dalia 164
    wheat-germ granules 165
    grain mixture 165
    Khichari 166
    Mustard greens 167
    Karela 167
    Loki 168
    Ginger root 169
Generic recipe for vegetables 169
Generic recipe for dry legumes 171
Raita 172
Combinations 172
Typical meal 173
Patzcuaro omelette mound for two 174

Unrelated spiritual connections 175

The human skin 176

Gonadic health and ambience 179
    Introduction 179
    Background facts to keep in mind 180
    Simple procedures and practices 182
        Structured breathing 183
        Blood circulation 183
        Massaging 184
        Prana shakti 184
        Physiological arousal versus sexual arousal
        184
    Advanced techniques 184

Genesis of evolution - food for thought 185

Bibliography 188

Index 190

Foreword

Dear aspiring savant,

Over the recent years, many stock phrases have come to describe the modern human condition and the countless demands made upon it by the complexities of a technological society into which we are being molded at an inexorable speed. Everyone faces problems and difficulties in life. Our management of and response to the problems can turn into a stressful personal tug-of-war. It doesn't have to be this way. Other options are open to us. They are easy to learn and they work without fail, because most of the time anxiety and tension are self-made conditions thrust upon the self.

First, a note of caution about relationships.

The tired and overburdened term "lack of communication" has been blamed for just about all the ills of society. It's the quality of a relationship that builds bridges; not the other way around. If you don't trust, you don't talk. You can talk all you want, but if there is no common ground, there's no relationship. Have a meaningful relationship and communication will follow.

Here are a few simple ideas beyond the well-trodden path.

An important factor in any equation is one's relationship with nature. Even at the superficial level, communing with open space, trees, streams and the freedom-imparting expanse of the rolling countryside can be a relaxing interlude during difficult times. It is said, the bigger the tree, the higher the mountain, the bulkier the rock masses and the wider the body of water you see around you, the deeper the sense of connection you develop for them. Make your actions accountable to nature. One cannot afford to lock horns with a difficult situation. A withdrawal into the fold of nature may inject the elements of grace and finesse which will work for you.

Make all your interpersonal decisions with only forty percent of the total energy involved in the equation working in your self-interest. Decrease the percentage as you grow older.

Another important factor is one's attitude to life. Philosophies were set afloat just for this choice. Life is like a garden. It has beautiful roses. But each rose comes with a bunch of sharp thorns. Did you ever see a rose without a thorn? In fact, the prettier the rose, the sharper the thorn! But then the garden pours forth a beguiling fragrance. That's the reward. It is possible to get to a state of mind where at first the thorn disappears, then the rose, and in the end, only the fragrance lingers. More about that later.

The fundamental good prevails all the time. It sees no change because it is beyond time and space. It is always present as a viable choice. Develop a mental frame of mind to harmonize with it. It will seek you out when you are ready for it, for it is omnipotent and omnipresent. It is the superior attachment.

Think about your feel for outer excitement and inner excitement. Outer excitement or exuberance smoothens the surface wrinkles. Inner excitement or motivation is the subtle force that impels us on. No matter what your primary pursuit in life, the "unmanifest forces" or environment may be favorable, unfavorable or neutral at any given moment. The window of opportunity opens for very brief periods but we miss it most of the time.

A conscious experience of silence practised regularly for a few minutes is rewarding. If you have been inside the pitch dark of a deep cave, you have probably experienced a nearly total silence. The quiet of the night under the dome of a star-studded blackness can be thought-provoking. You have probably noticed that the effect is not the same when the full moon is overhead. Silence in blackness and silence in light are two different things, but silence, nevertheless. Being near a silent monolithic dark mountain, shrine or temple at night gives a new experience of the feeling of self.

Much has been said about laughter and humor. The most relaxing laughter is when you laugh at yourself. Once in a while think of all the silly things you've done and have a good laugh at yourself. Your world will change very rapidly as your sense of vulnerability diminishes and your response to the daily difficulties and problems will become balanced.

Being yourself - your very sincere-self to your true-self - when you have a moment to reflect, will put you in a natural mood. You can make a list of your artificial postures and insincere stances taken for whatever reason; you know what they are. Recognize and acknowledge them. This will draw you closer to your real nature. If you manage to reach it, you will not experience stress under any conditions, no matter how frustrating. The closer you get to your real nature, the lesser your tendency to think of your needs first. You will become more giving, forgiving and a superbeing!

Think about the habit of "linearity" in thinking and doing things in everyday life. Make conscious efforts to break routine and add variability to thinking and doing standard things. Question yourself on how you may "think" and "act" differently.

Fight the herd instinct. It takes a strong character to be different. Sometimes the exacted price may be high. Is it too high for the end result - finding your real individuality?

Think about your biological roots. A steady stream of truths and gifts have been passed on to you for safekeeping. Take good care of them for you are a member of relay race.

The usual human mental state and response is to feel "burdened". How do you react when a difficulty or a problem arises? Do you feel challenged, threatened or distressed?

Shyness is associated with being in a "place" where you are out of "place" and cannot find your bearings. Some people never grow out of it. They feel shy at home and even in the most intimate relationships. Think about where they are coming from? Think about your extrabiological roots in terms of the present window of the earthly life given to you on the continuum of your personal evolution. Think about the three dreadful destroyers of faith in yourself. Their workings in your present life are a consequence of the burden of your past actions. The three dreadful destroyers are:

Doubt: You may intellectually discuss concepts and ideas to explore and clarify to get the other point of view, but never fall a prey to 'the tyranny of words'. Above all, don't let doubt and mistrust enter the debate. The moment they come in, out goes your chance to connect with the new concept. Doubt is the single most potent obstruction in the mind's opening to new beginnings, new ideas. It usually comes in when a bias - a social construct - against the person of the messenger makes itself known. Irrational emotion has now invaded the picture and muddied the waters. Think about who is the loser in this case.

Guilt: To miss a mark or to let someone down is a common human failing. If your effort was sincere, you will feel responsible and you should make a genuine attempt at making amends. If a wilful intent to harm or hurt was involved then you will answer to your karma. This can be counterproductive in the extreme.

Lack of conviction: Under normal circumstances, a reasonable amount of self-confidence will always manifest itself as a well-founded trust in the self. A fine line of distinction separates being inspired by your sense of conviction and being driven by it. If it drives you blindly, you have gone too far, which is as obstructive to growth as not having any conviction in the first place.

Don't get too hung up on your present age. Your real age is not the number calculated from the date on your birth certificate.

In nature, there is no such process as "teaching" per se. The only natural stream flowing eternally is one of learning. Everyone experiences, assimilates, learns and adjusts all the time. Even when a wise master stands in front of a class to "teach", he is learning as much as his students do. We are engaged in a personal self-realization at all times, especially during deep sleep. We just have to become more aware of this progress in our minds.

If science were to build a plant to duplicate the "aliveness" and functioning of the three solitudes of a human being, it would be the size of the universe.

The principle of learning by seed-ideas, marked by gradual change, is used in the book to project key concepts into the *savant's* mind. Memory-joggers appear in three strategic places in the book in compliance with this requirement. This has been scaled down from five to avoid the risk of excessive repeating.

People talk about seven spiritual laws because they are looking for a crutch. Would you like to be spoon fed all your life? How can anyone assign a number to spiritual laws? There is but one spiritual law and it defines what you feel in your heart about your relationship with everything else in the universe. This is your magic wand, by which you can shower a gift, a boon, a favor on everyone else. Now you are on your way to the human mission. You are saturated with immeasurable benign energy, both physical and extraphysical. The key to the secret is within you. Only you can reach inside and touch it.

Ravi Sadana
April 26, 1999

The living health model
The sensitivity of the human health to even minute shifts in the environmental, nutritional and internal body factors is very high. When the need for preserving health along the three broad physical, mental and spiritual disciplines is considered, the subject becomes inordinately complex. The three parts are closely interlinked, feeding each other back and forth, forever seeking to attain a balance with respect to each other. Any one of the parts can not stand on its own. It is the relative position of each with respect to the other two in a stable state that determines the overall health of the individual. An exemplary fit body without the buttress of adequate mental and spiritual well-being is a recipe for failure. When this equilibrium is disturbed, a person can become spiritually impaired, mentally disturbed or physically sick in any combination of the three.

In the beginning conventional medicine was only concerned with the physical health of the body. During the last thirty years or so, behavioral sciences have come into their own and mental disorders have been accepted into the fold of medicine. Because of the misplaced historical association of spiritual well-being with religion, the concept of spiritual health or debility does not even cross the threshold of a modern mind.

The motive force for the balancing of the three components of overall health derives its strength from the imperceptible nuances of one's spiritual health, the root of one's overall well-being. Why are the three disciplines necessary for the overall personal health?

The three components
Physical health
Because of the quick-to-appear flags of pain, bleeding and suffering calling immediate attention to physical damage or sickness, it is by far the most easily recognized and sought after goal of most people. It is everyone's top priority because without a fully functioning body that is also free of disease, all else in life seems less relevant. Fear of death is rooted in the loss of physical health, thus making it the most visible part of the holistic model, the mainstay of the modern medical investigative endeavor. It is medically treated as if it is dependent on factors lying entirely within the bounds of measurable processes of physiology and bodily

chemistry. A sense of urgency and immediate relief are associated with it.

Let us assume that the organisms of the body are purely chemical in nature and that their well-being and functional attributes are controlled by the intricate workings of molecular physiology alone. Following cues from the brain's biological clock, the control glands - pituitary and pineal - initiate the production of key hormones that flow through the blood stream to target glands in the body, such as the thyroid, to trigger reactions in causal sequences. The second order glands then produce their own hormones which flow down to a select group of cells in the internal organs triggering the release of site-specific chemical compounds for quick action. The local processes are then set in motion and the related circadian rhythms control the working of the inner reactions of the body regulating metabolism, temperature, digestive and respiratory functions and life goes on happily.

Two principal features of this model appear to be that its command structure is hierarchical in nature and that its operation is continuous, for the bodily functions must go on during sleep as well. The top level "timekeeper" seems to relate to the brain and it is arguable whether the brain orders the "timekeeper" or the other way round. Either way, the model seems to point to a level which has to be higher than the brain or the "timekeeper" to complete the upward reach of the hierarchy. It would also be reasonable to infer that some kind of a supervisory vigil beyond the body's feedback system to sustain a round-the-clock operation is required, again pointing to a higher level in the hierarchy.

If the processes of molecular physiology rely solely on the chemical reactions to produce a predictable result at a specific site in the physical body, then the outcome of an administered medication for a given set of symptoms or a given "chemical imbalance" or pathology at the site must always be same. It must be precisely predictable in every case. Chemistry works like that; for instance when you add sulphuric acid to lead plates in a car battery, the same thing happens every time and the outcome is measurable to the last molecule without any allowance for tolerance. But the same doesn't hold true for the human body. The effect of medication or chemical compounds introduced under controlled conditions into the body varies from person to person. The main effects vary by a wide margin and side effects are vastly different. The results are subjectively personalized.

More specifically, a sound body enables one to experience everyday events meaningfully to derive the maximum benefit through an exchange of perceptive nuances in the three solitudes to further the cause of individual evolution as described later in the book.

Mental health

Closely embracing emotional health, this part complements a fully functioning body, although the body by itself can function normally to a large extent even when the mental health is impaired. A great deal of effort has been recently directed at understanding the physical brain, its molecular chemistry and related functional attributes to gain an understanding of the neurochemical basis of mental health, both sound and flawed.

Let us once again assume that the key to behavioral processes, both sound and impaired, lies in the intricate chemical reactions and molecular balances that are presumably maintained in the different functional sections of the brain. When we are sad, a specific molecule is produced in a specific part of the brain; likewise for happiness and other sensations that occur in everyday life. Modern behavioral sciences tell us that most behavioral processes are initiated by related neurochemicals, and mental disorders are a result of chemical imbalances in the brain in direct causal relationships.

Stepping back from the arena, let us consider how the presence of a specific molecule(s) in a specific section of the brain - usually in the terminal sac at the synapse - translates into a literal, intellectual, emotional or perceptual ideation, the precursor of awareness or consciousness. All brain functions are thought to be electrical pulses racing along the lengths of neurons to their terminals at synapses or gaps separating them from the limbs of the adjoining neurons. Synapses may or may not activate an

The Latitude Syndrome

intersynaptic hormone - also called a messenger or neurotransmitter - to bridge the gap to complete the circuit to "encourage" or "discourage" the signal to pass on to one or more of the down line neurons. The scope of interneural connectivity is difficult to grasp as a neuron may be receiving signals from hundreds of synapses and if it fires, that is, it completes the circuit, it may be redirecting the pulse to hundreds of neurons along the path. Considering that the brain has billions of neurons of various types, the total number of active synapses in the brain is of the order of trillions. After receiving the pulses, a neuron may or may not fire, i.e. pass the signal along. This leads one to conclude that neurons possess aggregating or evaluative qualities.

As an example, the retina in the human eye converts the light pattern or image of what the eye is "seeing" into specific molecules which generate the electrical signals that pulse along the optic nerve to the sensory cortex in the brain, where, having delivered the goods they presumably end by grounding into the surrounding fluid. However, in a cause and effect sense, the presence of a molecule(s) can either generate an electrical impulse on its own which can run along a neuron or it can act as a messenger to bridge the intersynaptic gap to enable the pulse to travel further. Wherever the pulse ends up, it can produce a molecule which can either generate a pulse of its own or it can serve to bridge the synaptic gap for some other pulse on a different neuron coming in for aggregation at a neuron as pulses come and go along complex interconnected networks. Failing this the pulse grounds into the fluid and dissipates. A working example of this may be when a pulse on the optic nerve reaches the visual cortex on the sensory side, the visual cortex may respond by sending a pulse to the motor cortex to take defensive action by relaying a motor pulse to the muscle to close the eyelid. This is an oversimplification of the basic electrochemical processes of the brain. Remember that there are billions of neurons connected to billions of other neurons and billions of molecules of complex neurochemicals bonded into hormones, enzymes and neurotransmitters appearing and disappearing at strategic spots to make things happen. A neuron can be small enough to be invisible to the naked eye or as long as three to four feet with a well-defined structure. The role of molecules is to make possible a pattern of pulses through a pattern of interconnected neurons or network in the brain. This ephemeral pattern is pre-ideation, the forerunner of the awareness of an experience. Thus "happiness" is a coursing of specific patterns along neurons which wouldn't have been there if the right molecules were not present at the preceding synapses. The same goes for "sadness" and other behavioral attributes.

Brain's complex circuitry is forthrightly dynamic. Pulses are moving along millions of neural pathways even when the brain is seemingly inactive and neurochemicals appear and disappear in hundred-millisecond time frames. The pulsing action never stops. The brain has no static parts where pulses can be registered, counted or stored. It has no memory of its own. It has no screens on which sensations or perceptions can be flashed, the pulses assembled into patterns or the recall of past events displayed. It has no fixed surface on which the chemical compounds can be aligned or aggregated for a perceptual effect. Every single ideation of a literal, intellectual, sensational, emotional or perceptual fragment of an event is nothing more than a pattern of electrical pulses racing along networks of interconnected neurons which may last no longer than milliseconds. This short-lived frame of the pattern of pulses represents a fragment in a *tanmatra* - the minuscule "iota" between two gaps. The snapshots of the altering pattern of pulses through the neurons are played progressively like the frames of a film. These frames of pre-ideation are assembled into a whole through the agency of *prana* or consciousness and the very personal perception of the event "dawns" on one's awareness where it is assimilated. Now you have cognised the meaning of the event as it relates to you. When you later recall the event, the same patterns of pulses pass through the neural pathways and you relive the event passively. A critical question arises at this point. Is it the pattern of pulses coursing through the neurons or is the combination of neurons that get fired in complex sequences that constitutes a frame in the *tanmatra*? Where is relevance held in the ephemeral drama of the dancing pulses of the signals? Is the process similar to the concept of time, which lacks substance but provides a meaningful reference to zero-in on one linear sequence in a sea of simultaneity surrounding us? The answers to these questions are not easy to find.

Mental health is an expression of the flow of *prana* in general throughout the astral or ethereal body, which is superposed on the volumetric outline of the physical body. *Kundalini agni* or fire - the agent of transformation, localized on the anterior of the spinal column is a supercharged form of *prana* that plays particular roles in key mental functions like awareness, libido and psychological integrity.

Spiritual health

Conceptually it is a difficult notion to come to grips with because its effects are extremely subtle. Yet it forms the foundation for the other two disciplines, but it is not seen as such in the modern society because of the religious connotations wrongfully associated with it. It has nothing to do with one's religion or its practices.

A strong will to live with a passion for life, moral vigor for the common good, inner strength to struggle for just cause and the practising of altruism are some of the manifestations of sound spiritual health. A sense of contentment and inner happiness without the stimulus of a material gain, ability to derive inspiration from nature's inexhaustible store of art forms also point to good spiritual health. Aspects of shyness felt by a person are bound up in it.

In a simple analogy, if you place physical health on one end of the plank of a see-saw and mental health on the other, then the fulcrum about which the plank balances is an expression of spiritual health. The subtle forces inherent in spiritual health energize inner vehicles which make the physical and mental components of well-being more adaptable and less prone to aberrations. Since all change constantly happening at the minutest level is driven by subtle forces preceding it, the predispositions inherent in the spiritual health can be pointed at the "mind over matter" nuances. In this context, it can be regarded as the system of roots of the tree of health. Without these underpinnings, physical and mental components of the integrated health would deteriorate instantly. In the case of the everyday death, survivors acknowledge this fact by using phrases like "he lost the will to live", "the spirit gave out" or "the body succumbed". Structured breathing and sound clustering techniques can be used to perceive the faint workings of spiritual health. After a period of practical training accompanied by the subtle gains made by a regular contemplation of the two sets of seed-ideas described further on in this text, one can begin to appreciate the supernormal phenomena during quiet moments. One immediate effect is a sense of contentment and heightened perception.

The layered health model
A simplified plan of the health-related details is presented to make the understanding of the obvious complexities associated with the subject of health, a less daunting task.

Holistic health may be considered as the continuous outcome of effects and interactions of factors which can be differentiated along five layers. Starting with the most difficult to work with, the layers are described in the next section in the order of increasing flexibility and ease with which a person can understand and employ the factors to improve his health on his own. For ease of understanding consider the first layer as the foundation upon which the subsequent layers are superimposed in such a way that the influences of its factors can reach down and interact with the fundamentals and bring about changes affecting all aspects of personal health.

On a scale of one to ten, the number beside each layer stands for the degree of difficulty with which its factors can be used to advantage by a person on his own, to improve his overall health.
- The biogenetic layer   (9.5)
- The microbial layer   (7)
- The life style layer   (5)
- The nutritional layer   (3)
- The Latitude Syndrome layer   (4)

A brief discussion of the influences of the factors contained in each layer follows.

The Latitude Syndrome

Biogenetic factors

Factors, templates and codes governing a person's development and the foundation upon which the edifice of his physical, mental and spiritual health is erected are inherited from his inviolable biological roots. The understanding and manipulation of the key genetic sequences is a relatively new development and the complexities of the technical information are beyond the reach of the common man. It is obvious that a person is solely dependent upon the expertise of a highly trained medical worker to derive benefits in this area. Other than seeking expertise in exchange for payment, there is little a person can do on his own to use the knowledge to his advantage.

Microbial layer

Round the clock, all forms of life are incessantly bombarded by multitudes of invisible viral, bacterial, fungal and other microbiological particles casting very serious repercussions on a person's health. These, air, water and soil borne cells are forever on the prowl for a food-laden warm host - such as a human body - where, given the slightest chance such as a wayward kiss or an innocent walk through the woods, they can make a home and start to multiply by using the body's resources. Luckily for the humans, most of these particles are harmless, some beneficial and helpful in many ways inside the body and others so toxic and infectious that countless human diseases, from the common cold to the deadly bubonic plague, have been traced to them. In its protective role the human body's immune system is in a constant state of war with these particles, winning most of the hourly battles to maintain a state of well-being by keeping their numbers in check. But every once in a while a battle is lost with consequences of disease and suffering with which we are all too familiar in daily life. One never takes seriously the effects of the microbial layer all around us, until one feels unwell, but its pervasive effects are forever imprinted on the canvas of one's health, changing from minute to minute, making us feel dull, lethargic, weak or downright ill. We are forever compromising our state of well-being because of their ceaseless assault on our person. But the long-range effects of the microbial

The Living Health Model

invasions may be more beneficial than harmful to one's health as they keep the body's defences in a ceaseless battle-ready state. The effects of this layer are difficult to visualise but they can never be underestimated.

When long-established wind, rain and temperature patterns on land change on a large scale, such as those caused by the el nino effect, different microbial materials appear in the lower atmosphere exposing the local populations to infections and reactions that their bodily defences are not accustomed to. Waves of allergic reactions and unexplained infections like cold, flu and influenza sweep through the regions affecting everyone. Such is the intensity of war waged on the person of the unsuspecting by this invisible layer with very potent effects.

Some points to ponder in the endless war against them.

- Many animals such as monkeys, rats and squirrels maintain a state of healthful coexistence with some of the deadliest microbes in their blood streams.
- Many human beings maintain a state of peaceful coexistence with many deadly bacteria and viruses coursing through their blood streams or sheltered in different parts of the body.
- The range of human response to viral and bacterial attacks is very large. Are some "nonscientific" or supersensory factors involved? Many deadly viruses like HIV and bacterial particles like TB survive in the human body. Yet, they become active only in some people in time frames that vary from a few days to as long as thirty years. In some they don't become active in a lifetime.
- What forces cause the single-celled organisms to genetically mutate to thwart mankind's efforts to medically control or eradicate them?
- What is the role of the organisms in human evolution? Why are they there? What is there place in the grand scheme of things?

The Latitude Syndrome

The lifestyle layer

Numerous factors based on the persistent undercurrents of cultural, civilizational and medicinal changes impinge on the health in slowly emerging long cycles. Compare the present day, with its processed food industry developed in response to the demands of the evolving economic requirements of the society, to the day when mother used to cook all family meals on the kitchen hearth. New eating disorders seem to be a reflection of the modern culture's obsession with female thinness. Medical care has improved a hundred-fold with a dramatic rise in the life expectancy of the common man. Advances in molecular medicine have added a new dimension to fighting disease. In the new era of commerce-driven medicine rather than health-driven medical care, many unknown factors may have been introduced into the melange of long-range effects of this shift on the overall health of the future generations. Creature comforts have added to the material well-being of the body. Are the benefits negated by the injurious effects of the hidden cost of production in the form of air, water and soil pollution? What are the long range effects on the health of man, who, in his preoccupation with the efficiency of the industrial conglomerate seems to be distancing himself further from nature? How are the effects of the severe ecological changes going to play on the individual's health?

What about the status of the mental and spiritual health of man? Have they kept pace with the advances in the physical well-being of the body? Does anyone think or care about spiritual health, even as a plausible concept? Stress and strain seem to be more prevalent than before. Alienation of the individual and breakup of the traditional family value system seem to be on the increase. New workplace order and intergender mistrust and rivalries seem to have detracted from the atmosphere of relaxed cooperative feelings that used to prevail in the past. Many other similar factors have come into play because of the march of high technology into our lives. It is reported by industrial psychologists that people feel threatened by the introduction of the newer "artificial intelligence" robots and machines in the workplace. Will living near high voltage cables or working for hours in front of video screens gradually impact the human nervous or immune system? Has the sum total of all of the above added to the quality of overall health of the individual? Are we becoming a happier and healthier people? Is the march of modern civilization making us healthier physically, emotionally, mentally and spiritually? Our individual health weaves a fragile web through the dense forest of the many pluses and minuses present in this layer.

The nutritional layer
Of all the factors in all the layers affecting overall health, a person's eating habits are the easiest to understand. With a minimum of effort at self-education, they are most readily prone to change to promote personal overall health. It is quite obvious that constituents of what we eat have a direct relationship with our bodily health. It is a truism that we are what we eat, up to a point. A person has maximum control over what he may include in his diet.

The Latitude Syndrome
The factors in this layer, described further on in the text in some detail, blend the physical with the extraphysical needs of the overall personal health. It is hard enough to maintain a reasonably healthy body. If you include the mental, emotional and spiritual components of the integrated health for consideration, the overall picture becomes daunting for a person. We all seem to be dazzled by the allure of the body and drawn to it. Recall that like an iceberg, the visible part of the total human being is only one-seventh of the whole.

Conclusion
A snapshot of health at a given time in a person's life is the compounded result of the factors in the five layers which are in a constant state of flux. A closer examination of the elements in the five layers reveals that a person has a vast array of choices at his disposal in eighty to ninety percent of the total number of factors at play, giving him virtual control over every aspect of his health, a

The Latitude Syndrome

prospect that can only be regarded as very promising and favorable. Only the ingrained genetic factors in his biological roots lie beyond his immediate reach. The procedures outlined in the latitude syndrome section have a bearing on the esoteric components of his extrabiological roots.

Yet, if you examine the march of medicine over the last few years, it seems to be developing a very sharp focus on mechanical and chemical procedures. It is obvious that mechanical surgery is the only answer to correct a faulty heart valve or a plugged-up artery. But the vast majority of patients go to their physicians with symptoms of strangely moving pains, puzzling feelings of discomfort prone to quick changes, and other undefinable distresses which are very real. The simple "pill approach" will not serve them well.

It's only appropriate that the common man arm himself with the knowledge and understanding of all the components of his health.

The Traditional Model
My early childhood afforded me the golden opportunity to learn the Vedic tradition's practices first hand from very close quarters. My father, his ascetic friend Hira, and a host of other wise masters and swamis on occasion used to come to our house to perform religious functions. They became my unofficial *gurus*. The swamis also presided and lectured at the annual festivals and formal Sunday *havans* - prayer and study-group meetings with a ritual fire - at the Aary Samaj temple in the lower bazaar at Simla, the summer capital of the then British Raj.

A note of caution is called for. The perennially poor and historically tragic land known as India has a unique virtue of richness running in its veins. It is to interpret, practise, and live by Hinduism in a personal way which makes it more a way of life than a prescribed religion, thus giving it a diversity of interpretation which varies dramatically within short units of distance. From any geographical point in India, if you travel fifty miles in any direction, you will end up in a province with its own language, cuisine, religion, dress code, customs and work ethic. What follows is the version in which I grew up.

The old Vedic teachings for spiritual enlightenment or self-realization were based on the five principal pillars of a rigorous way of life to be studied and followed with a strict code of adherence to *dharma*, discussed in a later section.

The birth-rebirth cycle
The *atma* or soul is immortal. When a soul takes on the garb of a body, it becomes a microcosm with consciousness - a *jivatma*. So soul and consciousness are related. The sole purpose of the microcosm is to progress toward and unite with the *Paramatma* - God, macrocosm, or Superconsciousness, to attain *mukti* or liberation from the anguish of the cycle of reincarnations. This may take many births to realize. Microcosm's progress is charted through daily experiences and good or bad deeds in compliance with the laws of karma. The soul by itself cannot experience anything. It must have a body to live through life's up-and-down relationships for its evolution. Remember, it's relationships where it's at!

What happens in this and the following life depends, to a large degree, on your actions in the present life, given the freedom

The Latitude Syndrome

to choose and act. This privilege was bestowed by karma when it gave you a conscience before your conception. Over the years, the sages and wise *gurus* around the world in different faiths and in all periods of human history have discovered techniques which may decrease the number of birth-rebirth cycles or reincarnations required to speed the microcosm along the evolution of his personal consciousness to attain *mukti*. Many techniques work at the form or body level, some work at the content or emotion level and a very small number work at the substance or spiritual level. The practice of altruism, praying in earnest, meditation, chanting hymns or *mantras*, humility and developing an intense feeling of *bhakti* - selfless joy and devotion - are some examples of the well-known techniques.

The oriental cultures have attained astounding results with the practice of the "martial arts" - a technique originally based on form. *Hatha Yoga*, based on exercising and controlling the physical form, initially operates at the form level. The Buddhist sages have amassed a plethora of prescribed courses of practice. Over the years they have mastered and further refined the techniques for maximizing the effect in the right direction for the microcosm. A majority of the techniques operate at the form and content levels. The ultimate objective is to subliminally feed the "substance" to the spiritual aspect of the microcosm to help it evolve along the path. For most people, this can only be done through the form and content levels. When practised sincerely and selflessly, in the long run, the right techniques speed up the normal growth of the microcosm thus reducing the number of "organic experiences" or life-cycles on earth, required to achieve the final union of the *atma* with the *Paramatma* to attain *anand* or endless bliss.

In the short run, some practitioners have come to develop amazing powers for the purposes of demonstration and initiation of others. Examples abound in all religious faiths of avatars or prophets, like Jesus Christ, Mohammed, Krishna and *Guru* Nanak. Buckminster Fuller, Gandhi and Mother Theresa are examples from modern history. These powers can only be used for selfless purposes and at times can be so persuading that common scientific rules of measurements are transcended beyond the two well-known

The Traditional Model

dimensions of time and space. As such the *savants* become the object of ridicule and disbelief at the hands of the scientific community. Even then the prophets, who operate at subliminal levels, do not use their powers for punishment and revenge, as it was in the case of Jesus Christ, who died at the hands of violence, yet maintained a completely nonviolent and humble posture to the end. What a remarkable example, set for mankind to emulate for ever!

Duality and reflections of duality in nature
Throughout the universe, an entity by itself cannot exist without a pairing with its exact opposite. If you grasp the physical phenomenon first, say through a study of the laws of Physics, it can then be extended to apply to the unmanifest aspect to shed light on the concept of duality. I am suggesting this strictly as an aid in grasping the concept because the physical laws and their language, per se, do not apply to the unmanifest phenomena. Another major departure in the invisible reality is the absence of the concept of "critical mass". Each *tanmatra* - the indivisible speck of a knowable like "sound" or "touch" between two gaps - comprises critical mass, meaning that it fully functions on its own. You have to concentrate on this concept to grasp the meaning, which is not fully contained in the words I am using to describe it. It is postulated that at any given time when any event or mutation, howsoever minute in size takes place, the potential for a like event with opposite effect is also created. Another analogy from the physical world, to illustrate this point is the concept of hot and cold. Actually only the element of heat can be manipulated by adding or removing physical energy. The absence of heat automatically leads to the element of cold. Cold, per se, cannot be created in the way heat can be. Similarly, the absence of light is darkness. Darkness by itself, per se, cannot be created in the way light can be. Darkness *is*.

The fundamental duality of reality is a pairing of a manifest state and an unmanifest state for all constituents of things. What is perceivable through the five senses is the manifest part of the world. This is the gross matter level of reality. An unmanifest or hidden counterpart of each and every manifest part also exists. The hidden

The Latitude Syndrome

part can only be realized by the mind as it is beyond the perception of the senses. It is supersensory. It lies in the spiritual domain.

It is said that all progression takes place in cycles or repeating patterns throughout the universe. There are achievements points of going forward but they are never connected in a straight line. If you look at a tiny bit of matter, like an atom under a microscope, or at matter at its grandest scale, such as a far out galaxy in space with a powerful telescope, one observes fundamental properties which are common to all matter. One property is the cyclic nature of all processes related to matter as well as life forms. Everything happens in cycles. The Earth rotates on its North-South axis to form periods of day and night. The Earth moves along the same orbit around the sun, year after year, to ultimately get to where it is destined to go. Our solar system rotates around something else in its corner of the Milky Way Galaxy. In the vastness of the space continuum, Galaxies rotate around other Galaxies. In an atom, electrons move in cycles around the nucleus. Even the propagation of energy takes place in repeating wave motion. Light, heat, sound and radiation waves move in this way. When a weather-beaten rock disintegrates into finer particles, it enters a different phase of evolution which, again, follows in cycles. This quality is essential to any form of evolutionary change.

The evolution of a person takes place in life-cycles of bodies, our complex of ultra-sensitive antennae. The soul must seek one to become a viable consciousness for an earthly sojourn as an evolving microcosm. To move forward to its goal, it will bring together an appropriate set of parents - biological roots - and a "set of experiences" - extrabiological roots - assigned by karma before conception. The person will "live-out" the experiences through her relationships in life, mostly by repeating her actions and decisions. Hard habits and "resistance to change" are rooted in this match or mismatch of the two sets of roots. Each "live-out" cycle yields a changed set of trials and tribulations, highs and lows, successes and failures as the personal consciousness evolves and the pattern of "visible personal traits" may harden in some (a negative). The person usually doesn't realize that she is "repeating" her actions and decisions because her perception is tied to her consciousness, which is always evolving. How many times has a fifty-year-old said: "If I *knew* when I was twenty, what I *know* today," or "no matter how much *things* change, they remain the same." It may take many births, or it may take only one, but without the earthly experience, the soul by itself is not capable of evolving. The death of an infant at birth or during the embryonic term is explained by the reasoning that the specific experience was required by the occupant soul for the evolution of the microcosm. This subject involves intangible themes and constructs of a philosophical nature about abstract objects which are not easily understood, unless one has studied the subject at length and has developed a genuine interest in it. Conceptually, one has to become familiar with terms like "conscience", "wilfulness", "inborn guilt", "motivation", "inner pride", "self-esteem" etc and then try to assign a source to the origin of these attributes. To the uninitiated, these descriptions may sound meaningless. But I will try to describe the concepts in simple terms as they relate to the human experience, so that you will be able to understand the essence of key points.

Discipline and Puritanism
The Sanskrit word "Aary" means an upright person with an unimpeachable character who follows *dharma* and is aware of the laws of karma at all times in spirit and deed. In the beginning, a very strict code of discipline was written down for a yogin entering the path of meditation and yoga. Ascetism was advocated on the belief that the senses needed to be deprived of pleasurable experiences and tamed. Rigid definitions existed for "good" and "evil". The concept of "nipping the evil in the bud", any undesirable cause or effect of any phenomenon, howsoever caused, was actively promoted. The approach was that of an ascetic, who briefly surveyed the given situation and came up with a quick therapeutic action or a mental response. In the case of death in the family one observed, it was a "fait accompli", so one must endeavor to recover from grief by sheer will. After all it's only a gateway, a rite of passage.
Let me digress in the interest of diversity.
Lord Buddha is a well-known example of a microcosm, who, through his own personal efforts attained the union with the

The Latitude Syndrome

Superconsciousness during his lifetime - Nirvana to a Buddhist. How is the self-realized or recognized by the practitioner? You may ask. This is where intuition comes in to play a part. The subtle knowledge comes from within. The Sanskrit language has a word to describe it, it is *"Buddhi"* - enlightenment from within or divine intelligence, and this is the root word in Buddha's name. Let me tell you about one aspect of a unique technique uncovered by Buddha.

Lord Buddha was born a prince who turned away from the rich royal life after marriage (a key 'relationship' decision!). He learnt meditation techniques from many *gurus* and he was able to get in touch with his inner reality, entirely through his own efforts. He meditated under the *bodh* tree at Gaya in a *samadhi* or deep trance and eventually wisdom came to him from within. His joy knew no bounds as he felt he was very close to realising the ultimate enlightenment and the microcosm would empty himself into Superconsciousness and attain the eternal bliss. For a long time, the final union did not happen. Lord Buddha meditated on this inability but the answer did not come to him. He decided to go on a tour to seek help from the older *gurus* who, he thought were more advanced in the art of meditative yoga.

"No, we cannot help you. You have attained a very high level of spiritual development. At this level, no one can guide you. Your path is so unique that you alone can fathom the twists and turns in it. If you rely on outside help at this stage, you will not be able to achieve Nirvana because your yearning is not strong enough," he was told in no uncertain terms.

He went back to the spot under the bodh tree and meditated in a deep *samadhi* again, seeking the ultimate truth about his reality. After many months, the truth still did not descend upon him and he became discouraged and despondent. He searched his conscience again and after some time an idea came to him. He guessed that he still harbored a residual wisp of false pride in him. Soon he left his sanctuary and went on a two-year tour, begging and seeking alms to rid himself of any vestige of false pride. During the tour he went begging to his childhood palace where his own wife took him for a beggar and turned him away without giving any alms. After the tour, when he resumed his *samadhi* under the *bodh* tree, true

The Traditional Model

enlightenment was born in his mind and Lord Buddha became an avatar. He founded and preached the religion of Buddhism. This ritual is now a part of a Buddhist monk's training. They live off the avails of alms for two years and in the process, cleanse their minds of the last traces of false pride.

As a child I used to watch my aunt greet some beggars with reverence and then invite them in the house for a meal or refreshments. Now when I think back and recall their faces in my mind, I recognize the shine of health and wisdom on their faces and incisiveness in their eyes.

My father's ascetic friend Hira told us about himself one day. During his college days, his professors regarded him as a promising and brilliant scholar who would go places. He was studying the subjects of philosophy, theology and the ancient religious scriptures of the Christian, Muslim and Hindu faiths. With the open mind of a serious intellectual, he had sought the essence of religious teachings to enable him to spiritually develop on the inside. After many years of study, he came to the conclusion that practised religion was a man-made, politicized institution, contrived to exploit the inborn human spirituality to entice people to a given brand of faith. He felt, perhaps with some bias, that Hinduism offered him the best choice of freedom. There were no Hindu missionaries out in the world converting people to Hinduism by using the standard cliches built around guilt and and the inevitable human mortality.

Hinduism, he discovered, was not a religion but a way of life, absolutely democratic in theory and practice. It offered everyone the freedom to explore a wide range of paths and techniques to realize one's innate potential. Hira also discovered that, being interpretive, the level of freedom in the practice of Hinduism varied from community to community and from one town to another. Hinduism incorporated foreign ideas into its fold. Many other sects and branches of spiritual practices had evolved out of Hinduism, such as Buddhism, Jainism, Sikhism and Aaryism. In his years of study and research, he could not find one standard description of Hinduism. In fact he had heard so many different versions that it convinced him that within a broad framework of

The Latitude Syndrome

underlying pacific principles, a scope for a rigorous dynamic exploration existed for anyone willing to inquire and innovate. This freedom appealed to his emerging intellectual idealism since he studied at the college. One day he could even start his own path with his own following. The concepts of reincarnation and nonviolence, the two fundamental underpinnings of Hinduism, fitted his notions of continuity and simplicity of life.

He settled on Aary Samaj - assembly of Aary - as his chosen religious practice, as it was a relatively new offshoot of Hinduism. Swami Dayanand, the founder of the faith was born in the year eighteen hundred and twenty-four and founded the faith in eighteen hundred and seventy-five at Bombay. What appealed to Hira was the simplicity of the practice. Aary Samaj teachings, although puritanical in outlook and highly structured in practice, were concise, uncluttered and free of rituals. A book of about three hundred and fifty pages, spelled out the ten essential fundamentals of the Swami's teachings. It preached that there was but one God. Idol worship or any worship of a plurality of gods was an attempt at making a mockery of man's intrinsic need for spirituality. Precisely described paths of practice for self-realization were based on the principles of self-application, adhering to strict discipline and the mustering of a conscious will to change. He learnt *Mantra Yoga* or recitative meditation based on the abstract relationships among sound, object and idea constructs. These abstractions are difficult to grasp, but when mastered they offer a veritable gallery of "knowables". He learnt the principles of *pranayam* or structured breathing from a *guru* while he was studying at the college. This gave him an intuitive insight into life.

Every morning he would sit in the lotus position and chant the *Gayatri mantra* - the cardinal *mantra* - and meditate for many minutes on the idea of *om* - the wordless syllable encompassing the powerful idea of universal consciousness in its compact form. This practice gave him a measure of control over his ability to concentrate. He could fix his gaze on a dot on a wall, unwavering for minutes on end, emptying his mind of thought processes, achieving a state of desirelessness. He taught himself to exercise the power of mind over matter and the ability to present a willed

The Traditional Model

response to a stimulus. Over a period of time he gained some control over those of his faculties that were at once, extraintellectual and extrasensory. Methodical and precise, his understanding of the universe of the human condition was that of a purist. On an austere face, his deep-set, ultrakeen eyes dashed back and forth as he spoke of the inherent wisdom in the verses and *mantras* in the Vedas, which he described as the ultimate storehouse of all knowledge, both physical and spiritual. He firmly believed that like the Bible and the holy Koran, the Vedas - Hindu scriptures - were divinely inspired and uttered or written by wise beings of unknown origin.

Ownership of a thing or idea is not important. What is precious is the legacy left behind for everyone to study and benefit from the knowledge. Hindus make a big fuss over the Sanskrit language, because it is the language of the sacred Vedas. The origin of the language could very well predate the Persian era. The Vedas could have been written by the Persians or by the original Aary in central Asia and brought into India when they migrated in the fourth millennium before Christ.

This statement upset many orthodox Hindus because they consider themselves to be the masters of Vedas, the source of original knowledge. Their pride did not allow them to consider any suggestion casting doubt on the origin of the sacred Vedas or their language. Their Hindu ego could not bear the thought that the Vedas and their language might not have their original source in ancient India.

Continuity of life is based on the immortality of the soul. The body is a discrete but a disjointed entity in the scheme of higher things and is of little or no significance beyond providing a platform for experiences. The soul is the basis of spiritual continuity as it progresses along the course. But the soul needs the body to become an individualized atma or *jivatma*, a minuscule part (microcosm) of the *Paramatma* (Superconsciousness) which pervades the whole universe (macrocosm). Call it what you will, God or Force of Creation or Holy Ghost, whichever term you felt comfortable with while keeping the potential of "the tyranny of words" always present in your mind.

Dharma

Like the word *"darshan"*, *"dharma"* defies all attempts to simply translate it into English. It appears that the word has been given a range of shades of meaning in the usage in the Vedic scriptures. Based on the Sanskrit root *"dhr"*, meaning "to uphold", "to sustain", its principal meaning seems to be "fixed rules of conduct". From this base meaning, its multifaceted usage seems to take off within the framework of related context. It stands for "standard of conduct to qualify as a member of the Aary community", "virtues to be inculcated", "duties and obligations at stages of life", "relational duties" as a father, as a teacher, etc. *Dharma* and truth are considered equal. Practice of nonviolence and moral code of the Aary community is *Dharma*. It encompasses everything that one must do in obedience to one's conscience to uphold virtue in daily life. In Buddhism *Dharma* means the complete set of religious practices to attain enlightenment or Nirvana.

Karma

A *guru* once told me:

In reality you are already what you seek to become. Why do you toil so hard and worry so much? Conduct yourself like a decent and reasonable person. Sit in a lotus *aasan*, practise *pranayam* and chant *om* with devotion. Karma will take care of the rest.

What is karma? O! You great one with the shining eyes.

First remember that all matter exists in two states; manifest and hidden. Physics tells us that it is made up of invisible building blocks called atoms and molecules. Atoms themselves are made up of even tinier parts called electrons, protons, neutrons, positrons and others. These building blocks, bonded and extended in different combinations, make up all the known elements of matter in the universe. Physical laws govern the manifestation of matter in all its forms. Elements come together in many combinations and make up all forms of visible matter.

Karma is a similar concept, except that the basic building blocks of karma are our daily actions and deeds, great or small, important and unimportant, all alike. Every act performed by a

The Traditional Model

human being generates subtle expanding reflections of concentric rings around them, very much like what a stone does when it hits the surface of a still pond. The effects of the actions result in subconscious and unconscious impressions, which follow the feeling created by the experience of the deed itself and remain rooted in the the person's mind. Karmic impressions diffuse through the universe, touching every other object in the invisible world. They do not interact with physical matter, but each and every act performed by a human being during day-to-day living, makes a contribution to or detracts from an aggregation governing the quality of an individual's life and his environment, both directly and indirectly. The adjudged essences of our actions, referred to as "latent impressions" in the scriptures, are accumulated as discrete, unaggregated entities in our own mind. They are carried forward from birth to birth. The positive and negative essences cannot be redeemed. However, balancing and countervailing influences can be cultivated through the quality of one's actions and by removing ignorance from the mind. The latent impressions can fructify in the short, medium or long term into real consequences for the individual in this or a future life, the future life itself being a consequence of previous deeds. A very complex set of cosmic rules controls the timing of the delivery of a consequence to an individual. And considering the infinitely large variety of actions, situations and interactions possible in a lifespan, no one fully understands the resolution of the application areas, i.e. which original deed or misdeed impinges on what target result or how the advance-regress - the actual words used in scriptures are black-white - pairings are made or, if they are made at all.

Common sense tells us that good deeds bring us positive feelings and bad deeds make us feel guilty and insecure. The inborn feeling for justice, fairness and equality is rooted in our conscience. Through a complex process of aggregation, the seemingly uncompromising and unforgiving karma fashions a finely tuned conscience and places it in our pure I-Sense (spiritual part) at or before conception. Throughout the lifespan of the microcosm, conscience rules as a mediator between the good and vicious forces and the far-reaching limbs of karma caution the wary in the

The Latitude Syndrome

language of subtle hints, coincidences, gentle revelations and watchful prudence. For the unwary, interminable doubts, questions and a profound sense of guilt rule their lives.

Through the freedom to act, a gift given to us by karma - and it is an elegant trap! - if we want to, we can intellectually turn karma off or pretend that it doesn't exist. But the action is like turning the power switch to "off" in your house. We know very well that, ceaselessly "the potentials are always present in the wires" and that the same currents are running everything else in the whole world. Denying it doesn't remove it.

The physical analogies are so appropriate at times to get the point across! So, do not allow yourself to be fooled by the temptation. No form of life can be immune to the effects of karma, because no form of life, howsoever primitive or advanced, can survive on its own without interacting with other life forms, the ecological unity. The spirit and force of karma is omnipotent and all-pervading.

The karmic essences are continuously deposited in the mind and diffuse through the void of the universe. This arrangement is at the core of the working of karma and explained by the most fundamental of a set of seed-ideas related to the working of karma. The first set defines the mind: Mind is the power and capacity to know. The stream of mind flows in both directions, downhill for evil and uphill for good in the pursuit of knowledge to satisfy curiosity. Mind satisfies itself by exerting itself through the three channels, namely, intellectual thirst, emotional passion and spiritual devotion. The fountainhead of experience can never be shut down. Because knowledge is limitless, mind has to be everywhere. Like knowledge, mind has no beginning. Mind has no end. It *is*.

I suggest that you read the above paragraph again and again, dwelling on the concepts to grasp the inner meaning. You will find the subject to be irresistibly fascinating. It adds episodes to a current life. It gives one a feel for the continuity of personal evolution.

In dealing with guidelines for good action, the Vedic scriptures speak of volition and deliberate acts of a willful nature. It is thought that willful acts to hurt others, deliberately devised selfish acts of deceit and cunning directed at others, and ignoring

The Traditional Model

cries for help from those in genuine distress when you are well equipped to provide same are very low on the totem pole. One can try to argue through circular logic that the karma of the recipients justifies such acts. The prevailing wisdom is, of the first part that one does not become a willing agent for the delivery of pain and suffering to any form of life, under any circumstances, and, of the second part that you are allowed consultations with your conscience at all times. What can be simpler than this?

Now remember that karmic aggregations are stored in the mind, which is everywhere. If somehow you can reduce the influence of the empirical Ego on your daily actions and deeds, it is easy to see that the effects can be beneficial to mental and spiritual health. That is why unselfish acts, deeds of service to mankind and an outlook of altruism in day-to-day living are held in high esteem by most people. These practices defeat the working of the empirical Ego. Meditation is one of the many techniques that enables us, in addition to other benefits, to perceive the workings of karma around our present life or the series of reincarnations we will inevitably pass through on our paths. At the advanced stage of self-recognition by meditation, through the agency of the realized *Buddhi* - intuitive wisdom - one can perceive the details of the universal aspects of karma. This is Discriminative Knowledge, the lowest common denominator of all the variables operating in the universe.

I will now define the second set of seed-ideas.

In the universe each object, each entity, each thing and each idea like "time" is passing from "future" to "present" to "past" in subtle frames called *tanmatra*. Only the "present" is recognizable by the human senses. Another way of saying this is that the "present" is manifest. The "future" and the "past", by definition, are not manifest but they do exist. Anything that has come into being can never be totally annihilated. Anything which has not existed before, cannot come into being. It's only change and transformation.

By applying this logic, one can see how the "future" and "past" states of a thing exist, albeit in hidden states. Things in hidden states cannot be grasped by the human senses. But they can be perceived by the human mind. The specific term for this experience is "realization".

The Latitude Syndrome

Intuitive knowledge of the hidden parts of things can be gained by meditation. A person trained to "realize" invisible states of things is a self-realized person. Meditation enables a person to become self-realized. He is also said to have attained self-recognition. Remember that pure I-Sense is nonmanifest.

Now the term "self-recognition" is being explained.

Most religions of the world agree on an important point of reference. They all say that "man was created in the image of God". What does this statement mean? Simply that, at preconception in mother's womb, the proximity of the ovum to the chosen sperm personalizes a pure I-Sense, a core spiritual particle, under the supervision of the mother's spirituality. Pure I-Sense holds all the virtues and supersensory powers which it bestows upon the new life.

At conception, the "physical presence" of the new life is layered over the pure I-Sense and the microcosm is launched as an entity unto itself, distinct from the mother's entity. Karma thus has prevailed upon the scene. It has tempered with the prospects of the forming life in many ways.

- It has superimposed the empirical Ego on the pure I-Sense.
- It has planted its servant watchdog, the conscience, in the forming life.
- It has given the sense "I am the body" and "freedom of action" to the new life.
- Most importantly, it has given a "set of experiences" to the new life to live and relive through 'relationships' at different stages in life.

These events dramatically change the state of affairs of the newborn. The good news is that some actions of karma are reversible. The better news is that the effect of karma's actions can be erased by the microcosm himself. No other person can do it for him. The empirical Ego can be lifted off the pure I-Sense and dissolved. To regain the original state of pure I-Sense is every person's birth right, for it bestows universal love and bliss upon the person. The term "self-recognition" therefore means that you have recognized your pure I-Sense, implying that you have risen above the "I am the body" feeling. The temporarily felt out-of-body

The Traditional Model

experience is a short-lived decoupling of the empirical Ego from the pure I-Sense. It can be made to last longer.

To understand the concept of the "set of experiences" ("set") assigned by karma, regard your biological roots as giving you the field of play in the short-term, that is, over one birth and your extrabiological roots in the long-term, that is, going from birth to birth. Derived from your extrabiological roots, the "set" provides the means of the brightest beacons of progress along your evolutionary path because you relive the decisions and actions at successive stages of the ever-changing panorama of your relationships. An automatic learning process for all levels of intelligence is inherent in the scheme because it is based on the "incremental change" principle. Sooner or later the differences will be perceived and used to "learn" and modify behaviour. Given the freedom of action, especially for intelligent humans, it offers opportunities for experiential gain limited only by the imagination of the participant. Karma is like mother, who, even in punishment has your best interests at heart! Does karma drive evolution?

To highlight a point in passing, closer to home, many mathematical techniques used in research experiments employ the same principle of measuring "incremental change" or "deltas" in different settings. Successive approximations are calculated from repeating iterations and the decision to include a given number of terms in the series is made. Remember there are no absolute values anywhere in the universe!

It's worth noting that for the humans, the basis of personal change in a relationship has to be first realized in the spiritual space, i.e. in the self. The three verbs play a crucial role in how the change will find expression through the emotional and mental spaces and become a practical reality in the interaction.

Regarding karmic consequences, one enlightened swami of the Aary faith realized the existence of a connection between extreme willful selfishness and diseases of the body. He perceived activation of viruses and bacteria by mutation, where originally a state of active coexistence or passive dormancy had existed in the host body.

The Latitude Syndrome

A *guru* once told me a simple story to illustrate the subtle working of karma. A *gharra* is a common sight in the households of rural India. It is a fired terra-cotta brittle sphere used to store drinking water in poorer households. Every poor man wants to own a *gharra* of his own. The tale is told of an ambitious laborer who found a *gharra* lying by the roadside. He was happy with his newfound fortune as he walked to his hut. He set the *gharra* down on the floor and lay down to rest. He took off on a jubilant spree, building visions in his mind of how he was going to fill the *gharra* with drinking water from the well and sell the water to people who had no *gharras*. From the profit, he was going to buy another *gharra* and carry the two on a pole on his shoulder. From the profit, now he was going to buy a cart and two more *gharras*. Before long, he had visions of his young employees pushing carts and selling water to all the villages in the neighborhood. "The women wouldn't have to go to the well to fetch drinking water; I will become prosperous." He screamed out loud, his arms and legs flailing wildly in excitement, accidentally kicking the empty *gharra*, sending it rolling against the wall where it broke into many pieces, as did his dreams!

Now the importance of seed-ideas is being explained.

Seed-ideas are the working models of aphorisms, which tend to be tersely worded or condensed statements of first principles. They appear to be simple and straightforward in their import on the listeners. Upon acceptance by the pupils, they operate on their belief systems from the inside. Over time, they can change their fundamental attitude to the philosophies of their lives.

I urge you to recall the two sets of the seed-ideas with a quiet mind at least twice a day before going into meditation.

Mind over matter

We can appreciate the fact that all change in nature begins at the imperceptible level of the subatomic particles in a cumulative manner. In broad terms, ceaseless change is of two kinds. The first kind is the effect of a cause for which a physical basis can be defined, such as an exchange of energy, chemical reactions etc. Even a nuclear explosion starts out at the subatomic level and quickly builds up as more atoms get involved in the process. A volcanic burst is the sum total of the minute shifts in the trillions of atoms making up its mass. We are surrounded by a very large number of energy waves in the universe impinging on our nervous system networks affecting us in many ways, but we do not immediately feel their effect. But that does not imply that they are not there. This is because most of us operate at the gross matter level most of the time. This is the nature of man. By definition, any change must pass from the "future" to the "present" to the "past" to announce its presence, of which the "present" is in a manifest state at a given point in time. A snapshot can be taken of the "present" state of a thing and studied for its details of structure, properties and operation.

The second kind of change is mutative and evolutionary in nature and may not have a physical basis for it. This change also passes from the "future" to the "present" to the "past", but all three temporal phases are hidden. They cannot be seen but they can be realized and influenced by the mind through meditation or sometimes by sheer coincidence for which no apparent scientific basis can be offered. A spontaneous effect has no cause. The workings of thought and consciousness and the Cantilever Effect - discussed later, are prime examples of this phenomenon.

This is how mind over matter can be realized and made manifest in physical form. Sai Baba's materialization of *vibhooti* or holy ash from thin air is an example of this phenomenon because there is no physical basis for the ash's appearance.

Continuity and Spontaneity

When and where did the universe begin? The original (generative) cosmic processes didn't have a beginning and don't have an ending in terms of our linear thinking. They have been spontaneously ongoing. Man on the other hand has been conditioned to think, act and behave in small steps that have a beginning and an ending. This is man's most fundamental incompatibility with the natural order of things, because he limits himself by thinking "I am the body".

The Latitude Syndrome

Imagine standing on a point surrounded by thousands of trains whizzing by in different directions. Man gets on one, travels a bit, and then gets off. He is now surrounded by thousands of trains. . . and evolutionary life goes on. Most of the time he goes around repeating his actions and decisions, but in altered settings, and arrives back at the same point without knowing it.

It is quite probable that all events in the universe have always been spontaneous, discrete and ongoing. The boundless mind gathers the relevent ones and then arranges them in sequences to satisfy a given need or picture and the human experience of the need or picture is perceived. The model seems to lend support to the theory that all knowledge and perceived 'memory' are there, side by side, in *akash* (out there). Perception of an event then becomes a mere replay of a pattern of pulses on certain neurons in the human brain which could vary by a wide margin from person to person. We do not know that two people watching the same green tree have an identical perception of either the "tree" or the color "green". They use similar words to describe them because they have been taught to follow verbal codes - the tyranny of words.

The spiritual aspect of man is continuous and in harmony with the natural order of processes in the cosmos.

Darshan

Darshan is a particular term for a specific set of nuances attached to its import to give it an all-encompassing sense when one person visits or meets another. Let us first begin with the physical presence of each other. Add the emotional ambience of projecting goodwills, a sense of humanistic caring and reverence the physical presence brings with it. Further add the subtle expression in the eyes and an inclination to accept and cherish the beauty of human dignity. Further add the most significant element of the invisible spirituality which prevails between two Aary people. Lastly, surround the two in the language of silence. A flow of elemental nuances is implicated.

When one pines for the other for no obvious cause, one is missing the other's *darshan* in a spirit of self-surrender.

The Traditional Model

The stage for the subtle effects to take root is set by the exchange of the greeting of *namaste* at the beginning of the visit. When properly executed, it can set the stage for meditative silence.

Namaste

In the Sanskrit language, the language of *gurus* and meditators, there is but one form of greeting for all occasions. It is made up of three syllables, "na", "ma" and "te", literally saying, "I bow to you". In the context of the all-pervasive unity of things, the "you" represents the spiritual-self rather than the body. So the real meaning is "I bow to the divine in you".

Pronunciation and effectiveness of *namaste*:
The "a"s are short in sound, "s" is short and crisp and the "e" at the end is a long "a".The greeting is usually followed by "*ji*"- a syllable of reverence. It is designed to create an atmosphere of mutual respect and goodwill, which is further reinforced by assuming a posture while exchanging the greeting. The palms of the hands come together in front of the chest. The head is bowed such that the chin is above the thumbs. In a reverential relationship, the *chela* or pupil fixes his eyes on the feet of the *guru*, a gesture of acquiescence. Why?

It is based on the phenomenon of transference - how we all continually reinvent each other according to our nonbiological blueprints or roots. This phenomenon is said to have been discovered by Sigmund Freud in the eighteen-nineties in Vienna. But the *gurus* have been using it for thousands of years in a two-step relationship, chela-*guru* and chela-goddess/god. It works quite effectively in both cases.

Why Om is indispensable to the practice of meditation?

A parable "Try Softer" must be told first. A young boy travelled across Japan to the school of a famous martial artist. When he arrived at the *dojo*, he was given an audience by the *sensie*.

"What do you wish from me?" The master asked.

"I wish to be your student and become the finest *karateka* in the land," the boy replied. "How long must I study?"

The Latitude Syndrome

"Ten years at least."
"Ten years is a long time," said the boy. "What if I study twice as hard as all your other students?"
"Twenty years," replied the master.
"Twenty years! What if I practice day and night with all my effort?"
"Thirty years," was the master's reply.
"How is it that each time I say I will work harder, you tell me that it will take longer?" the boy asked.
"The answer is clear. When one eye is fixed upon your destination, there is one eye left with which to find the way."
- Anonymous (courtesy of Chris Vedeler)

Commentary
We spend most of our lives focussed on gross objects in a world where we have been trained to be goal-oriented. Cause and effect has been drilled into our minds. For every action we take, we are conditioned to expect a reward or at least a tangible result, from which we can derive a material gain . We are trapped in this mind set.

Om is the ancient mystic symbol of pure energy. The universe is said to have started with two ingredients, the *akash* or pure space and a pinhead of *shakti* or pure energy symbolized by the mystic *om*. In Sanskrit the sound is made up of three letters a-u-m. It has no cause and it has no source. It *is*. By unifying our thoughts with devotion, and then by meditating on the sound of the syllable *om*, we are seeking to free ourselves from the bondage of cause and effect, which hinders self-recognition. *Om* is the perfect sound syllable. It is a complete sound-object-idea entity. It has a deep inner blessing for the *chela* or pupil. It never fails a true *chela*. It ushers a feeling of universal love and joy into the heart. It helps in setting up an inner altar at which nonoptical luminous perceptions are presented to the *chela*.

The Traditional Model

Creativity Consciousness

Our most fundamental drive is to express our inner reality through whatever means, in whatever form, at whatever opportunity that presents itself to us. This drive is latent and a meditation-like technique gives us the insight to awaken it and get in touch with it. Every decision, every action of our everyday life is given to improving our chances to give expression to our reality. This is the basis of personal evolution.

When we make a new friend, we are giving expression to a facet of this reality, from both sides. That is why some friendships prosper and many do not.

When we choose a partner or a mate, we are seeking to express our spiritual-self through the other. The other may bring out the best in us or he may not. One has to think about the yardstick being used to measure compatibility. Therein lies the enchantment of the painting we call life. Superficial compatibility can be misleading.

When we read a book or study an object, it may not be obvious, but we are expressing ourselves by preparing our mind to absorb the "color" of the object of study in a selective manner. The expressing part is subtly embedded in the selection process.

When we write, cook, sew, knit, paint or build a house, we are expressing our inner reality. Think gardening.

When we laugh or cry, we are expressing ourselves in a language of our own. Through the pronouncements of the wordless syllables in laughs and cries, we express the inexpressible in sound-object-idea combinations. These combinations are unique to a human being for they are the vocal strokes of the invisible brush painting personal objects pertaining to the situation at hand with subtle ideas. Think about the possibilities here!

Mutation

Every object, entity, thing and idea like "time" or "space" mutates. Characteristics of objects, entities, things and ideas mutate. They all pass from the "future" to the "present" to the "past". Therefore they mutate. But their substance or reality remains the same.

The Latitude Syndrome

Mutation takes place in the *tanmatra* interval and is cumulative within the sphere of its influence, for example a preserved seed will sprout in the presence of warmth and water. By the time we see it at the gross matter level, its most telling effects are gone.

The mutations of the mind are its modifications. Because the source of experience can not be turned off, mind prevails every where. Mind is unstoppable, but its modifications are stoppable.

Sound Constellation

It is thought that the precursor of the literary language Sanskrit was an unwritten language of pure sounds and embedded ideas for introspection and study used by the religious elite, the forebears of the Brahamins of present day India. Afterwards, syllables and wordless expressions came into being, ushering it into the era of elaboration for *mantras*. Much, much later, it evolved into a literary means of communication for religious purposes.

Also known by the traditional Sanskrit word, "*mantra*", sound-constellations are made up of sounds, wordless syllables, syllables, words and sound clusters. An enlightened master in a *samadhi* or deep trance can put together wordless syllables, point them to an object and then add an idea entity to form sound clusters. The power of prayer may be added to the cluster. A certain feeling and rhythm are incorporated into the sounds. By reciting the sound-constellation with devotion, the practitioner can realize the specific idea entity embedded in the sounds by the master. The idea is realized from the feeling present at the time of composition. This can help the *chela* in overcoming barriers on their path to awakening the artistic Creativity Consciousness or realizing self-recognition.

How does it work? Here is a little bit of background theory.

By convention, a word, that is the sounds its pronunciation makes, points to an object and has some meaning attached to it. To understand the relationships between the sound, implied object, and idea, consider the word "table". When the speaker pronounces the word "table", each letter is converted into a corresponding sound. The speaker has an object in mind, that is, the thing the sounds refer

The Traditional Model

to. The idea part is subtle. It incorporates the feeling and spirituality of the speaker. In the example, the sounds can point to a dining table, a picnic table, water table or any of the other doable things related to table. But the speaker had a specific idea in mind when he pronounced the word. The reference is to a table. It exists. But where? And for what purpose? What was the idea behind the sound?

Sound clusters of wordless syllables which do not point to any material objects but incorporate powerful idea entities are useful in achieving self-recognition. Because there is no implied object in the sounds, the idea entity becomes a powerful vehicle. Elements of prayer and rhythm are added to give them harmonizing and purifying qualities to hasten the *chela* around the obstacles and barriers on his path seeking intuitive insight

Orchestral music

When the sound-object-idea model is extrapolated to instrumental music without vocalizations, we discover that they work in the same manner as they do in a sound-cluster. A master composer can incorporate the subtleties of one, two, or all three components - sound, object, idea - in a skilful manner to create a range of musical moods, effects, and tantalisations, pointed at the physical, emotional, and spiritual sensitivities of the listeners. Sounds can paint scenes as well as tell stories without speaking words. They can be programmatic, shifting mental sets from scene to scene in the manner of a staged drama. Sounds can induce a dialogue between the composer and the listener. Results can be similar to the effectiveness attributed to the practice of sound-constellations. The underlying principles are the same. This is the basis of the meditative-listening technique described in a later chapter.

Cantilevers

Cantilevers represent unceasing modulations of "potentials" in the Physical-mental, the Emotional-astral, and Spiritual solitudes of the person. They are immaterial projections or spurs that roll out of a solitude in all directions and then loop back. They seek a

The Latitude Syndrome

receptive, compatible "morsel" of ideation which gives birth to a premonition of "expectation". When the expression "pregnant pause" is used, it is understood that the pause is pregnant with cantilevers. Strategically placed pauses between notes in a musical composition are the principal sources of predictable responses in listeners' Emotional-astral and Spiritual solitudes. The musical pauses are so saturated with cantilevers that, in effect, they are not pauses or breaks at all but powerful fountainheads gushing with object and idea entities which cannot be conveyed in any other manner. In this manner the ideas encoded in composed music, the musical hieroglyphs, are realized by listeners. Some composed music can be a very powerful vehicle of spiritual give and take.

When a certain advantage in consequences in one direction or the other is gained by manipulating the "influences" in an extraphysical space, it is said to be the outcome of the cantilever effect. When emotions impinge on the spirit, extraphysical cantilevers reach into the Spiritual solitude. Worship, prayer, music, exercise of will, healing, and Sound-clusters work through this effect.

It is said that a "pre-idea" or a "pre-thought" is a horseman riding a cantilever seeking germination. Mind is but a maze full of colors of objects, entities, things and concepts like "time". Respiration is said to be the underlying catalyst that completes the picture and a thought appears. Without cantilevers the "pre-idea" or the "pre-thought" would have no scope for association in the mind. Without being born it has no chance of finding expression. A very boring world, indeed!

Monks and yogins practise silence as a part of their training. Silence appears golden on the surface. But it is very powerful because the projecting cantilevers prevail in profusion in the three solitudes. Not every period of silence is golden.

The process of mental sublimation is thought to be based on the cantilever effect.

Akashvani or clairaudience is a common, everyday occurrence among at least ten per cent of the population. It is the direct result of the Cantilever Effect and the phenomenon is realizable through meditation.

The Traditional Model

The cantilevers sired by an intense feeling of universal love are so profuse and pervading that the person is transported beyond himself. Spiritual passion or devotion are a part of this phenomenon. Intuition comes to fruition as a result of the Cantilever Effect. Cantilever Effect is responsible for the transfer of knowledge into awareness as a microcosm learns from the cognitive elements of perception.

How cantilevers work?

The "mechanism" of cantilevers is based on nonmaterial projections or spurs that occur in two phases; the outbound phase and the inbound phase. The meditator can exercise a measure of control over the first phase by building an intense emotion and a sense of devotion to, say, *om* or other object of worship while focussing on an object or idea entity associated with it. This capability can be easily learnt. Remember that you are working to enhance the ideation of "expectation". The payback, the realization, is bound up in the second phase, that is, the nature of the "morsel", which comes back with the retracting cantilevers. In the case of an art form, it can have many consequences for the audience, depending on what they set out to achieve, which, in most cases, may be a deeper appreciation of art, universal love or a personal feeling. Serious meditators and artists can touch the inner depths of their latent artistic Creativity Consciousness in this manner. The creator and the practitioner set their internal horizons. Consider the case of master composer Beethoven after he became tone deaf. He continued to compose heavenly music without the benefit of audible sounds. Because he was a masterful practitioner of clairaudience, he could conceive and musically express objects and ideas without the help of audible sound. He was able to attain the musical pinnacles that he did, because he could influence the cantilevers in his Emotional-astral and Spiritual solitudes with the intensity of his spiritual convictions. He was an adept at setting his internal horizons. We will find out in the future how other players were involved at other levels in Beethoven's music. The point to note is that audible sound is not always present in the sound-object-idea propagation.

Consider a person in prayer, an everyday occurrence. Spoken or silent words are intellectual events taking place in the Physical-mental solitude. They give rise to feelings which are impressions or sensations recognized in his Emotional-astral solitude. Feelings lead to spiritual nuances - entities registering in his Spiritual solitude - which was the object of prayer. How did this happen? Simply put, the transfer of "essence" from one solitude to another is brought about by the Cantilever Effect. It is worth noting that most people pray without even realizing it because that is their nature.

My guess is that modern science will start talking about cantilevers in their theories in the coming millennium.

Interconnectivity (unity) of all entities in universe.

First a few memory-joggers:

Source of experience is infinite. Mind is simply the power to know. Gathering impressions - color and characteristics - is the object of mind. Knowledge is limitless. Mind does not need space to exist. It has no beginning. It has no end. It is everywhere.

Anything which did not exist before cannot become viable. All minds are everywhere. This is the supermind, the Superconsciousness, the macrocosm, the holder and giver of all knowledge, universal love, bliss and truth. Individual consciousness of every entity, object, thing and idea like "time" is interwoven into the Superconsciousness. This is how all things are connected.

Immediately before a microcosm is conceived, the proximity of the ovum to the "chosen" sperm first personalizes the pure I-Sense with all the knowledge and all the extrasensory powers of the macrocosm. The empirical Ego is superimposed upon the pure I-Sense by karma, the essence of past actions. This obscures the real nature of the microcosm. But the doings of the empirical Ego can be undone by clearing the barriers and obstacles from the path. The pure I-Sense can be regained. This is *mukti* or liberation from the empirical Ego and the anguish of suffering.

The Traditional Model

During life as the microcosm grows mentally, reads, listens and learns by cognitive elements, specific elements of knowledge and truth are moved from the supermind into his awareness. Another way of saying that is that a cantilever "link" is established between his solitudes and the supermind, making him aware of and in possession of that truth and he can recall it at will. This transfer is cumulative and persists across incarnations and ultimately becomes his wisdom.

Good and Evil
In the interconnectedness of entities and objects in the universe, the outcome of a very large proportion of connectivity is beneficial. Most of the time, Good, Knowledge and Truth prevails during transfers into the awareness of the microcosm. However, the outcome of some connections may result in "potential evil". Along with Good, Knowledge and Truth, the "potential opposites" can also be transferred into a microcosm. The freedom of action given to a microcosm can fructify the potential evil into physical evil.

Meditation
When the mind is not under the influence of the empirical Ego, it is in a natural state of expanding consciousness and bliss of the pure I-Sense. During deep sleep, during realization of spiritual hieroglyphs expressed in music, during solemn deliberations and other periods, the mind automatically enters the natural spiritual state for brief intervals. Meditation enables the *savant* to prolong the period of separation of the pure I-Sense from the empirical Ego. Persistent and earnest meditation can lead to a permanent removal of the empirical Ego, the final stage of attaining liberation. Then microcosm and macrocosm become one. The birth-death cycle comes to an end. The rose disappears. The thorn disappears. Only the fragrance persists. This is the ultimate goal of natural evolution. A person may take many reincarnations to achieve this state. As a foretaste it is possible to perceive and see the luminosity of the cantilevers and the two synapses in the three solitudes through devotional meditation. These nonoptical perceptions appear at the inner altar of the *savant*.

The Latitude Syndrome

There are countless dissimilar paths to explore and rejoice in the royal realm of one's inner being. Ultimately the *savant* finds the one most suited for him. The only criterion is that the *savant* is sincere and true to himself. I have developed specific meditation and meditative-listening techniques set to classical music which enable a *savant*, after learning and practice, to actually perceive the outlines of his three solitudes and the cantilevers around them. The bliss and heightened awareness brought on during the "sightings" are beyond description. The effect persists for days.

Prana shakti

The universe began with *akash* or void and *shakti* which is symbolized by the mystical *om*. As the universe grew and came to be populated by material objects like the galaxies, *shakti* pervaded everything in it. It pervades the human body and vitalizes each and every cell in it. Our bridge to it is through *prana* or respiration. Its power is unimaginable.

- All forms of energy like heat, light, electromagnetic fields, radiation, gravitation etc are its physical manifestations.
- It runs everything in the body at the minutest level, giving each cell the vitality and the boundary of a self-sustaining life. Each living cell - invisible to the naked eye - is born, regulates, repairs and reproduces itself in mysteriously complex ways. It is capable of manufacturing complex chemical compounds within its small size. In a group of cells bound together as in the human pineal and pituitary glands, long-molecule chemical compounds and hormones are produced with amazing precision and regularity in mind-boggling sequences. A man-made facility to synthesize crude copies of the same hormones and compounds would take up a large laboratory full of complicated equipment. Just think about it!
- All sensory, inner organ signalling, behavioral inputs and other brain functions are nothing more

The Traditional Model

than short-lived streams of pulse patterns or frames coursing through specific interconnected networks of neurons in the physical organ. It is *Prana shakti* that assembles the pre-ideation frames into a whole and ushers the idea into a person's awareness for relevance and assimilation.

Time

Science has some difficulty in defining the true identity and nature of time. It is the fourth dimension, they say, extending from minus infinity to plus infinity; whatever that mean! Others say it is the duration of some physical event which has a precise beginning and a precise ending or the interval in which light or sound travels a certain distance. It is the period in which a certain type of radioactivity decays from one reading to another, with the radioactivity itself defined as a frequency based on time! It is always portrayed as an expression of an analogue of some physical process. It is used as a marker in our day-to-day calculations and dealings for measurements.

But what is time? And what is its true nature?

It cannot be visualized as the flow of a tangible entity like a stream of water or a waveform of particles in space. It has no form or substance. In order to give earthlings a sense of its nonexistent magnitude it has been given a relative size by the repetitive motion of the planet earth turning on its axis or going around its orbit in the solar system with realignments made periodically in order to synchronize events. It is expressed as B.C. or A.D. These events do not measure time or express anything about it in any way. Its usage over the ages has objectified it as an entity external to the human mind, thus alienating it from its true nature. If anything, it is the other way around. It represents the march of consciousness on a trillion fronts. So what is time?

Nothing. Yes, there is no such physical entity as time. By itself, it does not constitute a tangible or intangible thing. It is not an absolute scale. Neither is it a measure of any thing. Calibration symbols based on discrete physical processes have been devised to give its void form a visible garb. But the marks have to be realigned

The Latitude Syndrome

every so often to match physical states. It is not even a continuum. It is just a word. Occasionally the term is used as a substitute for space. It has no attributes. The concept has been formulated to mark and meter a short span of ongoing change. It is a cleverly disguised abstract gradient to serialize change. Imagine a statement like: In the space (of time!) the earth made a half revolution around its north-south axis, a Boeing 777 flew from Anchorage (Alaska) to Auckland (New Zealand), one million tons of solar particles entered Earth's atmosphere, the volume of my tomato plant grew by .0001 m3, a gene in the enterococcus bacteria altered once, the number of sequence repeats in a microsatellite of the DNA did not grow even by one . . . ad infinitum. See how confusing it all is. But the sentence makes a very crude attempt at describing the real world in which countless processes are at work simultaneously without end. At the present evolutionary state of the human mind, it can follow only one strand of cause and effect logic in its attention span. The human mind captures the essence of interactions in a linear manner, like a book, going from sentence to sentence, page to page, to the end of the story. Calibration marks on the conceptual scale we call time, enable us to concentrate on one progression in small steps. What a misfit! A linear square peg in a round hole of simultaneity!

Because time is not a real thing, our conditioned memory may not be serving us well because of our limitation in understanding simultaneity. How can we be certain that the "past", "present", and "future" states of an object do not coexist in the manifest state?

Perhaps it may be more appropriate to fathom "time" by genetic progress rather than the tics of a clock. Mutations are tied to the genetic code which presumably is tied to the march of evolution.

Duration of existence has something to do with the density of emotion and spiritual gravity in the existing life. Deeper the density of spiritual presence, the more quickly the body will lapse. A person with a very fulfilling life buttressed by ennobling deep emotions will have a short life span. The duration of a person suffering mildly for ten years may equal the duration of another suffering ten times more intensely for one year. When the *Kundalinis* of two perfectly matched soulmates conjugate, the

The Traditional Model

spiritual euphoria brought on by a dissolution of their duality is so intense that their bodies give out within a few years. Transcending time and space means that your consciousness has reached its peak and is beyond the sphere of change. A state of perfection is beyond change because incremental steps have ceased. How can one gauge such states?

By the way, what is the goal of evolution in scientific terms? Where is evolution taking us?

There is another circular model of time.

Humans can gauge "time" because of their capacity for "perceived memory" which derives its resolution from the concept of "incremental time" itself.

Origin of the swastica symbol

Throughout the recorded history of mankind, the symbol has sporadically appeared in varying forms to denote sun or fire or other mythological instruments in many earthly cultures. It has been likened to the Greek cross and has been ignominiously used by some to lend a false authenticity to oppressive military power. Although it has been used by many religions at different times for rituals and ornamentation, its most widespread use seems to have its roots in the region of India and Tibet from where it spread into the far east. Its most consistent feature is the "square" projection of its enclosure. It may be placed in a circle for contrast in a stylistic adaptation, but the swastica itself remains an occupant of square space, its limbs stretched along the vertical and transverse axes. Its intrigue lies in the depth of its mysterious relationship to the past. How did the form come into being and who first used it and for what purpose?

The origin of the phonetic word is in "*swasth*", a Sanskrit root meaning self-abiding or being in self. It has been associated with ideas of good luck, progress and steady development.

I list below some of the anecdotal sightings and interpretations given by their users during the course of my last three travels to that region.

- A large swastica of two to three feet square painted in "religious saffron" on the front wall of a temple

above the main arch signifies a place of worship of traditional significance.
- A border of small swasticas about one inch square around a doorway is purely decorative but "put there to arouse an ancient feeling". It appears frequently at the entrance door to the attached private quarters of a temple *pujari* or conductor of prayer rituals.
- A swastica carved on a marble pillar at the Birla temple in New Delhi is highlighted as the mother symbol of the script of the written Sanskrit language. It is written on the pillar that in the beginning a small number of the alphabet were derived by rearranging and redesigning the features of the swastica to produce varying shapes. Later the entire alphabet was attributed to its form.
- The believers of Jainism are its most consistent and ardent users. They have ascribed the eight parts of their meditative practices to its eight limbs. They place four dots in the four enclosures of the arms for special meaning. At times five small circles are placed at the bottom as a floating base whose purpose is unknown.
- In Buddhism the eight limbs of the swastica signify Buddha's eight right practices for a meditating monk in pursuit of nirvana. Buddhists throughout the far east use it as a symbol for good health and fertility and even place it on the head markers where their ashes are interred.
- Rows of small swasticas were observed at the two ends of some religious scarves in monastic orange colors worn by monks in Tibet and Leh. Only senior students who had attained high proficiency could wear such scarves. Swasticas with dots in the four enclosures indicated yet a higher status of achievement.

The Traditional Model

- The number of swasticas worn by a Chinese disciple indicates his spiritual status. A fully realized Buddhist sees the swastica twirling and synchronizes the rise and fall of his chants with the circularity of its mystical motion.
- I encountered seventeen other interpretations in Hinduism, all related to the meditative practices of yoga from the simple to the most sublime meaning assigned to the "implied motion" of the arms. Intuitively I am inclined to relate the "implied motion" to the very real perceptions of the cantilevers that I personally experience during meditation.
- Tablets bearing the swastica symbol were retrieved from excavations of the prehistoric sites of the Harappa civilization in the Indus valley, now in Pakistan. The civilizations covered the period 1500 B.C. to 4000 B.C.

One anecdote from Nagpur in central India is worth repeating; translated into English, it went something like this:

"*Pundit ji* - a common salutation for the religious head of a temple - you have two swasticas pointing in opposite directions painted on the front wall of your temple; is there a special meaning to the arrangement?" I asked.

"So you noticed the directions. You are moving forward when you are going in one direction. When you move in the opposite direction, you may perceive that you are going backward, but in reality you are still moving forward. It signifies that both directions point forward." the *pundit* explained. Then he went on:

"I notice that you are interested in the meaning of the mystical symbol; I am going to let you in on a well-kept secret. One of the most powerful forces to unleash the mysteries of the mind is embodied in the design and placement of the eight limbs in the *"akash"* of the frame of the swastica. After a serious *chela* has meditated for a year or two on his way to self-realization, he can find shortcuts to higher plateaus by meditating on certain sized swasticas arranged in a circle. Under the force of certain breathing

The Latitude Syndrome

sequences, the swasticas start to twirl and move along the circumference of the circle during a part of the meditation session. The *chela* can learn to use to his advantage the benign nature of the psychic forces locked in the ancient symbol which are proportional to the size, speed and direction of the twirling and rotary movements. I have to caution you that as the practise can be disorienting, dizzying and troubling in the beginning, it must be performed under the direction of a *guru*."

"But what is the mechanism at work in this exercise which sounds alarming, to say the least." I asked casually.

Pundit ji fell silent. Then he looked straight at me intently before speaking (I haven't understood the emotion behind the stare to this day except that it made me feel intimidated and ridiculed at the time). "It has to do with the resolution of the grain of the mind which guides our mental bearing at all times. This in turn controls how fine a perception one has. One can perceive electrons and atoms of matter this way. Physically too, one day, like this:" And he raised his hands in front of his chest, making semispheres with his taught curving fingers and twirled them as much as his wrists allowed, also bending and rotating his head at the same time while his eyes reached skyward with great concentration.

"I have never heard of this, *pundit ji*."

I think my remark offended him for a quick jerk of his head to a side told me that I was an ignorant man to be pitied and that I should shut up and not disturb him. But he resumed the pose, at least for twenty seconds.

"Organize your life, meditate, and when you become strong of mind, come back and spend a year with me. Results guaranteed."

Belatedly, now I realized that I was in the company of no ordinary temple *pundit*! I folded my hands and apologized to him.

"You know, you half-baked Hindus go to the western world and come back thinking that science has all the answers," and *punditji* grabbed my folded hands and held them above my head. Then he stepped back and looked up. A smile came upon his lips!

"You will be back, won't you?"

"Yes, *punditji*, I will try."

The Traditional Model

"You went to school and in geography they taught you that the earth rotates and also goes around the sun?"

I heard his voice but didn't pay much attention to the words. Thanking him profusely I begged leave. On the way back, the oddity of the episode got me wondering, especially his last sentence, which he put as a question to me. In the train ride back to Delhi I started to go over the details of the incident and how and why a chance meeting had turned out this way. I went over *pundit ji's* words again and again. Finally I understood the connection. The swasticas arranged in a circle for meditation, the electrons in atoms and the Earth-sun relationship, they follow twirling and rotating motions. That much he told me in plain language. But his postures and actions confounded me. Why did he appear to be annoyed? There was no doubt in my mind that he was a self-realized swami of stature who knew the subject. Was he trying to subliminally pass the secret of the origin of swastica to me? That is, if he knew it himself. His posture and his hands . . . and then I remembered seeing Ram Dave's hands in the same position at the Jakhu temple when his *shakti* had bridged the physical separation from Shona as described in The Three Verbs of Being. *Pundit ji* wasn't annoyed; I had disturbed his concentration!. I knew then why he raised my folded hands. He wanted me to look up to the sky with him! I understood the meaning of the chance meeting! What follows is based on the notes I had written on the train.

I think it can be reasonably assumed that the swastica symbol came into being long long ago, and somehow marks a significant point of transition in man's evolution. Its use is definitely not restricted to any one region of the world or to a specific ancient religion. I found a common thread in all the interpretations offered; it has been readily adopted and associated with human existence and has an air of uninterrupted history to it. Because of its mystical origin, it came to be revered and allegorically imbued by a host of anthropic themes at the hands of the peoples of the world who saw the simple but penetrating device and immediately recognized a sublime motif in it. They saw the images of their past in its form. It seems whoever first imagined or thought of the original concept wanted to leave behind an unmistakable clue for all time. Perhaps the world of "words", spoken or written, was not yet born. So it had to be a compact but indelible script of their rare insight with an unfailing drawing power.

A plausible idea

In my considered opinion, the swastica as we see it today is a nth generation revision of the original picture script of the most consequential event in the entire history of the *homo sapien*, namely, the transition of the "animal man" with a horizontal spine to the "spiritual man" with a vertical spine. Paleoanthropologists tell us that this shift began to gradually develop over four million years ago and perhaps took a million years to complete. The key indicator determined from the recent fossil finds of the prehominid era seems to be the size of the vault of the head and therefore the size of the brain in it. It has been established that the volume grew from a rudimentary size of about six hundred cubic centimeters to over twelve hundred cubic centimeters in the later *homo erectus*. Whatever evolutionary forces of nature or survival initiated this momentous adaptation of the prehominid to the vertical posture, they managed to accelerate the growth of the physical brain and set in motion certain developments of earthshattering proportions bearing on the very nature of the *homo erectus*.

Now imagine the offsprings of the hundreds of generations who were in the vanguard of the prehominid transition from the horizontal to the vertical posture. Being the most advanced verticals, they could see the gradations in the lineage of intelligence of those behind them all the way to the lowly "animal men" who were still horizontal. From generation to generation the proportion of the verticals to horizontals increased as their numbers increased. Eventually this progression of the different stages of intelligence became homogenous as all horizontals developed into verticals and the "intelligence" revolution took hold in the population of *homo erectus*, whose nature before this point had been "animal", that is, a form of life who had a spirit in him but was devoid of the awareness of a "spiritual something" in him.

The Traditional Model

One day a strange heaviness settled in the region around the heart of the *homo erectus* man. He noticed that his wild and vicious instincts were abating. He fought and hunted with diminishing ferocity over the next few centuries. Strange dizzying and disorienting impulses started to race through his head intermittently. He would scream wildly, make a quick dash and come to rest against a tree and beat his chest and press his head and bellow endless guttural sounds. His woman would follow him and look at him, but he would growl at her trying to chase her away. But she would hold her ground and continue to peer at his face with wondering eyes. When he got wounded in a fight, his pain was no longer the old physical pain alone; it was accompanied by new hurting sensations racing through his nerves and he would thump his head and shake it violently. One day his eyes moved nervously in circles, disorienting him even more as he fell to the ground, writhing and groaning, rolling over and over till he was exhausted and sleep overcame him. Laying on the ground when he woke up, momentarily, the "horizontal spine" instincts regained the upper hand and his agitation subsided for a while. Later when he stood up and went about his business, the sweep of transformation strengthened again in favor of the "vertical" and he went through the disturbing tussle back and forth for many a generation.

Soon after on a momentous day when his woman came close to him and peered at his face, he made momentary eye contact with her and the impulse to growl didn't overcome him. He saw something in her eyes and was held by it. His hands reached up to her shoulders and she became frightened and ran away. He caught up to her and again held her to look into her eyes, moving his head from side to side. When she wanted to free herself, a moan came to his throat and her ears perked up as she had never heard the sound before. She was solaced and drawn to his moan. She didn't want to run away anymore and he held her for minutes peering into her eyes, his head tilted to a side, his nose almost touching hers. Now when he wanted to part from her, a pleading moan sang in her throat and he was solaced and drawn to it. They fell into a clumsy embrace and the sensation of touch made him smile and bare his teeth with a guttural sound rising from his chest, and she pulled herself away. Days later he let his young ones come close and nudge him.

The strange disorienting impulses racing through his head started to settle down and he was no longer howling wildly. His savage temperament had mellowed down. He wasn't as much terrorized by fear as before. For the first time, his ears perked up when he heard the wind whistling at the front of his cave. He concentrated on his ears when he heard the distant rumble of thunder. A knowing was in the making. He moved his head to and fro with his eyes now opening wider than before behind the veil of coarse hair falling from his bristly forehead. He felt there was an inside to his body. Falling drops of water from the cave ceiling caught his attention and his gaze froze on them. At first his eyes smarted and turned red and then tear drops settled on the rims of his eyelids and the trace of the first human primitive feeling was born in him. Newborn pulses travelled over the neurons in a part of his brain for the first time ever, pushing out new branches. A new evolutionary note, the precursor of the civilizing force, had been struck which grew louder from one generation to the next. The wild and vicious expressions on the faces of the following hundreds of generations of the *homo erectus* became softer under the influence of first feelings. Their women, who were also evolving alongside, became less fearful of them. Longer periods of eye contact came about and eventually a closeness grew between them. Instinctual imprints in their primitive brains started to fade as the sentient forces gained ground and the first stirring of a heartfelt caring, sensitivity and affection were felt by them. They started to become aware of their hearts. In due course the tempest of feelings gained the upper hand and passion was born in the heart. A full-fledged cry was let out and the panorama of the full range of human feelings came into its own.

Now when the elements threatened him, a tempered fear rubbed against his heart and he didn't automatically take to flight. He started to look around and wonder about the things surrounding him. Eventually bonding and galloping emotions would lead the man to look tenderly into the eyes of his woman and along the way

The Traditional Model

the first shadow of a spiritual feeling crossed over the bow of the evolving species.

In a million years, the evolutionary progress made him a thinking, feeling, and experiencing human; that's us today, the end product of five-million years of evolution. During the last period of spiritual enlightenment, about five to seven thousand years ago, some very bright people, either singly or collectively, connected with the immense significance of the event and attributed it to none other than the singular feat of transition in human's posture from the "horizontal" to the "vertical" - time zero of human spiritual evolution - and they drew a picture on the cave wall to record their insight for posterity.

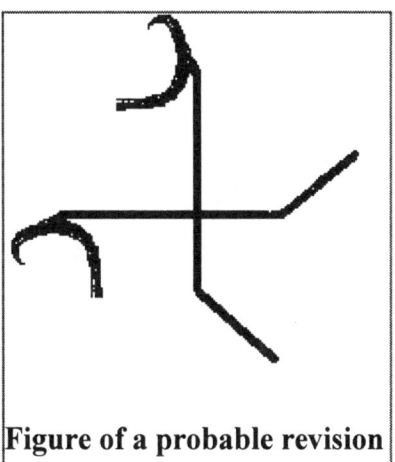

Figure of a probable revision along the way

The original script of the drawing on the cave wall might have started out as shown in the painting on page 52 and passed through many revisions over the centuries. It may have passed through the shape of the figure on page 51 on its way to the final symmetrical shape that we see around the world today.

It is noteworthy that the essential meaning of the original script was not lost on the intervening generations. The fact that they were able to interpret it correctly, connect with it and modify the shape of the limbs within the boundaries of the accepted elements of the historical truth, points to the inherently mystical beginnings of the symbol. Was it ever worshipped by some? Why were people drawn to it? What were its magnetic qualities? How has it managed to last through at least five thousand years of history when it has not been linked to a specific meaning by any culture?

Meditating monks have much to tell of its spiritual reach.

The Latitude Syndrome

Had the symbol not been jinxed during the thirties and the forties, what would its status be in the western world today? Let your mind wander back and forth as you think of what the *punditji* in the Nagpur temple had told me of its psychic powers. I have spoken with Buddhist monks who swear to its twirling and energizing effects. You be the judge!

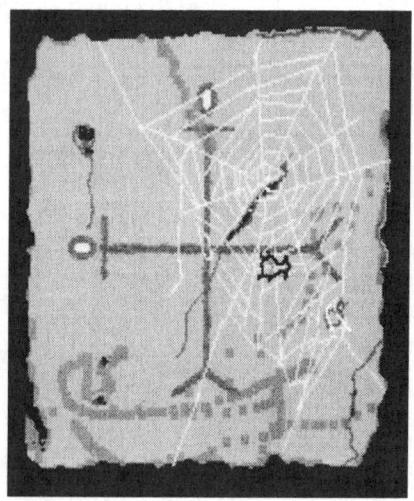

Script on cave wall

Hybrid Model of Human Evolution

I will begin by stating three universal laws applicable to human evolution. During the discussion of the relevant details, I have included the most frequently asked questions during the introductory classes held over the years.

The first cosmic law states that all objects, entities, things and ideas like "time" have a paired set of manifest and nonmanifest states associated with them. The manifest state is an embodiment of the dynamic individual flux or a measure of consciousness associated with the unmanifest state.

The second cosmic law states that all associated fluxes evolve in their individually unique ways to form a union or yoga with or merge into the superflux or Superconsciousness.

The third cosmic law states that the higher the level of the individual flux, that is, the more it is in harmony with the nature of the superflux, the faster it evolves towards its union with the superflux for *mukti* or liberation from suffering and anguish.

Throughout the universe the cyclical nature of processes related to evolution is fundamental to all matter and life forms. Celestial bodies go forward in cycles. The propagation of energy takes place in repeating wave motion. Vegetation evolves in cyclic patterns. This quality is essential to all evolution, including human. The evolution of man is predicated on the concept of the immortality of the soul. It takes place in life cycles of births of different bodies. The soul must seek a body to become a viable *atma* or *jivatma* for an earthly experience as an evolving microcosm. Yes, we do choose our parents! Our soul does it on our behalf. Depending upon the experiences the soul seeks to go through during an incarnation, it will elect an appropriate set of "parents" to start a new cycle, under karma's direction. During its earthly sojourn called "life", the experiential being goes through the highs and the lows, the successes and the failures to evolve towards its goal. It may take many births, or it may take only one, but without the earthly experience, the soul by itself is not capable of experiencing and therefore evolving.

The Cosmic laws apply equally to animate as well as inanimate objects. Since object is object, nature has no way of telling them apart. The difference between inanimate matter like a piece of rock and animate matter including higher life forms is the level of evolution, that is, the stage they have attained in their

The Latitude Syndrome

pursuit, relative to the superflux or macrocosm. In this context, you may be curious as to why a human "dies" sooner than a rock disappears from the face of the earth. The answer lies in the third cosmic law. The human being, on the whole, is on a fast track because he has evolved to a higher level. On a slower pace in its evolution, the rock may take the course of first eroding into fine sand particles. The sand may breakdown into different kinds of particles, eventually evolving to the level of the first "live" cell. It happened in the primordial sea of burning hot liquids and gases in the presence of lightning strikes and stellar explosions, when presumably, the carbon atom bonded with the inanimate sand particle to become an animate cell - the first living cell on the face of the Earth. Over time the living cell evolved into different forms of life. Modern science acknowledges this fact and Darwin built his theories of the survival of the fittest to explain the phenomenon of the evolution of the species. In practical terms the vitality or the motive force for the evolutionary push comes directly from the level of consciousness associated with the object.

The subject has implications at stages which precede the finite atomic interactions in matter, e.g. organic change, degradation of matter and energy etc. Over the past hundreds of thousands of years, evolution has taken mankind to the present stage of development. The implications for the intelligent life relate to the effects in areas commonly referred to under the umbrella term of "mind over matter". We know that change at the minutest level - mutation - is going on continuously. This affects us in many ways, but we do not immediately feel the effects because most of us usually operate at the gross matter level while the critical elements of mutation appear at the subatomic level, guided by forces that lie in the hidden or spiritual domain. It may be possible to influence the outcome of the critical elements of mutation by following certain "mind over matter" procedures.

The Three Solitudes

The present makeup of a microcosm may be described as being composed of three invisible solitudes - layers, spaces or domains, namely the Physical-mental, the Emotional-astral and the

The Hybrid Model

Spiritual. Everything on the face of this earth is at their own stage of development with their unique mix of these three solitudes. In real life, there are sublayers within each one of these elements, but to keep the concepts at an uncomplicated level, let us concentrate on these three solitudes for now. A unique word exists in all languages to describe the operative verb at work at each level. These are "to experience" for realization at the spiritual level; "to feel" or "to emote" at the Emotional-astral level; "to think" at the Physical-mental level. Every form of microcosmic existence is intimately involved in these living-verbs in a unique mix at a given point along the continuum of their evolution taking place when the spirit has a physical shell, i.e. body for humans, embodying it. In their makeup, human beings on the whole, may fall in the range of, say, fifty to seventy per cent for the spiritual component, ten to twenty-five per cent for the Emotional-astral component and thirty to fifty per cent for the Physical-mental component of their being. A devout Christian monk may be at seventy-five, twenty and five per cent respective levels of makeup. Even inanimate objects like a piece of rock may be at one, two and ninety-seven (mostly physical) per cent respective levels. A tree for example, may be at thirty, thirty and forty per cent levels, respectively.

"What? A tree? Absurdly non-scientific." You might ask.

Yes, trees have volition. They have been known to send messages to the surrounding kin on impending danger, such as poisons, bugs, and fire. We all think, feel, and experience during our lives and thus provide the all-important dynamism to the life-force to strengthen or weaken the effect. The *shakti* or life-force is a flux, an invisible unfeelable field of influence pervading our being. We can bear upon it through some practices in a "non-cause-and-effect sense" for a beneficial effect.

There is another word in the human languages that describes the rare state of spontaneity; but it is not a verb because it defies a conscious effort on the part of the microcosm. It is intuition; one cannot "intuit" at will. It is nonscientific and not consciously doable. But it exists and operates in all microcosmic embodiments. It is related to the concept of cantilevers - another example of "non-cause-and-effect", touched upon in a preceding section.

The Latitude Syndrome

A small digression follows to highlight key differences. Following the logic of "cause and effect" as embraced by science, in broad terms every observed effect has to have a cause, which may be quantifiable by mathematical approximations. This works very well in areas covered by Physics involving big objects or things. As the size of the particle under study becomes smaller, approaching submicroscopic dimensions, quantum Physics observes behavior in them that on the surface seems impossible in scientific terms, but very clearly resembles the "non-cause-and-effect" phenomenon.

The endeavors of the disciplines of science have a very serious limitation. Under a set of given conditions, science is incapable of observing or studying anything in its natural form because it is not experiential in nature. Science always and under all circumstances, studies or observes "analogues" or "modelled replications" or "contrived simulations" of a random sample or a small part of the real thing. After measuring the samples, the outliers or values that are either too high or too low are cast out. But every set of samples has outliers. If outliers are invalid then some of the values in the middle are also invalid. But the middle values are included in the study without question because they don't make life difficult. In other studies science attempts to make measurements of the extent of the effect, using a range of suitable processes which change the very nature of the effect being measured. This works very well when the "real things" are big, because the proportion of change or aberration in the effect to the physical size is insignificant. When the size of the thing under study is reduced - as it happens in the case of small particle physics - a corollary of the first Cosmic law, fundamental to all objects, entities, things and ideas like "time" comes into play, namely, the manifest state of the object approaches its unmanifest or hidden state. When the two states or realities superpose each other, new conditions arise and the particles appear and disappear in spontaneous reactions. Something can exist and not exist at the same time! When an "effect" appears spontaneously, it is said to have occurred without a "cause". That is something scientists are not equipped to explore or investigate. Some lacking humility, they shake their heads and rub their hands and use expressions like "bizarre" and "weird". Einstein called it

The Hybrid Model

"*spooky action at a distance*" - an apt spiritual lingo! Progressively, the use of more sensitive experiments in the multi-billion dollar linear accelerators around the world lead them to the same scenario. Because of their training, they are so hung up on entities like "femtoseconds" and the "collapse of the wave function", that the truth of the moment escapes their curious minds. So probabilistic models are conjured up and new "universes" are set afloat to explain how the subparticles can exist in many states simultaneously. The subject is discussed further in the memory section. Let's return to the three solitudes.

Consciousness and spiritual intensity are esoteric concepts. Emotional intensity, physical pain and mental processes like thinking and absent-mindedness are commonplace even though we do not know how a thought originates in one's mind. In order to get the essence of these concepts across to you, I will attempt to illustrate some of my points by using analogies and terms of descriptions from the physical principles or Physics. Consider the three solitudes of the microcosm as bands with surfaces at which they sit adjacent to each other and touch each other like a layered cake, so to speak, forming an interface, where the synapse is the thin edge at which there are two "presences". Imagine that the Physical-mental layer is at the bottom, the Emotional-astral layer is in the middle and the Spiritual layer is at the top. You have five distinct entities, three in their relatively pure form and two in interactive form at the synapses.

Let me postulate that spiritual progress or gain is a unidirectional occurrence and has a permanent tenure in the being, persisting from birth to birth. By contrast, physical and mental gains are ephemeral and end with the demise of the body. Let me further postulate that the mind, in its relentless pursuit of limitless knowledge through everyday experiences, utilizes one of its three channels - intellectual thirst or emotional passion or spiritual devotion - engaging one living-verb at a time, to feed the essence of the experience to one, two, or all three solitudes. Essences arriving in the Physical-mental space will enhance or retard the mental capacity of the microcosm and they will also act on the Physical-mental and Emotional-astral synapse. As a result of this interplay, emotional consequences, if any, will percolate into the other side of the synapse and feelings of "love", "hate", "anger", "jealousy" etc will register and create an emotional intensity in the Emotional-astral solitude. In this way physical-mental experiences can have physical and emotional consequences for the person.

Essences coming directly into the Emotional-astral solitude will register as feelings appropriate to the event and they will create an emotional intensity which will act on the two synapses on either side of the solitude. A consequence with an enriching or maturing quality from a happening with a potential for spiritual gain arises out of an interplay of the emotional intensity acting on the Emotional-astral and Spiritual synapse. An intense feeling, such as joy, pain, or grief may create a "must" for the Spiritual layer on the other side of the synapse just like some seemingly superficial physical experiences create emotions like joy or sadness at the Physical-mental and Emotional-astral synapse. One can observe how in this three solitude arrangement, something happening in the Emotional-astral layer can "feed" the other layer at the synapse, in both directions, Physical-mental at the bottom and Spiritual at the top. This is how the three verbs of being - "thinking", "feeling" and "experiencing" - reinforce or hasten the pace of personal evolution. It is a feat of assertion. The intensity reaching the Spiritual layer at the top evolves the consciousness and becomes the raison d'être of "change" in the person. Remember that the person is repeating her actions and decisions under the umbrella of her "set of experiences" given by karma as mentioned in the earlier Karma section. This is the only basis of "behavioral change" in a human being. This is why it's so difficult for a human being to achieve this state.

Imagine the three layers as compartments in which all daily experiences of an individual microcosm - no matter how insignificant they may appear on the surface - are "treated" at the two synapses to sift out and then to pass on the "abiding effect" - the real consequential stuff. Inconsequential physical-mental happenings and events will disappear during the "treatment" whereas some events will dovetail with others and, depending on the level of intensity in the particular layer of the microcosm, their essence will feed the other compartments through a "flux osmosis"

The Hybrid Model

or Cantilever Effect. Many emotional-astral happenings will similarly vanish. But some of consequential "weight" will feed the other compartments through a "flux osmosis" at the two synapses. The driving force behind the "flux osmosis" is the strength or intensity associated with the personally unique and internalized meaning of the experience - earnest prayer, inspiration, pain, craving for infancy or artistic creativity - happening at one, two or all three levels at the same time. In this way, each act, event and experience may have some consequence for the person's consciousness. This is spiritual evolution and anybody can learn the procedures to guide it.

Since each microcosm is a singularly unique case trudging along its path at his own pace, seeking experiences whose "weight" or "essence" is ultimately assimilated by the consciousness pervading it, a set of standard rules to apply to each case cannot be devised. This is the basis of embedded individuality in each microcosm, including inhibitions and idiosyncrasies, and an absolute democratic fair game is in play at all times. Furthermore, in real life the three elements are not linearly connected like a layer cake in the earlier example. The "treated" events feed the other layers in complex ways. I have noted before that there are sublayers within each layer. This happens in a cumulative way over lives and can be "enriching" or "neutral" in the spiritual direction and "enriching" or "diminishing" in the other direction in its ultimate effect. The freedom to interpret occurrences and the active flux in the Physical-mental layer of the microcosm create an abundance of choices of personal decisions and actions available to a person, each, with a positive, negative or neutral outcome. To put it simply, even though a specific "set of experiences" has been given to the microcosm to "live-out" through an "organic episode", the freedom of action that goes with the Physical-mental solitude of the microcosm creates many opportunities for positive or neutral effects on the evolution of the individual consciousness. But it must evolve in its eternal craving to unite with the superflux. It is like a meandering river flowing through different terrains, rubbing past obstacles and barriers, correcting its course often, and, eventually emptying itself into the sea, forever losing its visible identity and becoming one with it. Over the years, the sages and wise *gurus* around the world in different faiths and in all periods of human history have discovered helpful techniques which increase the chance of a positive effect on the evolution of the personal consciousness. Many techniques work at the Physical-mental or form level, some work at the Emotional-astral or content level and a very small number work at the Spiritual or substance level. But the essence from the other two levels, if any, percolates upward towards the Spiritual solitude. Different forms of meditation and *yoga* employ the techniques in different ways. Some of the proven age-old concepts are evident in different forms of activity given to spiritual fulfilment. They are all geared toward either creating an intensity in the first place, or increasing its strength in the layer to influence the outcome in the right direction for the individual. The practice of altruism, praying in earnest, meditation, chanting hymns or *mantras*, humility and developing an intense feeling of *bhakti* or selfless joy or devotion are some examples of the well known techniques. The oriental cultures have attained astounding results with the practice of "martial arts" which first influence cantilevers in the Physical-mental space. *Rajya yoga* - a blend of *Hatha yoga* and *pranayam* exercises the cantilevers in the Physical-mental and the Emotional-astral solitudes. The Chinese sages have amassed a plethora of prescribed courses of practice. Over the years they have mastered and further refined the techniques for maximizing the effect in the right direction for the microcosm. A majority of the techniques operate in the Emotional-astral domain. The ultimate objective is to subliminally feed the flux to the Spiritual solitude of the microcosm to help it evolve along the path. For many people, this can only be done through the two lower layers. When practised sincerely and selflessly, in the long run, the right techniques speed up the normal growth thus reducing the number of "organic experiences" or life-cycles on earth required to achieve the final union of the *atma* with *Paramatma* leading to enlightenment and bliss. In the short run, some practitioners have come to develop amazing powers for the purposes of demonstration and guiding of others. Examples abound

The Hybrid Model

in all religious faiths of *avatars* or prophets like Jesus Christ, Mohammed, Krishna and *Guru* Nanak. Buckminster Fuller; Gandhi and Mother Theresa are examples from modern history. These powers can only be used for selfless purposes and at times can be so miraculous that common scientific rules of measurements are transcended beyond the two well known dimensions of time and space. As such the *savants* become the object of ridicule and disbelief at the hands of the scientific community. Even then the prophets, who operate at subliminal levels, will not use them for punishment and revenge, as it was in the cases of Jesus Christ and Gandhi, who died at the hands of violence, yet maintained a completely nonviolent and humble posture to the end. What a remarkable example set for mankind to remember and emulate for ever!

How is the "self" realized or recognized by the practitioners? You may ask. This is where the fourth word - the nonverb - "intuition" comes in to play a part. The subtle knowledge comes from within. The Sanskrit language has a word for it; it is *"Buddhi"* or enlightenment from within and is the root word in Lord Buddha's name.

How does one know that the second cosmic law is operating?

Microcosm's inexorable yearning to become one with Superconsciousness and thus attain liberation is reflected in the uncertainty felt by everyone when the question of the purpose and meaning of life comes up for discussion. In the course of his life a person may concentrate his efforts on achieving material gain or professional recognition, the love and respect of their fellowman and the financial independence that may go with the success. These are great ego-boosting accomplishments. When the early preoccupation and the temporary sense of euphoria - the Adrenaline fix - eventually subside, a sense of loneliness, a burnout feeling or a loss of perspective may pervade his being. Many turn to philanthropy and humanitarianism and devote their lives to helping the less fortunate and the handicapped to fill the emptiness. The void they feel is the chasm that separates them from the union with the macrocosm. At one time or another, everyone has felt the existence of the chasm in the form of an ambiguous feeling of "nonbelonging" when they are in a reflective mood.

Attainment of sublime tranquillity is coveted by the poor as well as the rich. The innate[1] longing to get in touch with one's inner reality and gain a measure of spiritual awareness is felt by everyone. These are all manifestations of this longing. It can be covered up for a long period of one's life through different pursuits that focus on the physical and ego gratification in the short term. One can ignore or coverup this inner need but it can never be eliminated because it is the principal characteristic of one's spiritual reality. To deny it is to deny one's innate spirituality. Lack of recognition of this fact can only serve to increase the number of rebirth cycles one must go through to evolve spiritually. But many people do spend their entire lives focused on the lower two domains of their being.

How does this apply to infants and children, who are presumably pure and uncorrupted? What prevents their microcosm from forming the union with the macrocosm? A purist might pose the question.

The moment of conception may lead to an entry point into the physical world for the would-be infant. More importantly, it can be viewed as a supreme event of immeasurable proportions. The symbiosis results in an instant metamorphosis into the three solitudes of the microcosm that I have described earlier. At birth, with some rare exceptions, an infant's consciousness prevails at

---

[1] AS THE EXISTENCE OF SEEDS IS INFERRED FROM THE SPROUTING OF VEGETATION IN THE RAINY SEASON, SO FROM THE TEARS FALLING FROM THE EYES AND HAIR STANDING ON END ON THE BODY OF A PERSON (DUE TO ECSTASY) AT THE MENTION OF THE PATH OF LIBERATION, IT IS INFERRED THAT THERE IS ROOTED IN HIM THE SEED OF PREVIOUSLY ACQUIRED DISTINCTIVE KNOWLEDGE WHICH LEADS TO LIBERATION . . . . VYASA'S COMMENTS ON THE SUTRAS, PATANJALI IV.25, PP 438
"NOTHING WHICH DID NOT EXIST CAN COME INTO BEING . . ." COMMENTARY IV.11, PP 405

The Hybrid Model

about twenty-five per cent in the Spiritual domain, about seventy per cent in the Emotional-astral domain and about five per cent in the Physical-mental domain. This dominance enables the baby to receive information about its immediate environment through "feels" which are interpreted by the parasympathetic nervous system. The biggest "frustration" it feels is the inability of those around him to understand the messages it is sending through feelings - his unspoken language. This frustration leads to the reflex of crying and lo and behold, it has discovered a way to communicate with those around him who don't know its true "language" of "feels". It is the parents and the siblings around a new infant who fail the language test for it takes them a few days to interpret and "read" what the baby is telling them. The infant has no verbalisation skills, but the wealth of "set of experiences" it brings and the rush of cantilevers reigning supreme in its solitudes, make it more than an equal of an adult because the medium of communication through "probes" is far more sophisticated than a communication system based on language skills alone. The newborn has a decided advantage because its solitudes are not yet cluttered with the demands of the Physical-mental domain. Who has not seen a baby skilfully prevail upon and exploit the parent who is more likely to give in? Don't forget the microcosm in the infant's body has a mission to live out its span of life - thinking, feeling and experiencing - to enable its Spiritual layer to attain its determined point along the course of its evolution. If only we could understand what the "natural" infant is trying to tell us, we could help speed it along the path of evolution because of the proportionately high concentration of cantilevers in the Emotional-astral space feeding the Spiritual layer. Instead, let me review with you the series of regressive steps we put the infant through.

    The need to sustain the physical body is paramount and all our logistics are in the form of material systems. Since no one around understands the "feels language", in due course, the baby looses touch with this unique capability and forgets the language. What replaces it are sounds and verbal skills, absorbed from the environment all around it. Names of things and set routines of doing "things" are slowly learnt. The inevitable linearity of the time line

The Latitude Syndrome

starts to take hold. Soon, it will be launched on a course of "education". Physical-mental growth spurts along and for a while it may even become the dominant flux of the three solitudes. The material world unfolds and its powerful symbolism runs away with it. Everything has a name; and there are set rules for everything represented by the name or the symbol, like a chair has four legs; two plus two makes four. If you think about it in absolute terms, what is the relevance of "two" and what does the name "chair" stand for and what is the true meaning of the numeral "4"? Aren't these prearranged symbols that have been given an agreed-upon meaning by age-old convention so that we can communicate with each other and physically survive? With rare exception, the masking process begins and the child's Emotional-astral reality is covered by layers of the learning events in the Physical-mental space. The spiritual reality becomes dormant. The relative proportions of the three domains change. Don't misunderstand me. I am merely describing the processes as they work at the present level of our civilization and not passing judgement on mankind. This is the best capability we have developed so far to enable the microcosm to realize the potential richness in his "set of experiences" through the vehicle of his body. And in terms of material abundance, the present society has an unchallenged record. We could not grasp and retain the sophisticated communication capability we came equipped with at birth. Perhaps, as evolution proceeds, microcosms will be able to develop the skills to reduce the level of masking in the Physical-mental context by balancing the emphases placed on each of our three solitudes. An increasing awareness of this fact is appearing in the minds of those who care about such things.

    The net result is that the seventy per cent level of the Emotional-astral reality of the infant is reduced as the Physical-mental reality unfolds during physical development. Depending on the mission of the microcosm, the appropriate mold descends on the microcosm before adulthood is attained and the organic journey, in the end, accomplishes its task of spurring the spiritual reality to enrichment. This is a necessary step, for without it, the evolution of the microcosm would not be possible at all.

The Hybrid Model

These esoteric topics can be received with a sense of feeling and probing by some or with the pointed keenness of intellect, weighing and cataloguing the abstractions in one's head, by others. A student with feelings may only half-understand some concepts but he will accept them in good faith. Whereas a student who is regarding the concepts purely in an intellectual light may find the ideas very difficult. In either case the abstractions deal with structures which are not easily understood, unless one has studied the subject at length and has developed a genuine interest in it. To the uninitiated, what I am describing may sound meaningless. But I will try to describe the concepts in terms as they relate to the human experience to highlight the essence of the key abstractions. The descriptions may give the mistaken impression of "cause and effect" of science. But since there are no obvious units of measure; how does one know that one is making any progress at all?

Spiritual progress is not measurable in a scientific sense, because it is extraintellectual. During growth, if you are at a plateau "A" of achievement, you cannot read about what it is going to be like at plateau "B" in any book; you cannot imagine what it will be like being at plateau "B", and you cannot feel your way to the higher plateau. It can only be attained through tiny experiential steps, one leading and unfolding into the next. For example, at this very moment let your mind focus on the present instant. As you are reading the material, the words may be registering in your mind in the "present". Moments from now, they were being understood as "immediate past". A little later yet, the meaning will be in "recent past". Tomorrow, in a few days, in a few weeks, in a few months, as the meaning will be further assimilated - at this stage, involuntarily - it will reside in the form of recallable knowledge. Over a period of years, seeds of judgement are founded in this storehouse of knowledge. If you put the results of mental, emotional, and spiritual activities cumulatively in this context over time, even though your memory cannot recall individual incidents from the past, the sum total is available to you as experiential knowledge which, during the course of your life, you will use to appraise situations as they arise in the future. This is happening at the Physical-mental level (fully aware) as well as Emotional-astral

The Latitude Syndrome

level (partly aware). The secret to rekindling the dormant spiritual cantilevers lies in reducing the intellectual ("tyranny of words") component in favor of the feeling component or "advancing" back to your natural ratios of infancy. Meditation has the ideal features to achieve this.

How do the yoga practices help a person?

Yoga practices are not the only methods available to us for spiritual growth. Among the many known techniques, yoga practices of meditation have been used by serious scholars for a long time, possibly over the past five thousand years. One begins in a simple way, by making one's body strong through *aasans* or postures. Extraintellectual exercises based on structured breathing and sound clusters help build a focus for the ever wandering mind. *Mantra Yoga* uses the principles of the sounds, embedded ideas and prayer to clear the mind of the unwanted thought processes. This all takes time and a strong sense of devotion is required of the *savant*. Perseverance and persistence are the key rules here. Then little miracles start to take place. One swami told me that on an average a human being spends about half of his mental energy in defending himself against real and perceived threats. The threats come from within in the shape of inhibitions and idiosyncrasies, and from without, as a result of the interaction of the three verbs of being in the competitive social milieu. As one makes progress toward self-recognition, the fears, doubts and inhibitions start to disappear. The new reserve of freed-up high-spirited energy has to be discreetly directed at other channels and pursuits. The psychology of this gain is so overpowering that a practitioner is frightened by the changes occurring in the mind and the new feeling about self and self-worth. This is the reason for having a good *guru*'s guidance along the way, especially at the advanced levels of one's work.

You may be totally captivated by the subject. At other times lingering doubt in your mind may give you an uneasy feeling which may or may not develop into a question. Many have shaken their heads in disbelief during my introductory classes. A clinical psychologist found the fascinating topic to hold immense potential, and he wanted to know the origin of the knowledge.

The Hybrid Model

As we know it today, the source of the traditional knowledge was in the form of ancient aphorisms passed on from the *rishis* or masters to pupils by word of mouth. It is believed by some scholars today that *rishi* Kapila was born with eclectic knowledge and a spirit of nonattachment to the world. He attained spiritual heights through his own efforts by meditating to attain *samadhi* and then he passed on the practical knowledge of *Yoga Sutras* - aphorisms and doctrines - to his disciples. In this regard, names of Manu, Vyasa and Patanjali are also mentioned in some literature. It is not possible to ascribe a date to their work, which may have been all verbal or partially scribbled down in rough sketches and diagrams. Some estimates place them well before Buddha, for he learnt by the practice of some of their techniques. Later *rishis* and scholars wrote them down in the Sanskrit language in expanded form in the scriptures called Vedas and Upanishads. These topics are described in verses and cover thousands of pages. Although it is believed that the knowledge was divinely inspired, the authorship and chronology based on the linguistic styles has not been determined. Through the ages, many theologians and *gurus* have studied relevant portions and translated them into practical guides for spiritual guidance. Learned academics in many universities have spent their entire lives in unravelling the meaning of many verses. The true meaning of the written words is not obvious. Serious students like Vyasa and Achaary meditated on the words in the verses and the meaning then came to them through intuition. They bore out the realized meaning by devising their own techniques which they practised and revised through trial and error. *Mantra Yoga* is based on this principle. For example, the *Gayatri mantra* - the most fundamental of all the *mantras* - on the surface, appears plain and modest in its arrangements of the words in its syllabic structure. But taken altogether it is powerful in its self-initiating and regenerative effect on the mind of the practitioner. One *guru* has described it as "benignly insidious", implying that gradually it establishes itself as a shrine or inner altar of total supplication in one's heart and as such it becomes capable of bestowing miraculous results upon the practitioner. When *mantras* are composed, the inner seed word or syllable with no specific literal meaning is born in the

The Latitude Syndrome

minds of advanced yogis when they enter deep *samadhi* or trance for long periods of time. After waking they dress the seeds in simple words to give them the appearance of a modest prayer or a single syllabic sound. They use the *mantras* to teach worthy *chelas* or disciples in the science of meditation. The *guru* teaches the *chela* a predetermined *mantra* and if the *chela* can subjectively realize its inner seed, the *guru* knows that he is on the right track. A new *mantra* is then given to the *chela* and the training program is carried forward. It is said that when a *chela* meditates on the *mantra* given to him by a *guru* and realizes the seed, the two may communicate with each other despite large physical distances separating them. In this way a *guru* always knows the level of attainment of his *chela* who can get the needed direction from the *guru*. The necessary condition for this to work is that the *chela* unquestionably surrender himself - an act of acquiescence - to the master and have inviolable faith in his teachings. It is not easy for an advanced *chela* to find a *guru*, because prominent *gurus* take a *chela*'s failure as their own and take it as an imperfection in their technique or the selection of the *mantra*. The *guru* wants to be absolutely certain of the burning desire in the *chela*'s heart and puts the latter through a rough entrance test. Swami Dev Anand, the founder of Aary Samaj, personally went through this stage of his development. At each instance the *guru* asked him why he considered himself worthy of his time. "What makes you think that I am capable of teaching you"? One *guru* asked modestly. The higher the level of attainment of the *guru*, the more difficult it is for a *chela* to win him as a teacher. It is said that in order to convince his future *guru*, Swami Dev Anand momentarily levitated for the first time in his life. He was inspired and enthusiastic enough to pull it off and he won the right to be taught by the master. Such was the ardor in his determination to learn. The *guru* could not turn him down.

Most of the verses attributed to the Vedas and Upanishads are *sutras* or definitions of principles and *mantras* which were developed by a number of *rishis*, the spiritually advanced meditator-masters. This is the reason for the immense amount of meditative study performed by the advanced scholars to perceive their inner meaning. In the first to second century AD, Patanjali, (different from the earlier Patanjali, it seems there were more than one) a great Hindu theologian made a major breakthrough. He personally realized and interpreted most of what is practised and understood to date. Somewhere along the passage of time when the spoken word also became the written word, monastery *rishis* or monks started to write them down in Sanskrit verses. It is proposed by a school of philosophy that a later yogin Achaary also conceived original principles and taught them to his disciples. Eventually six Vedic Philosophical systems were written down, *Yoga Sutra* being the oldest work. The *Sutra* encompasses but a small fraction of the knowledge embedded in the Vedas. The complete picture is not clear and the factious debate continues to this day.

To fully understand the basic concepts in this discourse it will probably take an initiated and well-read student with a few years of university-level instruction in philosophy, psychology and theology courses. Is there a simpler description which could be understood by a simple mind who did not know a word about Vedic spiritualism? Yes, there is:

A human being or microcosm is a "g(od)" who is born in the spiritual mold of the "G(od)" or macrocosm and has the potential to realize all the qualities and virtues inherent in "G". The limiting factors, barriers and obstacles are in the very nature of "g". A person starts out by being the "pure I-Sense" with supernormal powers at or before conception, when karma, the impartial great judge that it is, superposes the empirical foolish ego on the "pure I-Sense", the result of past deeds and misdeeds. The important thing to remember is that "g" also has the inborn capacity to undo this masking, if he wants to. Given the freedom of choice and action it is entirely up to the "g" to realize the "G".

Relationships

The happiness of any society is founded on the quality and integrity of relationships its members enjoy, may it be at home, at work or for serious romance. Lately the subject has been analysed from many angles and many functional models have been postulated. It is clear, perhaps more from a feminine perspective, that it is very difficult in these days, first, to develop a meaningful

The Latitude Syndrome

relationship and second, to nurture and maintain it at its fulfilling pace. The following brief comments and suggestions are germane to the specific area of interpersonal relationships where personal growth and harmony are the key objectives of the two partners.

First an overview:

The seeds of all relationships - personal, family and business - first spring into your spiritual space as offsprings of your philosophy of life or concept of spirituality. Please reread the sections, Darshan (page 30) and Darshan revisited (page 140) for background information.

For a relationship to become important and meaningful it has to transform itself into a workable model. It does this or the subject moves it into her emotional space where it is massaged by considerations appropriate to the situation. You start to develop nebulous feelings (reinforcing or rejecting) for the other person but still cannot express them into words. Now you move them into your mental space where a big debate follows in which physical appearance, emotional factors, charisma, charm and cultural-social factors play a part. A clearer picture starts to emerge and things can now be expressed by speech from the mental space. Interaction can now begin, and it usually does!

It is obvious that the success of this exercise depends on finding common ground in the three principal areas, namely, spiritual, emotional and mental (includes physical).

This is an oversimplification of a very complex picture. But it does cover the fundamental processes at work. People usually don't see things as black and white. Feelings can paint things in many shades of undefinable gray.

Three key elements to consider are:
- Relationship is founded in the spiritual space.
- Similar processes are going on in the other person's three spaces.
- The original "seed" in the spiritual space is a sublime element. It gets diluted when it moves into the emotional space and again, when it moves into the mental space. This is the nature of a human being!

The Hybrid Model

Basis of Artistic Creativity

One of the most fundamental functions of human existence is to express one's inner reality. "I have to find myself," they say. This function is as much a part of the living verbs as the microcosm's yearning to unite with the Superconsciousness in order to liberate itself from the cycle of rebirths and suffering. You recall my earlier descriptions of the three living verbs as they apply to the three solitudes or spaces comprising the microcosm, the Physical-mental, the Emotional-astral and the Spiritual. For ease of reference to solitudes, I will abbreviate the term "Physical-mental" to Mental and the term "Emotional-astral" to Emotional.

I invite you again to focus your attention on the synapse where the Emotional-Spiritual symbiosis takes place. Experiential events entering the Mental and the Emotional solitudes result in emotional consequences of some weight. The emotional consequences consist of two parts. One part is based on emotion mixed with the mental components or "attached" emotion. The other part is based on the fragment related to "pure" emotion or "unattached" emotion. As a result of the "pure" and the "impure" components of the emotional intensities acting on the synapse, fluxes are produced which flow upward and downward into the two spaces. The flux flowing to the spiritual space results in the microcosm's spiritual advancement. If a part of the spiritual component excited by the "pure" emotion present in the interaction, flows back across the synapse into the Emotional space from the Spiritual space, it awakens the Creativity Consciousness and may manifest itself as artistic creativity. All forms of intelligent life have a fundamental need to express themselves in their own way. There is an undeniably ever present urge to give expression to one's inner creative reality, because a fraction of the emotion present in an interaction, in spite of the constant exposure to mental influences in every day life, manages to escape them and retains its "pure" character. This phenomenon is personal. It is subtle and may not be realized by an individual unless he is finely tuned to his spirituality.

The drive behind this need stems from the Creativity Consciousness, which manifests itself at this synapse, and makes an incursion into the Emotional space seeking an expression. Art forms

The Latitude Syndrome

are mere tools for expressing the results of this phenomenon. The poet, the dancer, the painter, the sculptor have their fleeting flashes of creativity which they capture in their chosen medium. The word "inspiration" is commonly used to mark the onset of the creative impulse, which originates in the artist's spiritual space. They can create only when the creative phase is "inspired" by the Creativity Consciousness, and then it must flow back into the Emotional space to become tangible in order to find expression. They cannot express directly from the spiritual space. It is easy to see that creativity manifests itself at different levels in different microcosms. It is important to note that when great minds, artists, music composers, thinkers and true spiritualists create original works, they only express an aspect of their "inner being" through their medium. What is this "inner being"? You might ask. It is born of a Spiritual-Emotional - not Emotional-Spiritual - intimacy in which the artistic aspect suddenly descends into the Emotional space and craves immediate expression. The hallmark of the act of expression and the common denominator in the equation is "altruism" - a moment of self-negation because true artistic genius creates for "others". The artist "unloads" and posterity is the richer for it. The poet says, "I do not know whence it comes from, but comes forth it, in torrents, from within." Again, this phenomenon is extraintellectual because it is an expression resulting from "pure" emotion, conceived in the spiritual space. It cannot be willed or brought on through a consciously controlled stimulus or action by the individual. It is unpredictably spontaneous or altogether absent at a given moment.

Another concept to keep in mind at this time is that the genius is somehow "inspired" and perceives the spark of creativity at an intangible level, as an unfathomable "impulse". Interpretation and further expression of the intangible feeling into the tangible Mental space can be a frustrating experience for the creator. Therein lies the secret to a brilliantly glorious creation as opposed to a mediocre one. In fact, in most of us, involuntary flashes of creativity happen quite frequently but these flashes do not cross over into our Emotional solitude, for whatever reason, and they do not register as "inspiration". It is quite likely that this inability to consciously realize the crucial moment may separate the artist from the nonartist,

The Hybrid Model

brilliance from mediocrity. The involuntary germination of the original creative concept is strictly in the Spiritual space, and it can only be hoped that this capability can be influenced by the intensity of the emotional flux, which some lucky microcosms can muster in the right setting.

I will now describe another aspect of how the artistic expression may be fulfilled by giving an example. Examine a piece of rock or wood lying on the ground. It has the potential to assume many artistic shapes and forms. It can be said that all sorts of potential images are present in it all the time, waiting to be cut and chipped out of it. Same is true of a lump of pliable clay. Somehow the subliminal impression in the artist's Creativity Consciousness gets through to one latent image in the rock or clay and makes itself manifest. You might ask: "Does the rock or the lump of clay have a role to play in the selection of the image"? Very much so indeed! It is an extremely subtle point that has to be carefully realized. Think about the constraints imposed by the physical dimensions, color, texture and grain of the stone and clay. Now think about the spiritual-emotional constraints on what the image is supposed to evoke in the beholder. Similarly there are other artistic imperatives which are entangled with the artist's Creativity Consciousness in the most intimate way. Normally when an experiment or a test is made, (in our example, the subject is rock or a lump of clay) the experimenter (observer) thinks that he is in charge of the interaction. Little does he realize that the playing field is no longer level. The tables have been turned in the most subtle way. The subject is observing the observer! This is just one manifested interaction of Creativity Consciousness.

Some thought has to be given to the feeling present in the artist at the time of the formation and flow of the artistic expression. Specifically, what may be the role, if any, of sadness and tragedy in the creative process? It has been written in many accounts that the great geniuses produced works of exceptional beauty when they were in sad moods and feeling despondent. The most frequently cited story is of ustad or master Isa Afandi, the genius architect who was asked by the Mogul Emperor Shah Jahan to design a masterpiece to serve as a mausoleum for his beloved wife Mumtaz

The Latitude Syndrome

Mahal, who had passed away prematurely - after bearing him fourteen children! It has been recorded that Ustad Afandi presented many designs of the mausoleum to the Emperor, but failed to impress him. The Emperor wanted to leave behind for future generations to admire and behold for eternity, an unrivalled structure of high spiritual appeal, with an exceptionally high artistic beauty and worthy of his love for his beloved Mumtaz.

"Create me a wonder, O great master, go into a trance and communicate with your Maker and pour your soul into it," implored the Emperor.

After many more failures, Ustad Afandi became dejected at his inability to please the Emperor. He went into seclusion to reflect upon the commission at hand. The next proposal turned out to be a marked improvement over his earlier works, but still, it failed to satisfy the Emperor completely. Then an idea came into the Emperor's mind. Realizing that the Ustad was having a rough time, he got one of his ministers to spread the news among Afandi's friends that his *mehbooba* or fiancé had suddenly taken ill and died. When the news finally reached his place of work in seclusion, it cast a gloom over master Afandi's heart. He went into a period of deep mourning, during which, gradually, an image of Taj Mahal was carved out of sheer pain in his heart. In the end, Afandi was doubly rewarded for his work. First by the news that the Emperor was pleased with his design of the mausoleum and later when he returned home, by the revelation that his *mehbooba* was alive and well.

Not all masterpieces created throughout history have realized their conception in the womb of pain. It is true that a lot of them were conceived when the heart was filled with despair and anguish. Of all the emotions that a microcosm is capable of arousing, pain is the most effective agent to enable one to reach his inside. It mobilizes inner resources and strengthens the spirit. The reason for this is that suffering creates an intense emotional environment which can be induced to act on the Emotional-Spiritual synapse by the genius. It is particularly true of the great creators who can direct the inward focus of pain to bear on their Creativity

The Hybrid Model

Consciousness and on occasion, "inspire" themselves into creative action. But it is totally involuntary. We see a moderate application of this technique at the lower of the two synapses in cases where people face difficult situations in daily life to which an answer is not forth coming through a conscious mental effort, which is akin to increasing the intensity of the mental flux to bear on the Mental-Emotional synapse. When they turn their mental focus away from the predicament, in some cases a satisfactory answer may appear within a short period of time. Applied correctly the simple technique involves alternating between intensifying the flux for brief periods, followed by an appropriate kind of diversion. The phenomenon works at both synapses. Diversion enables a resolution of the interaction at the synapse. It provides a "hesitation" to the flux to assert itself at the synapse and eventually it may complete after many cycles of interruption.

Over the ages, numerous techniques have been devised by the great masters to intensify the flux and then break away from it. The subtlest and the least understood technique is one of alternating between despair and silly joviality. I will give you some examples of its application as we proceed further into the discussions of the subject. An important aspect of this phenomenon to note is that after using a medium such as despair or passionate excitement to intensify the flux at the synapse, it is not possible to easily disassociate from it at that stage. The diversion has to be a spontaneous turnabout into a seemingly neutral or coasting behavior involving frivolity and abandon.

Many techniques are available to achieve the shifting of gears and they can be learnt by the serious students. Toulouse Lautrec, Vincent Van Gogh and some of the great European music composers of the classical era provide shining examples of their methods, each refined to an idiosyncratic pinnacle to serve their purposes. When you study the details of their work habits in their biographies, the two phases of their efforts to glean the remotest vestige of creativity from the recesses of their Creativity Consciousness stand out in their uniqueness. Toulouse Lautrec, the great French painter used elements of personal suffering and pain to intensify the emotional flux and then used sexual indulgences

The Latitude Syndrome

with abandon as his diversion. Ecstasy is also a potent medium to intensify the flux, but its focus is outward and the result on the synapse is ineffective because it is short-lived. It is worth noting that when ecstatic joy is used by the artist to stoke the Creativity Consciousness, the most commonly used diversion is in the form of mild despair. This technique works well for poets.

Now, if you focus your attention on the microcosm, resourceful and ingenious though he may be in his ability to create, he is capable of carrying only one train of thought at a time in his mind. In his Mental solitude, in one attention span, one observes and understands the surrounding environment in a serial manner, like reading a book from one sentence to the other, following one word to the next, attempting to maintain a single strand of thought. Concentration is about rising above linkage by association, with some exceptions. At some stage or a series of ministages along the way, the mind pauses to form a partial "picture" of the bigger reality, which is also forming elsewhere, but let us not think of that for the moment. In the case of the book, the pause could be at the end of each page, each chapter or at the end of the whole book. It is the fundamental nature of human existence that we suspend one thought and begin another, for we consciously cannot carry two separate ideas in our minds at the same time. Try it as an experiment and you will discover how inadequate a microcosm really is, in this respect. But the reality around us is turning over in myriads of dimensions. Events are happening all around us simultaneously. Even after a very productive lifetime of training and study, a microcosm understands but a tiny fraction of the big picture, and that too only superficially, in an area of one's interest. What a misfit! It is in this arena, that artistic creativity - a servant of one's innate Creativity Consciousness and thus one's spirituality - in its myriads of art forms, plays the very important role of filling in the gaps between the partial "pictures" that we all form in everyday life when we pause and reflect. The serious artist, like a serious meditator, perceives the "grand picture" in its totality at the Emotional-Spiritual synapse in a spontaneous flash as an unfathomable impulse. He senses something is there, but perhaps a whisker away from his conscious reach. The true mettle of the genius shines in

The Hybrid Model

relation to the degree of creativity with which the "grand picture" is articulated through the chosen medium of the artist, back into the relevant context of the partial "pictures" to which the viewing or listening public can relate in terms of everyday life. Therein lies the success or the failure of the genius. Many an undiscovered genius perceived wondrous works of art which nobody did comprehend in their day and age. They were either ahead of their time or their medium of expression was inadequate for the mission in hand. The preferred medium of the artist plays an important part in the presentation of the finished work. Many derivatives of space and time and subjective assimilation come into play at viewing time.

    A painter uses colors, lines and contours on the flat surface of a canvass or cardboard and draws the whole painting and presents the completed picture to view as a whole. Although painted over a long period of time in linearly serial strokes, the viewer sees the whole canvass along its length and breadth as an integrated entity, and interprets it to fill the gaps between his partial "pictures" and may or may not see any meaning in it. The sculptor or the ceramist creates his vision of grandeur in stone, baked clay, metal or wood and presents it as a finished product which the viewer may take a little longer to walk around and interpret according to the gaps in his partial "pictures". The architect creates on a much grander scale but presents his design as a finished piece of work, set in the landscape very much like a precious jewel set in an ornament. The viewer may require a long time to view, interpret and assimilate the artistic aspects of his work.

    A poet presents subtleties of wit and aspects of meaning of things with a special coloration. Although the reader may read the poem one line at a time and read it many times over, the poem is presented to the reader as a finished piece of work - a whole. But it can never be assimilated as a whole. It has to be broken down into lines and words, that is, the poet invites the reader to take part in the recreation of the feeling inherent in his work at the time of conception. The author paints verbal and abstract pictures and weaves a story through many pages of the book which may take a long time to read and assimilate on the part of the reader. You will notice that, unlike the painter, the sculptor, the ceramist and the

The Latitude Syndrome

architect, the poet and the author present the aggregate pictures to the viewer in single threads of interconnected ideas, a quality with which the microcosm feels perfectly at home, in keeping with his inherent ability to carry one thought in his mind at one time.

There is another category of artists which enjoys an unrivalled position in the repertoire of the many art forms through which creativity is expressed. I am now referring to the members of an exalted club of rare geniuses, who were responsible for unparalleled feats of artistic creativity in the European Classical music development.

How does "flux-osmosis" act on the synapse?

It is postulated that a Cantilever Effect takes place at the boundaries of the synapses. Subtle-body spurs or probes strike out into the solitude and pull back with a "potential". This is how nonmaterial essences and influences pass from one solitude to the other or from space into a solitude.

How does the Creativity fragment come back into the Emotional space from the Spiritual space?

The cantilevers reaching out like corkscrews into the Spiritual solitude deliver the "essence" from the Emotional-Spiritual synapse. When the cantilevers retract, they may bring the Creativity "fragment" back into the synapse, from where it emerges in the Emotional space seeking expression through a medium of art form. The Creativity fragment cannot be expressed from the Spiritual space.

Memory

The puzzling subject of human memory along with the brain has been the object of study by modern science for many decades. Insofar as an understanding of the functioning of brain and the memory is concerned, it appears the reason for a delay in definitive progress may be the result of a lack of appropriate tools in the arsenal of the researcher. As the sophistication of high technology tools has increased over the years, the mysteries of these two subjects have been couched in the language of a high technology computer. So the currently fashionable assertion that the human brain has a memory system similar to a computer's, is

The Hybrid Model

tendentious, to say the least. Nothing could be farther from the truth. The computer memory is built on physical attributes while the human memory is strictly experiential. The best we have come to do is to fit the sketchy models of the brain and its memory system into the high technology operations jargon. I am not attempting to underestimate the grand progress made in the modelling and mapping of the brain structures by the application of computer simulation and scanning techniques and modern 3D graphics. Neither can the recent experiments on the oxygen uptake in the localized area of acute neurochemical reactions using designer isotopes and the Positron Emission Tomography scanning be taken lightly. These days hard research is so much more believable. But how can medicine justifiably afford to overlook the fact of "experience" in its study of human brain and its memory system?

I have read somewhere that we have a sense of "past", "present", and "future" because we have memory. I have also read somewhere that when a human being is conceived - read when the pure I-Sense is localized in the mother's womb - he has all the knowledge that can ever be known. All knowledge came into existence at the same moment the universe came into existence. Somehow, this vast knowledge bank is hushed into an "archival storage" as soon as the sense "I am the body" is layered over the empirical Ego, which itself gets layered over the pure I-Sense and the fetal homo sapien is launched. From this point on, human's learning becomes a simple exercise whereby the specific piece of learnt or discovered knowledge gets moved from the "archival storage" into his awareness for use and recall. If we cannot recall a piece of knowledge from our awareness, we usually refer to a record written in the past. Awareness manifested by linear thoughts can't hold or recall everything in it.

Then I also read in some old Buddhist literature that Lord Buddha did not have a formal education during his childhood. He got into the habit of thinking and contemplating. He became known for his "knowledge". He started meditating for longer periods of time and ordinary people were aghast at his explanations of day-to-day problems of life. He always came up with the right answer. He meditated for yet longer periods and his *gurus* were dumbfounded

The Latitude Syndrome

by his descriptions of complex phenomena, both physical and spiritual.

"Where did you learn this"?

"Nowhere, the knowledge came to me."

Soon Lord Buddha was on a lecture tour of the land. People discovered that his knowledge had moved up to a higher plane. It was no longer "knowledge" that he dispensed to them. His words became "words of wisdom". He enunciated first principles, aphorisms and seed-ideas touching on all aspects of their lives. When people thought of the first principles, aphorisms and seed-ideas, they realized that their knowledge and their belief systems started to change. Soon the quality of their lives improved as contentment came to them.

Buddha was so pleased with the results of his efforts that he decided to pursue the idea further. "Let me meditate some more". He said. He discovered that the more he meditated the more profound his wisdom became. Ultimately he became "enlightened". His *gurus* told him that he had managed to dissolve the empirical Ego and that all knowledge was within his awareness because he had regained his pure I-Sense. Wisdom came to him from within.

Many similar cases have been recorded throughout human history. Abraham, Mohammad, and Jesus Christ and many prophets in Chinese and Vedic civilizations knew this road quite well. How the potential of a new Dalai Lama is recognized in the solitudes of an unknown Tibetan child is based on this knowledge. Einstein learnt higher mathematics and quantum physics without the benefit of a formal college education in these two very rigorous subjects.

How is this possible?

I propound the broad outline of a plausible theory of human memory based on the principle of instantaneous communicability between two identical entities separated by large distances. The authenticity of the principle sits on the overwhelming evidence gathered by the recent wave of experiments in the field of quantum physics in the world's leading particle accelerators. The quantum physicists are not conducting these experiments to understand the why and wherefore of human memory. They have a different agenda, but they might have stumbled upon a momentous revelation

The Hybrid Model

in the annals of human history. They have not connected with its real significance.

First a few memory-joggers to set the stage.

Memory-joggers

Seed-ideas - set one

Mind is simply the capacity to know. Knowledge is the objective of the mind. Mind exerts its power through the three channels, namely, intellectual thirst, emotional passion and spiritual devotion. The fountainhead of experience can never be shut down. Because knowledge is everywhere, mind has to be everywhere. Like knowledge, mind has no beginning. Mind has no end. It *is*.

Seed-ideas - set two

In the universe, each object, each entity, each thing and each concept like "space" is passing from the "future" to the "present" to the "past" in subtle frames called *tanmatra*. Only the "present" state can be known to the senses, i.e. the "present" is manifest. The "future" and the "past" states are invisible, but they do exist. Anything that has come into being can not vanish entirely. That which has no previous experience of being cannot become viable.

Discussion

Memory of an incident is not directly contained or held in the brain; the awareness of the event is enacted at each recall because the brain is a dynamically interactive organ. For an internal memory system, a part of the brain would have to be static, which is contrary to its nature because the living brain never shuts down, not even during the deepest part of sleep. The awakening of the "memory" of a happening is preceded by a spontaneous connection between two identical entities sharing a common origin and properties, which, in physical sense, are distant from each other. Sometimes spurious connections come about for no reason. At one time or another, everyone has had dreamy recalls which they couldn't trace to a real event in life and they have been struck with its strangeness for days. This couldn't have happened if memory of an experienced event was stored locally in the brain with direct access to it. Possibilities exist to recall knowledge from any region of the space without actually sending a physical signal to it. When the same event is experienced twice, it doesn't get "memorized" twice by the person. The dynamic associating process registers the context twice; for this reason a monotonic event leads to boredom in a hurry if the context remains similar, although no two identical contexts can be exactly alike in a temporal sense.

Entity one
At the time of the "experiencing" of a happening by a person, one or more of the senses were involved in the sampling of the episode. The sensually-coded residuals and keys came into being, that is, they passed through the sequence of the "future" to "present" to "past" as the pertinent details of the incident were assimilated and the experience was "perceived" in the internal structures of the brain by the successive frames of patterns of pulses representing the experience. Soon after, the perception of the incident faded away as pulse patterns subsided in the neural pathways of the brain and newer events came into the awareness. The coded residuals and keys for the specific incident were "catalogued" by dynamic association within the structures of the neurons.

Entity two
Sharing common origin and qualities, the perception of the experience of the incident registered sensations, impressions, literal templates, images and fluctuations - evoked components of the experience of the incident - in the mind, which is outside the confines of the physical body. Mind does not occupy space and being external to the brain, it is all-pervasive in the universe.

Memory recollection
When we recall past incidents, we only zero-in on the coded residuals and keys which were catalogued in many different neurons by association, after the meaning and relevance of the original experience were assimilated in a personal context. The cellular parts

The Hybrid Model

of the neurons in the brain, where the coded residuals and keys were originally "catalogued" and their counterparts in the mind form paired sets of entangled entities that are in instantaneous communication with each other at all times. Association or context is dynamic and always alive in the "present" when pertinent. Memory is always in the "past" out there. The original components of the experience of the incident or its "memory" held by the mind are instantly transmitted or tunnelled to the same neural pathways in the brain for a replay of the original patterns representing the experience, which gets "restored" in the awareness because it has been passively reexperienced or relived by the brain. Even when not consciously recalling a specific event, neural pathways are always in a state of flux, enacting stray impressions from the outside mind which get filtered for relevance continuously by awareness.

At the demise of the body, and the ensuing destruction of the coded residuals and keys in the cranial cavity, the impressions in the mind linger on and become latent. During meditation, it is possible to intuitively recall the latent impressions from a previous life. The scriptures specifically mention this possibility.

Intuition

It is possible to access the all-pervading mind without the benefit of the coded residuals and keys. During *samadhi*, the yogin has a direct connection with all minds or supermind. He is capable of knowing anything by concentration. He is enlightened.

Now, let us go back to see what science is doing in this context.

Quantum Physics analogy
Entangled particles

When two subatomic particles or quanta of energy such as photons share an origin of common antecedents or parents, they become "entangled" particles. Entangled quanta continue to have an instantaneous connection with each other even when they are far apart from each other. Recent experiments conducted in the powerful linear accelerators in Geneva, Switzerland have proved the existence of this "weird" connection up to a distance of ten kilometers. In principle, the mates - they can exist and not exist at the same time - could be anywhere in the universe and the communication would be maintained. They continue to have a spontaneous "touch" with each other because independent movement made by one is replicated by the other. At all times, one mate "knew" what was happening to the other and it automatically replicated its course. Some newer experiments have suggested that it is possible to "entangle" or "correlate" bits of matter which do not share a common past.

Electron Tunnelling

When an impenetrable barrier is placed in the path of fast-moving subatomic particles, they get blocked. But some times, a few particles magically appear on the other side of the barrier. The weird part of this experiment is that as the thickness of the barrier is increased, so does the speed of the particles that appear on the other side. They make it to the other side faster than, if the barrier had not been there, even exceeding the speed of light! If the barrier thickness were to be increased to a large enough dimension, in principle, the speed of the particles could become infinite.

In quantum mechanics, the reality of wave-particle dualism is well-recognized. Both the "entangled particles" and the "tunnelling" effects are relatively new particle physics phenomena which are considered to be "unexplainable". Physicists say that for every particle of the physical world - the manifest reality - there exists a "shadow particle" - the unmanifest reality. The universe is full of visible matter. But it is also full of "dark or invisible matter". Heisenberg's uncertainty principle says that the very act of making a measurement of the "particle" changes its characteristics. In the case of "entangled particles" the act of measuring one particle, will cause both to collapse! Two messages coded with Quantum Cryptography keys based on the "entangled particles" principle behave in such a way that the reading of one message will destroy the other key or render it mute, a pilferproof coding system.

Some points to ponder
- What came first, mass or gravity?

- What is the source of gravity?
- Why doesn't gravity get used up? It is always there with its full force, a constant value. Who or what maintains it flawlessly? Does the mass of an object automatically convert to the gravitational force without affecting its physical integrity?
- What if the resultant of all the apparent movements of all the celestial bodies is zero? This means that in absolute terms everything is standing still and only the void of emptiness appears to be expanding taking the physical bodies with it.
- What happens when an electron in matter meets a positron in antimatter and they annihilate each other? Physics says that a burst of gamma ray of a fixed wavelength emanates from the annihilation process. So it's really not annihilated!
- Ordinarily, the lighter water molecule exists in a stable liquid form, whereas the heavier Carbon Dioxide molecule exists in a gaseous state. How did this anomaly come about?
- Did the water on Earth really come from outer space by a constant bombardment by icy comets, a phenomenon about which some scientific information has recently emerged?
- If the most abundant particles hitting the Earth are photons, is number two slot occupied by organisms like viruses and bacteria?
- What is the final goal of evolution?
- What forces or powers oversee the survival of the fittest?

Conclusion

Experientially derived and intuitively refined over the past thousands of years, traditional belief-systems relating to the duality of "manifest" and "unmanifest" states of matter are valid today. They can be studied, grasped, and personally experienced by anyone, regardless of the level of intellect, technical education, or

The Latitude Syndrome

the financial prosperity of the individual involved. Particle physics on the other hand, is a highly rigorous discipline available only to a handful of intellectual elite at a few universities around the world at prohibitively high costs which are borne by all members of the society. It is only fair to assume that unknowingly, the ultra-focussed scientific effort is furthering the cause of the traditional "experiential model". With the emerging dilemma of the recent quantum findings, many scientists in authority have observed that after reading the results of the experiments and studies in the scientific papers, one does not make one or the other interpretation, but rather that one derives a range of diverse meanings from them. Some scientists believe that quantum mechanics research will ultimately reveal the interconnectivity of everything, including the beginning of "intelligence" in the universe which, in my humble opinion, can only be couched in a spiritual language. The "experiential model" began with that assumption and its authors realized it again and again, personally and collectively, without the benefit of modern measuring instruments and at no cost to the society. I think this is a point of immense significance for the future of mankind.

Structured Breathing and Sound Constellations

These discussions and practicum are presented in the same form as they were taught by an Aary *guru* in a serene forest, thousands of years ago. The traditional techniques employ the seed-idea principle of introducing new concepts. The content, however, is proven knowledge tempered with more recent scientific findings.

Session one

Guru's initiation exhortation given to the *chelas* is very important.

Guruji greeted his *chelas* with bounteous cheers.

"I am glad to see that we are all here together ready to embark upon a journey in search of our inner selves. You are all very special pupils to me. All of us have had the opportunity to learn something of ourselves through personal contacts over the last few years. For some of you, specific personal experiences in your lives may have drawn you to this ancient body of rich knowledge. It is my privilege to be your *guru* and guide. I will cover the introductory phase over the next eight to ten sessions. Every session will begin with a fifteen-minute-long talk, followed by half-hour of meditation and *pranayam* practices. I encourage discussions, so feel free to stop me and ask questions at any time. These sessions will turn out to be the greatest personal revelations of ourselves to each one of us, including myself. You will learn and progress in personally unique ways because no two humans are alike, especially in the matter of personal growth.

Then *guruji* went on to describe some basics. He began.

"A true *chela* has an unquestioning faith in the *guru*. Not even the slightest aspersion on anyone's personal integrity must be cast by anyone. If a *chela* entertains a trace of doubt about the efficacy of the *guru's* technique or content, his learning ability will cease to function. The *guru*-chela interactions take place at many levels, some obvious but the majority take place at subtle levels involving complex psychological principles. A compatible fit is of the utmost importance. Above all, please be true to yourself."

"Today we will learn three essential elements; the underlying philosophy, the correct sitting *aasan* - posture - and the uttering of the *om* sound - the symbol of the underlying cosmic *Prana* all around us throughout the whole universe. One common theme binding all our work is based on the most fundamental of

The Latitude Syndrome

requirements, namely, *pranayam* or structured breathing. It will be present in all of our discourses and exercises. It is the foundation without which the temple we are planning to build will collapse. I urge you to pay special attention to it."

"You are all quite familiar with the ancient Vedic philosophy of incarnation and the cycle of rebirth of souls in physical forms. There are three extrasensory solitudes - spaces or domains - within each one of us, namely the Physical-mental, the Emotional-astral and the Spiritual. It is important to maintain a balance among these solitudes, as the associated capabilities with each one of them can bestow remarkable powers upon the practitioner. Later we will come to understand the unique nature of the potential qualities associated with each domain."

"Now for the first part, the *aasan*," and *guruji* demonstrated in three easy steps how to assume the correct posture. Within a few minutes all *chelas* were sitting in the *padmaasan* or lotus posture, with their legs neatly folded under the erect torsos and the backbones smartly stretched under their brain stems. The arms were bowed across the thighs, hands resting on the sides of the knees and the forefingers were folded under the thumbs as the three other fingers pointed forward with palms facing up.

"Now, close your eyelids with a velvet touch without causing strain in the forehead. The eyelids may flicker at first, but eventually, control of muscles will bring your eyes into a state of steady rest. Pull your tummies in and let your rib cage relax. Take a deep breath slowly, hold it for a few seconds and exhale as slowly as you can manage. Work on this *aasan* to hold your breath as long as you can and then exhale at the slowest rate possible for you. The assignment to work on has two parts. First, you have to be able to sit in the *aasan* without any discomfort for at least ten minutes. Second part requires you to lengthen the time of one inhalation-exhalation cycle to your maximum possible limit while exercising full control with your diaphragm. Let me describe the immediate objective of this exercise. Practise the *aasan* such that the audible airflow through the nostrils becomes barely audible. Breathing will get deeper as it will also become effortless. In the beginning, this form of breathing should be performed ten times after you have

Meditation

comfortably assumed the lotus *aasan* and settled into it. Within a few days you will start to notice the winding down effect of this form of breathing. Over time, you will begin to feel the viscosity of the air passing through your nostrils. When you have attained this stage, automatically, gentle grins of devotion will form on your lips and tranquillity will start to settle in your minds like a lingering veil of mist in a valley. Eventually you will begin to sense the *Prana shakti* or life-force component of the molecular flow of the air through the nasal passages. Keep your mind on the flow of the air as it rubs against the membranes of the nasal cavities at the base of the lower limbic brain and try to develop a positive feel for a subtle sensation. When the stage of the positive feel is attained by a disciple, the grin of devotion will automatically internalize and a state of deeper calm and relaxation will begin to germinate in his mind. Develop an image of the glorious orange-red of the rising sun disk at the horizon as you look straight ahead on the inside of the closed eyelids. Extraneous thought process will begin to diminish. If necessary, in the beginning , allow all thoughts to flow freely from your mind. The desired objective is to make your mind impregnable against stray thoughts without any effort on your part. This exercise is also described as reducing the modifications of the mind."

"I will now demonstrate the *pranayam aasan* and you can join in after watching me perform a couple of cycles."

Leading the group, *guruji* started the deep inhalation-exhalation cycles through his nostrils. The *chelas* joined in and the group was launched on their first *pranayam aasan*. After ten slow cycles, *guruji* opened his eyes to observe the group taking deep but faltering breaths. He corrected the *chelas*' postures, emphasizing the importance of the erect backbone and a slight lifting of the chin to ease tension in the neck muscles.

"Now for the all-important *om* uttering. At the end of the slow, long inhalation of the breath, blend the sound of the *om* with a long, drawn out "o" sound culminating in a continuous nasal "m" sound and exhale the breath at the same time. The vibration of the *om* sound should resonate in the nasal cavities. *Om* helps to stabilize the exhalation part of the cycle and adds the component responsible for the extrasensory effects by putting your supersensory vehicle in harmony with the natural vibration of the universe. The physical aspect of the vibration massages the lower limbic brain. After some practice, the *om* vibration and the *pranayam aasan* will start to relax the lungs and heart muscles. The heart rate and consumption of oxygen in the body will start to go down. A deeper sense of soothing and calming will begin to descend in the practitioner. You will attain the different stages at your personal rates of progress. There is no hard and fast timetable of the number of days required for these steps. Perseverance and dedication are the key operatives here. You will know when the changes start to occur. You cannot escape their effects."

"Two effects are defined for *pranayam*. First, it provides the necessary oxygen supply for the physical processes of the body - the manifest reality, that is, the world we encounter through our five senses. Second, the unmanifest effect is in the provision of the *Prana* which transcends the physical world. It is the latter that is responsible for setting the framework for more subtle effects to take place in the two other solitudes within our being, namely the Emotional-astral and the Spiritual. In fact, the manifest and unmanifest reality pairings are associated with all matter and phenomena. The manifest represents the physical aspect, while the unmanifest represents the other two solitudes in our being, the Emotional-astral and the Spiritual. A simple analogy might be the duality present in matter in its minute particles, the two states of energy and mass present in atoms. In the physical world, an entity by itself cannot exist without pairing with its exact opposite. If you grasp the physical phenomenon first, say, through a study of the laws of Physics, the knowledge can then be applied to the unmanifest or hidden aspect to understand the concept of duality. The example I am quoting is strictly as an aid in grasping the concept. The language and laws of the physical world, per se, do not apply to the unmanifest phenomena. It is postulated that at any given time when any event or change, howsoever minute in size takes place, the potential for a like event with opposite effect is also created at the same time. Another analogy can be borrowed from the physical world, the concept of hot and cold. In reality only the element of heat can be manipulated by adding or removing energy. The absence of heat gives birth to the element of cold. Cold, per se, cannot be created in the same way as heat can be. Cold *is*. Similarly, the absence of light creates darkness. Darkness by itself, per se, cannot be created in the manner of light. The effects of the manifest reality can be observed through the physical senses and the intellectually derived cause and effect relationships can be based on them. But the effects of the unmanifest or hidden reality are subtle and difficult to perceive without a period of rigorous study and training you are undertaking right now. This is all I have to cover for today. Do practise the *aasan* and breathing with *om* chanting everyday. I will expect you all back next week at the same time."

At this point the *chelas* get up and walk about, stretching their legs. They are pleased with what they have learnt on the first day. They walk about exchanging notes, admiring the ease with which *guruji* has introduced them to a difficult subject.

Session two

"Today, I will talk further about *pranayam* and introduce you to a technique which will usher you into a reduced rate of breathing. Let us, for a moment, think about the relative position of breathing as a provider of life-sustaining energy. A microcosm can survive without food for a few weeks, without water for a few days and without air for a few minutes. The sensitivity of the body to the need for breathing is very high. This fact makes breathing a key component in the sustenance of life, in that, the minutest change in the breathing technique can have a far-reaching effect on its outcome on one's state of wellbeing. *Pranayam* recognizes this sensitivity and provides an effective way to use this to an advantage. Remember that *pranayam* has two aspects, namely, the sensory and the extrasensory. Today we will concentrate on the extrasensory aspect. Let us now resume our *aasans*, close our eyes ever so lightly and breathe deeply and effortlessly as we utter the *om* syllable during exhalation of the breath for ten cycles."

A chorus of *om* sounds filled the open space all around. *Guruji* was in his fourth cycle of breathing when the others had

The Latitude Syndrome

finished ten. He opened his eyes and surveyed his pupils, smiling graciously.

"I will now teach you to inhale through one nostril and exhale through the other. Please make sure that your nasal passages are unobstructed. Hold your right hand in front of your nose with the palm towards the face. Develop a feel for the little finger pressing down on the left nostril and the thumb on the right nostril, closing the nostril in alternating manner, one at a time. Now, press the little finger and close the left nostril. Inhale through the right nostril as slowly and deeply as you can manage; hold the breath and press the thumb to close the right nostril and exhale completely through the left nostril. For the next cycle, inhale through the open left nostril, hold the breath, close the left nostril with the little finger and exhale through the right nostril. Remember, you can start with either nostril. Once having started, inhale through the nostril through which you have just exhaled and continue with the cycles, stretching the time as much as you possibly can, alternating between the nostrils. Again, the objective of the exercise is to prolong the duration of the cycle by breathing smoothly and effortlessly. As you develop this technique, your sensitivity to the molecular flow of air through the passages will further increase. With an enhanced sensitivity to the physical aspect, the extraphysical aspect of *pranayam* as the provider of *Prana shakti* to the microcosm will also be realized. This technique will enable you to induce a deeper sense of peace and calm in your mind. Your heart rate will subside and the need for oxygen in your metabolism will be further reduced. With careful practice over time, the reduction in the consumption of oxygen will enable you to prolong the inhalation-exhalation cycle without feeling discomfort. Eventually, each one of you will find your own level of balance. For the time being, concentrate the focus of your mind on the airflow through your nostril. Your mind will begin to empty of all extraneous thought processes. Goodwill and warmth will start to fill your being. When this happens, you will have taken the first, tiny step in the direction of de-emphasizing the physical aspect of breathing. Let us now practise this technique for a few cycles."

When the session ended, a *chela* asked why the eyes had to be closed during the practice of *pranayam*. *Guruji* replied:

"It serves two purposes. First, the sensory input of images through the eyes causes a lot of activity in the mind which is eliminated by closing the eyes, thus initiating the calming effect. Second, the ever-so-gentle contact of the eyelids on the eyeball acts as a catalyst for the relaxation to commence in the forehead. *pranayam* takes hold of this seed and helps in the propagation of the effect towards the rear brain. The rest is physiology taking its course. Try an experiment during practice at home by yourself. Shut your eyes tightly at the beginning of the session and see how long you can stand the strain of breathing."

Another *chela* wanted to know the physiology of inhaling through one nostril and exhaling through the other. *Guruji* explained:

"It helps to slow down the flow of air across membranes in the nasal cavities at the base of the lower limbic brain. The Vedic scriptures postulate that a precursor to a tiny electrical potential is created in the lower neural pathways by the air rubbing against the surfaces of the membranes. These minute potentials are transmitted through the *nadis* or subtle nerves of the astral body along the neural highway on the backbone. These potentials are contra rotating in character and breathing through the two nostrils - normal breathing - has a neutralizing effect. Breathing through an alternate nostril at a time achieves a resolution of these potentials into two separate channels. This differentiation of the potentials into two channels has implications in the awakening of the *Kundalini agni* or fire at the base of the spine. This flowing *shakti* is the vehicle of advanced techniques used by meditators to stimulate their *chakras* or glandular control centers or plexuses in their bodies. Suffice it to note at this stage of our work that *pranayam* lays the groundwork for inner growth to be realized by those who are in it for the long haul. It prepares the body and the mind to receive the *shakti*, if they are lucky enough to progress to the stage and have it awakened and flowing through their body."

Thus ended the second lesson. *Guruji* summarized two day's work into one practice session, consisting of three parts.

The Latitude Syndrome

Assuming the erect but relaxed *padmaasan*: one minute; taking five long, deep breaths through two nostrils: two to three minutes; taking ten long, deep breaths with *om* chants: seven to eight minutes and finally taking ten long, deep breaths through alternating nostrils: five to seven minutes.

"At the end of the practice, do spend a minute or two in developing a feel for the changes occurring in your mental processes and your feelings about yourself during each session. It will take a few sessions for the routine to smoothen out. Take your time in following the order of the exercises and I will see you next week at the same time." He reminded them.

Session three

"Today I will talk further about the concepts of manifest and hidden realities. Their relationship to each other can be likened to the relationship of the elements of hot and cold to each other. They coexist in the human body as two opposing qualities, except that emphasizing one is always at the expense of the other. Reduce one and the other automatically increases and the vice versa effect can also be easily appreciated. Right from the time of our births, we humans preoccupy ourselves with the physical - manifest reality - phenomena as it is the basis of our survival in body form and also because it is easily assimilated through our senses. Education of our children has a high content of the physical phenomena in it. As layers upon layers (some call them walls) of knowledge relating to the physical world are piled upon each other, the unmanifest reality gets buried deep inside and by definition, its emphasis is diminished. We are enamored of the immediate gratification quality of the material gains and the society in general admires such "successes" and rewards the achievers by heaping praise and special status on them. Based on this observation our ancient *gurus* have talked about de-emphasizing our focus on the sensory aspect of life. Imagine the effect of this seemingly simple exercise on the unmanifest reality of the practitioner. Just like increasing or decreasing the element of heat can de-emphasize (reduce) or emphasize (increase) cold, manipulating the physical emphasis one

Meditation

way or the other carries a reward or a penalty of a very consequential effect on the supersensory aspect of the individual."

"By de-emphasizing excessive focus on material gain the immediate psychological consequence is that the mind has less of the material possessions to "worry about" and less of an effort to "maintain" them and the inherent "fear of loss" is reduced. As the mind becomes "uncluttered", the disciple starts to feel a creeping sense of freedom. A soothing mental lightness appears in the mind. At this stage, the mind can be taught to concentrate on an idea entity. It can be taught to "meditate" and thereby unlock its immense hidden resources made up of the summation of the evolutionary cycles of birth and rebirth it has gone through. It can be channelled to transcend the imprint or confines of the physical barriers wherein, contrary to his true nature, it languished during its preoccupation with the manifest reality."

"Many forms of yoga have been developed to show us the different paths to the realization of the pure I-Sense resident in us. We will be following the path of *pranayam* and *mantras*; *pranayam* to tune our body and mind for the journey, and *mantras* to fathom our inner selves. Let us now assume our *padmaasan* and commence our exercises."

After about twenty minutes, when *guruji* opened his eyes he was greeted by the happy faces with bright eyes and expressions of beaming smiles on their lips.

"It is time now to introduce you to the *Gayatri mantra*, the cardinal *mantra* of all meditators, for without *Gayatri*, all other efforts are rendered powerless. So, repeat after me:

'*Om Bhoor Bhawa Swaha, Tut Savitur Varenium, Bhurgo Devasya Dhiemahi, Dhio Yonam Prachodayat*'."

Guruji led the group through the *Gayatri mantra*, taking a few syllables at a time as the pronunciation of the compounded Sanskrit expressions is difficult for beginners. Not only do the expressions have to be correctly pronounced and memorized, a certain pleading tone and rhythm have to be cultivated in the voice of the practitioner for maximum effect. The *Gayatri* was learnt and practised for many minutes after which *guruji* handed the *chelas* paper copies of the phonetically arranged *mantra*, to take with them

The Latitude Syndrome

to practise and to commit to memory. The *chelas* expressed their boundless gratitude to *guruji*.

Session four
"Today, I will talk about the role and effectiveness of sound in the *Mantra Yoga* practice. The underlying element in a *mantra* is resonance and through the sounds it utilizes the hidden *shakti* inherent in the subtle vibrations. It is known at the present time that vibration and wave propagation is the most fundamental process of the many forms of matter and energy in the universe. Light, heat, radiation and even the workings of tiny electrons follow well understood laws of Physics which are based on vibrations of different lengths and heights. A *mantra* may be merely a sound, or it may be a combination of sounds expressed by the words which may or may not have any meaning, or it may be a string of meaningful words with the power of prayer attached to it. It may also have a latent seed-idea embedded in it. Regardless of the structure of the *mantra*, three powerful qualities permeate its purpose: it has sound, it has an idea entity embedded in it, and it has a specific objective associated with it which is realizable by the mind. It takes a long practice to progress through the three stages of the realization of a *mantra*."

"In practice, one starts by speaking the *mantra* audibly to memorize the words and the sounds. A tone and associated rhythm are cultivated to blend with the element of prayer inherent in it. In the beginning the practitioner is lulled into a silent repetitive chant of the *mantra*. With sincere and unfailing practice, an internalized mental-chant stage is attained which acts on the mind in a predetermined way. Mentally, in the first stage, one is aware of the sounds and the meaning of words comprising the *mantra*. In the second stage, the embedded idea takes precedence and the practitioner meditates on it while the sounds and words recede into the background. This stage develops to the point where the practitioner is not aware of the words and sounds even though an internal recitation is going on. In the final stage, the idea itself submerges as the reality of the objective inherent in the *mantra* starts to unfold in the consciousness of the yogin. One begins to

Meditation

meditate on the unfolding reality within, which transcends the boundaries of the mental processes."

"Ancient Vedic scriptures are full of *mantras*, of which the meaning and purpose of only a few hundreds have been fully understood to this day. Most of the verses are narrative but appear to be disjointed, as such they are subject to reflective thought and interpretation. In addition, the richness of the language adds many combinations of diverse meaning to the compounded phraseology of the Sanskrit language, which have to be sorted out after a careful study and research effort. A psychology of secrecy, whether put there by the authors by design or unwittingly, surrounds some key elements. A limited amount of meaning is expressed in parables to arouse the interest of the new disciple, but many key relationships are only hinted at, perhaps, to challenge the seriousness of the intent of even an advanced student. Many Yogis have managed to master the art and the science of composing *mantras,* entirely through their own enlightenment, for which they go into *samadhi* - a state of one-pointedness in which the pure I-Sense prevails free of the empirical Ego - and all fluctuations of the mind have ceased. It is said that some highly advanced Yogis communicate with their disciples through *mantras* which they have specifically composed for this purpose.

"*Om* is the all-powerful pure *mantra* which bestows its *shakti* or energy inherent in the sonority of the mystic syllable. It is pregnant with the idea of the all-pervading Superconsciousness throughout the universe. By chanting *om* we prepare ourselves for the spiritual aspiration. It eases a passage through the gateway from the sensory to the supersensory self. Its main purpose is to help us empty our worldly mind and fill it with absolute tranquillity in anticipation of the union of the microcosm with the macrocosm (consciousness with Superconsciousness), the ultimate reality attainable through *mukti* or liberation. Hundreds of verses have been written in the *Upanishad* scriptures, extolling the virtues of *om*. One metaphor describes *om* as the *beej* or seed without which further flowering of the consciousness of the microcosm is not possible. Another hints at a probable technique by suggesting that the target first has to be placed in the heart, which then can be attained by releasing the arrow of self or ego over the bow of the *om* syllable. With the recitation of *om* at the beginning, one prevents the silent chant of the *mantra* from degenerating into a meaningless monotony; this is one of the reasons why the *Gayatri mantra*, or any *mantra* for that matter, always begins with the *om* syllable. Many virtues have been ascribed to the mystic syllable and they are all attainable through a reverent chant. Initiation into the esoteric *Mantra Yoga* is not possible without first understanding the significance of *om*.

"And now, let us assume our *padmaasan* and practise *om* with the breathing exercises."

For the next half hour the group filled the air with deep, long, melodious humming of the *om* sound. Later the *Gayatri mantra* was recited aloud, again and again, with *guruji* interjecting the pleading tone and the rhythm at the appropriate syllables to reinforce devotion. The disciples noted the inflections in the sounds and made the necessary adjustments in their recitations. They still had some way to go to polish up on the correct pronunciation of the difficult Sanskrit words. After a while, a contemplating *guruji* lifted his hands and massaged his face from the eyebrows down in one stroke, smiling in the process. He took a deep breath and nodded his head a few times and approvingly said:

"I am very pleased with the progress you are making. Remember, the key to success lies in your acquiring an ability to practice without strain and at your own pace, howsoever slow it may seem at first. At the next session, I will talk about the munificent *Gayatri mantra*, the cardinal *mantra* of the school of *Mantra Yoga* and its boundless power and effect on the faithful disciple."

Session five

"The *Gayatri mantra*, also known as the *Guru mantra* or the *mahamantra* (the grand *mantra*) has been the subject of study for thousands of years by serious *savants*. It has been translated by many wise men to show a variety of descriptions of its effectiveness and significance. Since the *mantra* was conceived by some ancient master(s) during a state of deep *samadhi*, its true and complete meaning was known only to the original yogin. It is simultaneously

Meditation

a pure *mantra* and a compound *mantra* consisting of the essential elements of sound, meaningful words (idea) and a beseeching prayer. Over time, different practitioners have seen diverse meaning and significance in its purpose, but they all have concurred in their summation of its effectiveness. It has been claimed that the *Gayatri* never fails the disciple. If it has not worked, then the *chela* has failed either in his or her resolve or in the technique of practice. Such is the sentiment of invincibility of faith in the *Gayatri*! So approach it with the same sense of veneration you have reserved for your deepest aspirations." As *guruji* pronounced these words, his voice broke down. His eyes became red and moist as he was overwhelmed by something stirring within his body. He felt a sudden jump in his heartbeat and he felt a whirring sensation at the base of his spine. He folded his hands in front of his chest and with his head bowed, started to recite " *Jai, Gayatri mata*; *Jai Prana mata*" (hail, mother of *Gayatri*; hail, mother of *Prana*) in whispers. He recited the hails as he struggled to regain his composure. *Guruji* closed his eyes and quietly relaxed in the *pranayam aasan* while at first, a blush raced through his cheeks, which was noticed by the disciples. Soon after, his normal skin color and poise returned and a glowing aura of serenity settled about his face. For untold number of minutes he sat meditating as his *chelas* watched him with unsubdued awe at first, which turned into a rampant fascination. His face broke into a blissful gentle smile. Then his eyelids flickered and the eyeballs rolled upward towards his forehead. A sliver of the white of the eye appeared in the parting eyelashes. He stayed in this posture for a long time. The *chelas* themselves fell into their *aasans* and commenced the recitation of *the Gayatri* in silent whispers. When they were finished, they realized that *guruji* had gone into a deep meditation for he was still in the same unmoved posture, with a crescent of the white of his eyes showing through the eyelashes. Very quietly they got up and in hushed tones they recited, " *Jai, Gayatri mata; jai, Prana mata*" just as *guruji* had done several minutes ago. Somehow they knew that a miracle was taking place right in front of their eyes, even though they did not understand the first thing about it. Gathering their belongings, they prepared to depart. From the descending road, they looked back for the last time

The Latitude Syndrome

and saw *guruji*'s body sitting in the same posture. A *chela* broke the silence.

"While he spoke he garnered so much yearning and devotion for the *Gayatri mata* that it induced the Divine Spark to burst into a roaring flame through the divine grace. I have read in a book that a ripple effect from a burst of energy can be aroused at the base of spine in disciples who are at an advanced stage of self-realization and who are in good health and genuinely meditate for self-realization."

Nobody said another word. Quietly, they slid down the slope in a single file.

Session six

The following week when the *chelas* arrived for their lesson, it did not take them more than a minute to realize that *guruji* was an entirely new person to behold and be with. A luminous radiance adorned his face and an aura of joy encircled his being. He sat down on his prayer carpet, cross-legged, in the familiar *aasan*, but the stiffness and the rigidity in his body of the earlier days was gone. His body appeared supple and more at ease and a plausible hint of an unusual *shakti* flowing through him was apparent. The previous determined facial expression and the incisive deliberate look in his eyes had given way to a kinder, softer, and almost ecstatic expression exuding magnanimity and grace. He began:

" Friends, fellow travellers, I apologise to you for my sudden preoccupation of the other day. I was called away by the mystical, sovereign power I have been longing to serve for the last ten years. *Gayatri mata*, in Her inimitable kindness saw fit to reward my humble efforts at last. I have been touched by the first rousing of the *Kundalini fire* in my body. It was through the grace of the *Gayatri mata* that Cosmic Prana, the subtle life-force sustaining Superconsciousness in the whole universe, awakened the *Kundalini shakti* in my being. I will, in due course of time, cover the topic in greater detail as it reveals its mysteries to me. For now, let me begin where I had left off in the last session."

Guruji reflected for a while, searching within.

Meditation

"Yes, I recall that I was singing the songs of glory of the *Gayatri mantra*. The masters composed it in three parts, each part setting the stage for certain, subtle psychological forces to come into play, without which the succeeding parts will not be effective. In the first part, *"Om Bhur Bhuva Swaha"*, the seed-sounds representing the three solitudes of the microcosm - Physical-mental, Emotional-astral and Spiritual - are invoked to harmonize the physical vehicles of the *savant*. The essence of the three seeds is represented in *om*. The middle part of the *mantra* stimulates the disciple's mind to a high pitch of assertion of will, in preparation for the realization of yoga or union between his consciousness and the Superconsciousness. The end part expresses obeisant self-surrender and an advocacy for mercy at the hands of *Prana shakti* which is aroused. The literal meaning of the syllables of the middle part is, "we meditate upon the effulgent Light of Divine Consciousness who unfolds our Buddhis (intuition)." To emphasize selflessness, the pronoun "I" is not used in the *mantra*, all verbs ending with the plural form. Egoism is brought to the surface through an assertion of the collective will and then neutralized through self-surrender, thus wiping out, in stages, the last vestiges of false pride in the disciple. In this way, *Gayatri mantra* prepares the practitioner for the ultimate union. The pleading tone and the rhythm have to be cultivated and internalized with the *mantra* through the same three stages, namely, uttering softly, repeating silently and concentrating mentally. The prayer part built into the *Gayatri* initiates the emotional earnestness which can be progressively developed by the *chela* at his or her own pace. The deeper the faith and the conviction with which the practitioner applies himself or herself, quicker will be the beginning of the transformation of their mental focus. So now, let us all recognize an immediate objective to work for." *Guruji* nodded his head, seeking acknowledgement from his *chelas* and continued, " let us now resolutely, resume our *aasans* and practise *pranayam* with the recitation of *om*, followed by the chant of the *Gayatri mantra*. It may be an opportune time to bring a little emotion in our chants today."

The *chelas* flexed their bodies and relaxed their legs and back muscles before settling into familiar postures. With closed eyes, for the next twenty minutes they breathed, recited the *om* syllable and fell into a melodic chant of the *Gayatri*. Gradually, their audible voices mellowed into inaudible whispers and later into the silent repetitive chants. The direction of the relaxation was set and unwittingly everybody dropped their shoulders and their hands came together in their laps. *Guruji* opened his eyes and observed that on the meditating faces of his *chelas*, their upper eyelids were uniformly stretched, revealing contours of the still eyeballs underneath. The eyebrows and foreheads were relaxed. The disciples are getting into the rhythm, he thought to himself happily. Later, when everyone opened their eyes, it was discussion time.

A question appeared from a *chela*, "what is *prana*?"

Guruji thought for a moment and began:

"Cosmic *Prana* is the immaterial, subtle, vital force which sustains Superconsciousness in the whole universe. It permeates every atom in the universe, giving it the physical force for the machinations of its parts, such as electrons and the nucleus. It permeates every cell in the organic world as well, giving it vitality and making it a complete life, capable of producing complex chemical compounds and self-replication. Because it is immeasurably subtle, *Prana shakti* is said to be the invisible part of breathing while oxygen is thought as the manifest part. With every breath we take in, along with the gases, we inhale *prana* and that is the basis of the technique of *pranayam*. Unfelt and unknown to us, *prana* flows through the body and bestows vitality upon each and every cell in our body, which makes them alive. In higher states of *samadhi*, advanced yogins can perceive *prana* consciously, alter its flow through their organs and modify their vital functions, such as pulse rate, blood pressure and temperature. Over the years, common adage has come to equate breath with *prana*. Actually it is *Prana shakti* or sometimes expressed only as *shakti*, which is responsible for all activity in the universe. Even modern science considers a type of energy to be the basic substance behind all physical phenomena. It is well known that the universe has manifested itself from the interaction between two constituents - *prana* and *akash*. The word *pranayam* is made up of *prana* and *yam* - *yam* meaning exercising or controlling. Whereas *Hatha yoga* begins by influencing the cantilevers in the Physical-mental solitude, *pranayam* works directly on them in the Emotional-astral solitude and produces quicker results."

At this point a chela's eyes lit up like two lamps in the dark. "Pardon me for interrupting, *guruji*. A certain basic understanding has just dawned in my mind and I cannot contain myself. For years, I have been playing music and wondering about the effect of the musical notes on my mood. My music teacher has been telling me about the different vibrations created by the different wires of the musical instruments when the hairs of the bows rub them. He is referring to the mechanical vibrations of wires. Today I can understand how this wave action landing upon my ears can be perceived as tonal sensations through the agency of the *prana*. Am I correct in my assumption?"

"Yes," said a smiling *guruji*. "The deepest mystery confronting us today is about the role played by the individual consciousness, which we know to be the result of the *Prana shakti* vitalizing every cell making up the body. Through his own consciousness, physical things like vibrations and electron agitation are felt as sensations or emotions by the microcosm. The physical body with all of its sensory apparatuses in good working order is an absolute imperative, for, without it there would no personification of the individual consciousness. Is there a physical or subtle connection between consciousness and body? If the answer is yes - and it has to be an unequivocal yes for the two work in close harmony with each other - where in the physical body of the microcosm is the bridge connecting the physical to the superphysical, the sensory to the extrasensory? Is it the physical brain itself or is there some other mediating praxis within the physical body? Is it outside the physical body? This question had been the subject of study by our ancient spiritual masters through the ages. Their laboratories were their own brains, minds, and bodies. Through introspective study and rigorous practice they uncovered the three instruments - contemplation, meditation, and concentration. A theoretical model of human evolution was written down. Based on personally achieved results, six practical models for human evolution were defined. They made other major discoveries.

The Latitude Syndrome

In the beginning, this body of knowledge was passed from *guru* to disciple by word of mouth and living example, as civilization had not yet discovered writing. Much later, some masters wrote down their mystical experiences using an all-encompassing philosophical-cum-religious way-of-life terminology, in the form of Sanskrit *mantras* and verses in four Vedas and six Upanishads; this body of literature comprises the ancient Vedic scriptures underlying Hinduism of today."

With these words, *guruji* ended the long session.

Session seven

Guruji started the session with a slightly different timetable. The *chelas* were to go through the practice part of the lesson first, followed by the discourse. The thirty-minute practice session had been ingeniously constructed by *guruji*. It had the basic elements of exercising *prana*, reciting *mantras* and setting in motion the requisite psychology for change. It was fairly easy to follow and did not involve strenuous work on the part of the practitioner. The parts of the routine subtly worked in setting the direction of the focus, ushering in the next stage until certain physiological modifications, e.g. less need for oxygen, took hold of the disciple. He continued:

" The contents of the practical part of the session will remain fixed for the time being. Please pay special attention to and concentrate on the individual parts and refine them to the level of a personal fine art, using emotion as the driving force behind your devotion and faith. Remember, *Gayatri* has never failed anyone!" He observed each *chela* throughout the session, as they went through their practical steps, making mental notes of where they might need further guidance. When they were finished with the practical part, he continued:

"Today I will begin with an explanation of the concept of '*mata*'. The word simply means, 'mother' or 'doctrine'. What is the significance of '*Gayatri mata*' and '*Prana mata*' and how the dynamics of the strongest of human relationships, one between a mother and her offspring, are used as a vehicle to enhance the psychological impact on the practitioner. In most cultures, the mother occupies a special place. More so in Hinduism. *Mata* is source. *Mata* is goddess. *Mata* connects with all physically, emotionally, and spiritually. *Mata* brings forth new life. *Mata* nourishes. A well-developed relationship, based on reverence and obedient love for *mata* makes the practitioner more receptive and sensitive to the prevalence of *prana*. Implicitly, it is a pregnant prayer that says, '*mata*, in you was my soul personified; you gave my physical body immunity to disease when I sucked milk from your breast. Pour forth *prana* and the glory of *Gayatri*, so that I may receive them'. By placing the self in a subservient position to the conceptual *mata*, the practitioner neutralizes residuals of hostility and eliminates aggression and false pride from the self. *Prana shakti* is considered feminine because the healing and the divination powers flow through the feminine channel of our feminine-masculine duality. This differentiation of the feminine principle has a positive effect as the craving of infancy is recreated in the disciple."

"The old wise masters developed elaborate methods to prepare the physical and mental vehicles of the disciple to experience expanding consciousness, if and when he attained those plateaus of progress along his path. Their descriptions were not precise, because, I think there are no precisely definable milestones along the way. Each case is so personal and different from the other that it easily repudiates any attempt at establishing a standardized vocabulary. An element of unpredictability of partial or full success for some, or any progress at all for others, is always present. For this reason an aura of veiled secrecy has surrounded the topic of transcendental meditation. But at a beginner's stage of elementary *pranayam* and developing a technique of concentration, the basic concepts work very well for most students. So let us be sincere and true to ourselves and put our hearts into our work," said *guruji* pleadingly.

Session eight

"Today, I will talk about the ever elusive bridge between the physical and the extraphysical in our body. It is called the *Kundalini agni*. The *shakti* exercises master control over all functions at all levels in the three solitudes of the microcosm. Normally it flows in

The Latitude Syndrome

imperceptible trickles in the astral body, spreading along the spine toward the head where it diffuses throughout the cranial cavity. When awakened, it has the power of supercharging *Prana* and bestows amazing powers upon the *savant*. It then gives the *savant* the capacity to perceive the physical world through heightened senses. Mechanical vibrations arriving at our eardrums turn into nerve currents, which in turn are assimilated as meaningful or superfluous by the consciousness given to us by *prana*. Symbols and pictures are seen by our eyes which are converted into neural currents by the retinas. Again, relevance, association and meaning are provided by the consciousness. A sense of time and space or depth has evolved into our consciousness. Without making any conscious effort and without interruption, the brain organizes day-to-day events into "associated keys" which we activate to recall memory of the present, immediate past, past, and long past from the ubiquitous mind. Over lifetime, the cumulative effect gives us referential judgement. Our capability to recall memory by activating the associative residuals in the brain is responsible for giving us a sense of delay or "elapsed time". In fact, we are conditioned by linear thinking to such an extent that we have difficulty understanding simultaneity, which is the prevalent reality around us. If you think for a moment along this line, you will conclude that there is no such thing as "time", per se. There is no particular flow on land or passing of waves in space associated with time. Events are simultaneously happening all around us throughout the whole universe. The concept of time allows us to understand our immediate environment through the sensory inputs and then with our limited grasp of events we sort things in a personal order. Through the awakening of the *Kundalini shakti*, we can free ourselves from this limitation, which exists strictly in the Physical-mental solitude of the microcosm. The freeing of the mind from the linearity of time in our daily experiences is the principal cause of disorientation when *Kundalini* first awakens in the *savant*. The *shakti* begins to guide the integration of the three domains of the microcosm into a sustaining whole. Science tells us that heat is nothing but a more agitated state of the electrons in an atom. How is this fact translated into a perceptive sensation of heat or cold, not

Meditation

in the brain, but on the spot on the body where it occurs? It is done through the *Prana shakti*, which also pervades the central nervous system, just as it raises flags of danger through an arousal of pain and emotions in our middle solitude.

"When the flow of *Kundalini* along the *nadis* in the astral body is regulated, for example in yogins who practise *pranayam* and other forms of *yoga*, the acuity of perception increases. It is postulated by the old masters that *Kundalini* rises through the *Sushumna* canal - a Physiological analogue in the astral (subtle) body. The movement of *Kundalini* is initiated when *prana* and *apana* at the opposite ends of the *Sushumna* interact in a certain manner. If it can be made to advance from *chakra* to *chakra* -six in all - in the subtle body, the corresponding plexuses are energised in the physical body. If and when the yogin succeeds in getting the *Kundalini* to awaken the dormant seventh *chakra* in the crown, he goes into *samadhi* in the spiritual domain, transcending time and space. You can see how the three solitudes of the microcosm can be harmonized by the practices I have outlined in these classes.

"I have been personally dazzled by the very first rumbling of the *Kundalini* at the base of my spine. I am now practising the technique to meditate on the *chakras* to induce the *Kundalini* to flow at will. In time, I will succeed in maintaining a stable flow after which I will be able to induce it to flow from one *chakra* to the next in my body. I am gaining control over the flow, albeit in minute measures. It may take me one year or it may take me several, but let me assure you from a personal experience that once you have enjoyed its pleasurable splendor, you are forever captivated by the magic of its effulgence," said *guruji*. His face was beaming with an unusual serenity. The sparkle in his eyes was vivid and his gaze was all-knowing.

"What are some of the telltale signs that a beginner can watch for?" a *chela* asked.

"Three well-known early stages have been described by many an aspirant, which I have personally passed through before the first faint arousal of a wave at the base of my spine. A progression of precognitive visions or flashes in luminous blue-white lines will appear on the inside of your closed eyelids during deep meditation

The Latitude Syndrome

in succeeding sessions. The jagged or smoothly curving lines may be two to five in number. They will appear and persist during meditation when the focus of eyes is shifted from the inside of the forehead to the inside of the upper eyelid. Depending on your progress, some future session may produce the outline of a feminine likeness of the image of *Gayatri mata's* face in luminous blue-white lines on the inside of your forehead. The face will be recognizable and the head will have a triangular or a semi-circular crown adorned with circles of iridescent polka dots. After the session try to recall and remember the number of circles.

"From this stage, you may regress back to a vision of jagged lines only. Do not allow this to discourage you because progress occurs in repeating up-and-down steps. In a subsequent session, sooner or later, if you are on the right track, jagged lines will become wavy and a male counterpart of the conceptual *Gayatri mata* will form out of the same luminous lines. The male face may have a crown of jutting rhomboids or squares perched on their corners. Again, try to recall the number of drawings. This is the beginning of the second stage. In some cases the male form may appear before the female counterpart appears. As a general rule a male disciple will see the female head first and a female disciple will see a male vision first. If this order is not apparent, it may point to conflicts of gender identity which may have to be examined by the disciple.

"You will at once realize that you are on your way to resolving the innate sexual duality in your being. I do not know of any words in any language which I can use to describe the beauty of the aura of inner tranquility that this resolution brings about. If you have succeeded in progressing this far, you are well on your way to realizing higher states of consciousness. In the third stage, during deep meditation, fixity is brought to bear on the cerebrospinal complex. Initially the complex is visualized as a bare thread symbolizing *Sushumna* along which the focus of concentration, visualized as a luminous point, is moved up from the base towards a spot in the region of the heart. The eyes are simultaneously rolled upward in an attempt to focus on the inside of the forehead bone. Eventually this form of meditation leads to an upward, sparkling movement of *Kundalini*. I use the word "sparkling" to suggest that a white radiance is felt about the head. Particles of nonluminous dashes and dots in blue and black colors emanate as *Kundalini shakti* bathes the rear surfaces of the retinas at the back of the eyeballs. After months of practice, a predictable sequence of patterns starts to form over which the practitioner gains mastery in small steps. Bliss and enrapturing visions of pure ecstasy start to take hold of the *savant*. Sometimes one gets stuck at a stage, for it appears again and again, a little clearer each time, but further progress is hard to come by for the time being. At other times, a momentary separation of body and consciousness is experienced. One's astral body can be felt as a distinctly separate entity and the phenomena of levitation and clairaudience can be realized. Such is the path of enlightenment! I do not want to leave the impression that one can realize all this easily and quickly. Only the determined few get to reach these stages.

"Usually three distinct areas of closed-eyes focus become established in the disciple. The internal focus of the eyes can be effortlessly moved from one to the other during meditation. They are:
- Inside layer of the forehead bone
- On the inside of the upper eyelids
- On the inside of the bottom eyelids as the eyes are moved to the tip of the nose."

Another noteworthy telltale sign is a developing feel for the vertical axis during a closed-eye *aasan*. You will actually perceive an imaginary axis formed by the brain stem leading down the spine about which you will feel your head floating. In the beginning the tendency is to move the head to and fro to align it to the axis. This can be a bothersome exercise as the axis will remain fixed at an angle to the axis of the head. This feel by itself is a remarkable milestone along the way.

Session nine
"Today, we will go straight into the practicum for half an hour. After the exercises, I will give you a demonstration of a cycle of *bhastrika*, as I think the time is right to rock the course of the

The Latitude Syndrome

routine with which we have become all-too-familiar." To demonstrate *guruji* went through the cycle of ten loud inhalation-exhalation cycles, pushing out the breath in three rhythmic thrusts. " We will add the *bhastrika* to our daily practice. You will notice the extra vitality it will bring to your faculties at the end of the session."

The group practised the *bhastrika* through the full cycle and they became dizzy. A disciple felt uneasy about it and remarked," I don't see why we have to add a storm to the tranquil waters of our fixated and calm minds, just when we are beginning to grasp the formation of an inner focus."

Guruji grinned. "If you want to climb a mountain twice, after reaching the summit for the first time, you have to go down to the valley, otherwise you cannot climb it the second time. In our case we want to climb the mountain a thousand times. With each successive climb to the top, you will find that the mountain has grown a bit higher and that you can see farther from the top, perceptually speaking. Try the *bhastrika* for a few days and we will take stock of its effect next week. If you become dizzy then you are doing it too violently. Slow down the tempo. You will soon find your tolerance level."

Session ten

"Today let us begin with our *aasans* and go through the practice of *pranayam* and *mantras*, following the routine we now know quite well. We will end with *bhastrika* for it is the last exercise we have added to our routine." For the next half hour everyone was absorbed in their yoga practice with unflinching devotion. It was obvious that rhythm and timing were becoming unified in their practices. They all arrived at *bhastrika*, more or less at the same time. Loud and airy bellows were at work now and pronounced hisses accompanied the expulsion of breath from the nostrils. The practice session ended with a flourish of unabated breaths.

"Well, who would like to initiate a discussion of their experience with *bhastrika* so far?" *Guruji* asked invitingly. A *chela* looked up and said, "my early fears have been laid to rest. At first,

Meditation

at about the sixth cycle it made a dizzy feeling in the head. I could feel blood rushing through my body. After the seventh day of practice, I started to feel a dilation in the respiratory track and the dizzy feeling in the head subsided. Then I worked with it several times a day and now I have successfully blended it with my breathing schedule." *Guruji* continued: "My *guru* taught me that *bhastrika* warms the body and enables one to know *Kundalini* when she arrives. Twenty doctors could not do what it does to purge disease from the respiratory system of the aspirant."

"Today, I will talk more about *Kundalini shakti*. It is the fountainhead of heightened consciousness and the regulator of personal evolution in man. It is a special case of *Prana shakti*, and it forms a link between the sensory and the extrasensory within the visible bounds of the human body. It is a manifestation of *Prana* in action in the body, but its effects are exhibited throughout the three domains of the microcosm. Unknown to the ordinary person, it is silently at work at all times furthering the cause of individual evolution. Its awakening and action in an accelerated mode can be achieved in many different ways developed by many diverse cultures utilizing techniques based on form and substance. *Pranayam* is one of them. Other Yogic, Tai Chi, Sufi, Inuvik and hundreds of tribal practices also speed up the process of evolution by bringing *Kundalini* into the subject's awareness. After *Kundalini* is kindled in the very few lucky ones, and this fact is realized by the aspirant, heightened awareness, the effulgent glow and the boundless joy associated with it make the subject spiritually enlightened. In this state, the aspirant can participate in the psychic phenomena and can perform *siddhis* or superphysical feats."

"What is the purpose in cultivating the image of the rising sun on the inside of the eyelids during meditation?" a *chela* asked.

"*Jivatma*, a unit of life when the individualized consciousness or pure I-sense assumes a body for the earthly experience, is considered to be a symbolic ray of the *spiritual sun*. The practice helps to form a bridge between the inner and the outer aspects of our consciousness."

The Latitude Syndrome

Guruji continued:

"A note of caution for the *Kundalini agni* flow in the astral or subtle body is appropriate at this time. As the *agni* makes connections inside the physical body of the *savant* between his physical and the extraphysical vehicles, some people have experienced discomfort, physical illness and persistent disorientation at the hands of the *agni*. Let me emphasize that *Kundalini* is an altogether benign *shakti*. If the physical vehicles of the *savant* are out of alignment because of lifestyle choices, violent and hostile attitude and mental anger and anguish, they don't mesh and integrate with the extraphysical vehicles when the *agni* makes its coveted appearance. If appropriate courses of preparatory attitude are not followed, the conditions can lead to disastrous results for the practitioner.

"A continuous meditative practice may be required to maintain the physical vehicles in alignment with those of the extraphysical. If the farmer doesn't remove the weeds regularly his crops will not get the nutrition from the soil and the result will show. In the absence of maintenance meditation, both sets of vehicles become dull in locked step, and no problems bother the realized person. This is the normal modus operandi. Very rare cases do exist where this does not happen, especially in women who can spiritually grow very quickly because of their natural inclination. The *agni* flows with unabated strength in their bodies with a physiology far more complex than man's and in spite of every precaution and living strictly by the rules, they do suffer through no fault of their own, e.g. the case of Shona in The Three Verbs of Being, after her *Kundalini* had locked with that of her soulmate and had to be tamed.

"Then there do exist genuine cases of incompatibilities and misfortunes where things don't go as planned. Karma may have a hand in this scenario.

"I have also had the opportunity to meet some noble souls who were naturally endowed with *agni* because of their advanced spiritual status from before. But in this life they showed no interest in either the practice of yoga or a wish for this "rare gift" to dwell in their person. Again, some went through cycles of excruciating

Meditation

suffering as they sought medical help and were treated for maladies they didn't have and symptoms that will not go away. If only they could see the benefits of learning a bit about this phenomenon and adjusting their lifestyles to realign their thinking with the great natural gift given to them, not only will their suffering disappear, they will experience the bliss and heightened awareness - they thought was only possible in heaven - with minimum work or practice on their part! Making a staunchly scientific choice with little room for "other possibilities", they became slaves of doubt and misgivings, forever doomed to their own self-fulfilling prophecies."

"Someone recently sent me a quip over the Internet: The human mind is like a parachute; it works only when it is open."

"To successfully bring the course of study and practice to a close, you may continue with your schedules at your own pace at home. The golden rule is to pay heed to what your body is signalling to you and to stay in tune with the changes coming about on the inside. Any sign of discomfort or ill-being should be investigated seriously. The limitless intelligence bundled-in with the miracle of life is on your side. Make use of it as much as you can. Allow it to guide you at every step of your path."

Meditative Listening
Please note that the discourses include the dramatizations of the questions raised by pupils in the teaching sessions of the past.

You are urged to reread the section on Creativity Consciousness before putting the procedures of this chapter into practice. This will only add layers of heightened enjoyment to the experiential miracles coming your way.

Introduction
There are many different ways and methods to attain inner tranquillity and contentment. They all start with an evaluation of one's attitude to and philosophy of life. Meditation and *yoga*, of which structured breathing and sound constellations are an integral part, train the disciple to seek a balance among the three solitudes where the three verbs of being reign supreme. A capacity to never stop wondering at nature's ability to reveal its innermost marvels at every turn in life is a prerequisite for this balance. An intimate communication with nature implies an intimate craving for the expression of one's inner reality through an art medium of one's choice. The technique of meditative-listening of music was developed by the author over a period of ten years in conjunction with traditional meditative practices. The method produced results and effects in a time frame which I believe could not have been realized through meditation alone. The bonus is an indulgence - with ennobling rewards - of an enjoyment of the spiritual aspects of something which only orchestral music can convey by its reach through an unrivalled sense of intimacy. Each and every aspect of the spiritual phenomenon described herein was personally perceived and realized to the accompaniment of deep inner revelation. The author was able to unravel the spiritual mysteries associated with the development of the Classical style of European music involving the golden triumvirate of Haydn, Mozart and Beethoven.

Hypothesis
It is proposed that the intimate experience and enjoyment of the creativity expressed in an art form is fundamentally evolutionary in nature for the subject. The structures and processes related to the three solitudes and the three verbs of being - described elsewhere in the text - play a part, integral to the evolutionary roles assigned to them. In the physical aspects of daily life, cause and

Meditative Listening

effect verbs like "observe", "run", "make", "take", "give", "do", etc produce a desirable sensory effect, which is measurable in physical units assigned to the properties of the effect. During the experience of an expression of a nonverbal musical art form, where the subject is a silent listener, powerful "musical verbs" are at play which compel the subject to respond in ways, predetermined to a degree, by the composer. Thus the silent "musical verbs" may give one the experience of sadness, ecstasy, being by a brook, being in the countryside, or by a mountain, or by the side of a damsel in a thunderstorm. This is achieved when the music at once transfers to the listener the artist's feeling of emotion or spirituality or an idea-entity present at the time of creation. Recall that a spontaneous effect has no cause. The musical sound is the medium of delivery of the immaterial verbs and not the cause of the effect perceived by the listener. Other examples of this phenomena may be the spontaneous effect perceived when a painting is viewed in silence or a poem is mentally recited, where even the medium of sound is not present. Mental chant of a *mantra* and silent meditative practices are other examples where spontaneous effects may be realized by the *savant*.

I will begin with the subject of how artistic creativity can be individually perceived by a serious practitioner in the manner of a serious meditator seeking enlightenment.

Before I elaborate on the topic, I must apologize for the analogies I must borrow from the physical world to formulate the basic ideas. I do not know of any language or of any other means with which to express the complex concepts related to the subject. I will be touching upon entities which cannot be measured on any scale. Their effect is more subtle than a vague feeling or the shadow of a dream. They can only be intuitively realized in the manner of the very personal experience of transcendence by a meditator after many years of patient hard work.

Let me begin with how masterfully composed orchestral music impinges on the devotee's Creativity Consciousness to produce the spontaneous effect. The mechanism is based on the emergence of an intimate relationship between the composer and the serious devotee-listener through repeated meditative listening of a particular type of music. It can be likened to a *guru*-chela

The Latitude Syndrome

relationship where the interweaving of the two minds in the *akash* creates an environment in which a spiritual give and take can materialize. It can be seen that it requires a long period of concentrated nurturing on the part of the listener, before the "pure" emotion present at the time of composing a musical work, can be realized by the listener as a "pure" emotion, fragment by fragment, leading to the emergence of a heightened mental state which sublimates the *savant's* level of self-recognition at that point. The aesthetics of the reality of the relationship are beyond description in any language. Remember that the operative spiritual hieroglyphs are masqueraded in the musical lacework, which the "musical verbs" carry forward, riding the tonal sound waves.

You have already read in an earlier section how artistic creativity is born at the Emotional-Spiritual synapse of the conceiving genius. Although most music consists of successive patterns of many sound-tones linearly propagating in space, the creative merit does not reside in the tones themselves. It is camouflaged in the ever present transients, the breaks, the pregnant gaps and the gradients adjoining two successive notes. A delicate lacework of punctuations is woven into the tones, the highs and the lows, the rhythm and the melody, the sonority and the slow and fast tempos of the sounds. The creative magic is divined into this lacework. How is this magic assimilated by a devoted listener? The series of modulations and synchronized intervals, occurring in parallel or offset repeating patterns act upon the listener's three solitudes, who is "stimulated" subjectively. Basically, the stimulating patterns cause a flux in the Emotional-astral solitude of the initiated listener which may progress to his Emotional-Spiritual synapse. If it reaches the synapse, the emotional inertia is perturbed by the minutest modulation in sound or by a break between two successive notes. A hesitation or a change in the course of the minute inertia gives rise to the projection of a probe or a spur into the "must" of the solitude. The Cantilever Effect brings a returning fragment from the artist's synapse at the time of creation to be "imprinted" upon the Emotional-Spiritual synapse of the listener. At this point, if the *savant's* synapse is spiritually mature to receive the potential "experiential plateau", the assimilation of the cantilevered

Meditative Listening

fragment takes place within the listener's frame of reference. Thus the subtle transfer from the artist to the initiated listener completes itself.

That is why enjoyment of music is so personal and varied. Now imagine the number of tonal changes occurring in rising crescendos, short notes followed by long notes in different keys, separated by scales of octaves in a hundred instruments following each other in a great composition. If you now synthesize the scenario, the different instruments joining in slowly, sharply, repetitively or not at all, and brief gaps, long breaks and pregnant pauses, you have created a mosaic of an artistic filigree just like the marble lattice work on the arched doorways of the Taj Mahal. The main difference is that the musical experience is progressive and the magic can go on for a long period, making it an unparalleled medium of artistic expression. Words like "wonder, enchantment and brilliance" merely describe the emotional dimension of the complex phenomenon.

Repetitive and concentrated listening can create a more earnest and diverse emotional impact at the synapse, in which the "pure" emotion component reaches into the spiritual solitude of the listener. With each successive episode of meditative listening, the cantilevers diffuse a little deeper into the Spiritual space of the *savant*, finally giving birth to an experiential ideation of the musical composition for which no descriptions exist in any language in the world. The complex of cantilevers in the "must" can cause an initiated *savant* to be "possessed" and they can "leave" the world momentarily or go through other ethereal experiences.

Such is the nature of the manifestation of the composer's spiritual ambience at the *savant's* Spiritual solitude. When one attempts to document the experience, the realized fragment has to be transformed through the Emotional space into a Physical-mental expression, fit for the senses to understand and relate to. There is an inherent dilution of quality in the transformation from the subtle to the gross elements. With training and practice it is possible to develop to this stage of musical experience for a composition of one's choosing. It becomes an intimate exercise in meditation and the embedded fragments of spiritual nuances and feelings, coded into the composition by the artist, begin to sublimate into the *savant's* reality.

At this point the musical experience transcends the intellectual and emotional boundaries of the disciple. The richness of the experience depends on the listener's ability to identify with and subsequently assimilate the "pure" emotion embedded in the composition. At this stage of spiritual enlightenment, you will actually see the luminous cantilever rolls around the shape of a void to the right of the right eye, or, to the left of the left eye. And after the meditative-listening session, if you sit down to meditate with a specific sound-cluster, you will also perceive the effulgence of your Emotional-Spiritual synapse along a black and blue demarcation boundary. Artistic features will be present at the synapse. This realtime spiritual enlightenment from firsthand experiences will overwhelm you and you will profusely weep with joy and gratitude. You will immediately shed antique baggage. You will feel light in body. The feeling of contentment and clarity of mind will dramatically surge at once. An ennobling sensation will pervade your being. Your consciousness will expand outward. You will not be able to contain yourself from an overbrimming feeling of universal love and bliss.

The "visual" perception of the cantilevers and the outline of the synapses occur at the inner altar in nonoptical effulgence. Passing your hand in front of the eyes or moving the head from side to side does not block the image. The crispness of the effulgence and the brilliance of the colors in the cantilever probes have no physical dimensions or attributes. Optical light of equal intensity will burn holes in the retina in a few seconds.

[See section on The Cantilever Effect in the Traditional Model chapter for details related to the phenomena at work]

Furthermore, orchestral music is not memorized in an associative manner which most humans use to remember mental and verbal details. An initiated disciple, untrained in reading music and having little understanding of the structural rules for music, will automatically commit to memory sequence of sounds after due practice. The phenomenon takes root in the Emotional-Spiritual synapse without any conscious effort on the part of the passive

Meditative Listening

listener. The cantilevers projecting into the synapse take care of this. This capability may take longer to develop in some listeners but, once there, the recall is spontaneous. Mozart possessed this uncanny ability to memorize music after hearing it once, even as a child. He was born with the gift of recognizing a fragment of "pure" emotion, which he readily put to music.

Now, think a little about the expressive power of nature. All around us throughout the universe, the ability of the natural phenomenon to reveal itself in countless ways is the ultimate expression of artistry. This is what Superconsciousness does all the time - reveal and express itself in absolute terms. At the physical level we may see beauty in it because our senses recognize forms, colors and symmetrical arrangements. Flowers, trees and plants are an example of this expression. A volcanic explosion is extremely destructive to many forms of life. But the artistic content of the flowing materials, colors, shapes and forms generated in the process is very high, although we do not have time or the presence of mind to appreciate it at the time of happening. But unknown to us, like an oil painting which an admirer scrutinizes in the tranquillity of an art gallery, the many visual frames of a volcanic eruption in progress, also impinge on the Emotional-Spiritual synapse in the same way. This happens naturally because emotional intensity is augmented in the beholder at the time of observation. But we become preoccupied with the Physical-mental aspects of the phenomenon and we stand there overwhelmed by sheer awe, in awe. This feeling of awe is what comes back into our awareness from the cantilever effect projected by the experience into the Emotional space. Extreme distress or loss of a personal nature in everyday life thrusts a similar set of conditions upon the synapse. Weeping is an expression of the disarrayed projections of the cantilevers into the Emotional space when a sudden burst of emotional intensity presents itself at the synapse. Unlike an ordinary person, an artist may not be overwhelmed by distress.

Over the ages, many artists have used sadness caused by distress as a subtle trigger to usher themselves into an "inspired state". The "inspiration" comes alive when the Physical-mental component - a distraction - is reduced from emotion, thus refining it and taking it in the direction of "purity". The intensity and the purity of the emotion at the Emotional-Spiritual synapse has a bearing on the Creativity Consciousness of the individual. But the inspiration cannot be willed through a conscious effort. The underlying phenomenon is the same for all of us. The outcome depends on the nature of the three solitudes making up the being of the individual. In this scenario, you can see that there is some scope for awakening the Creativity Consciousness of a motivated *savant*.

With this background, a person who has the following characteristics has a good chance to awaken their Creativity Consciousness. Inculcating an insatiable thirst for learning from nature at any age and any time, a longing to perceive change at the minutest level (Vedic scriptures call it Discriminative Knowledge) and an ability to mitigate the Physical-mental component from emotion. Practising of inner humility in day-to-day dealings is known to enhance the purifying process. One must have the capacity to be able to spend long periods of time in solitude, where somehow, the "pure" emotion component comes unbound, craving an expression. It is the last characteristic which prepares the listener to delve deeper into one's Emotional and Spiritual spaces. Remember, the purer the emotion, that is, the higher the degree to which you can refine it, the greater the chance to express the artistic treasures through an art form for which the *savant* has an inborn aptitude. Of course, it goes without saying that inborn natural talent to begin with makes the job easier. Everyone cannot become a shining genius, but one has the capacity to grow if one is well-motivated. An immense resource can be discovered within one's native spirituality. Meditation and meditative listening enable this possibility to come to the fore.

In the repertoire of different media (painting, writing, sculpting, composing, etc) used by the creative artist to transform the spiritual conception at the synapse into a presentation fit for the senses of the intended audience, instrumental music is an expression of a form which cannot be expressed or communicated in any other way. The basic building blocks of the material are abstract and formless. There is no formal language, other than to arrange sounds in unfathomable patterns following certain guidelines for structure etc. It has been described earlier how the grand design originates at the Emotional-Spiritual synapse of the rare genius. At the receiving end it can be perceived at three levels. In some listeners, it enters the ears and the response stimulates the Physical-mental space, going no further. In other listeners, the response progresses to the Emotional-astral space and arouses a complex of intense native feelings. In yet others, it makes inroads further in, to resonate in the inner mind after synthesizing with one's spirituality and this rare event - in those of us who are lucky enough to perceive it - produces a spiritual significance of immense proportions. In fact, the greater the degree of congruity between the nature of consciousness of the music's composer and the nature of consciousness of the devotee-listener, no matter how far apart in time and space they might have lived, the stronger the invisible but very perceptive bond that is established between the two consciousnesses. Through this accord, an imperceptible means of communication operating at a subtle level begins to manifest itself. It can only be realized after years of study and practice, just like the yogin, who begins to perceive the inner revelations after years of study and meditation. It can have a direct effect on a powerful center of *Kundalini shakti* in the listener. It can be used to awaken the *shakti* in a serious disciple. The processes set in motion by the two parallels are similar in their impact on the practitioner. If you are initiated in the fine art of music appreciation and you listen to Mozart's creations as a reflective person, after some time you will begin to perceive its impact on your Emotional-Spiritual synapse. Meditative listening by repeated playing of the same compositions will eventually draw you into their inner meaning, which was originally conceived at the Emotional-Spiritual synapse of the master, in the long-gone past.

    (At this point, a student's intellectual apparatus became overloaded and blew a fuse)

"Wait, wait, wait," she interjected.

"I don't see how this can work. I mean, are there some fundamentals at work here? What is the underlying theory? There must be some mechanisms in play here. I understand meditation a bit now. Even there, you must begin with a seed or a kernel to initiate the inner processes," she inquired apologetically. "I don't mean to be disrespectful."

I was hoping to avoid going into the details, because the subject area is horrendously abstract and requires an inordinate amount of concentration and study.

An idea has just entered my mind, yes, I think it will simplify things. But I must warn you that your mental faculties will be severely tested. O.K. Let us begin.

I will first enunciate underlying memory-joggers, so that you may not loose sight of the underpinnings.

Memory-joggers

- There is an intrinsic unity of all objects, entities, things and ideas like "time" in the universe.
- Anything which did not exist before, cannot come into being.
- Anything which has come into existence can never be completely annihilated.
- Source of experience can never stop.
- Mind is simply the power to know. It has no beginning. It has no end. It does not consume space. To know is the object of mind. Because knowledge is everywhere, mind is everywhere. Mind has intellectual thirst, emotional passion and Spiritual devotion.

Now I will introduce you to the sound, object and idea relationships to enable you to understand the internal aspects of sound, musical and otherwise. These first principles also form the basis of the workings of *Mantra Yoga* as defined in the commentaries in [2]Book III. Consider the spoken word and how it conveys.

---

2 PATANJALI YOGA SUTRA, 3-17, PP 317-23

Meditative Listening

Sound

Consider the word "table". It has five alphabets. The sounds remind you of a physical object(s). It points to a packet of knowledge. It carries a hidden message (idea).

At the source:

Alphabets are spoken sequentially making conventional sounds, lacking the nature of the complete word. Articulation causes an appearing and a disappearing act, creating present and past things of sounds. Each alphabet-sound is pregnant with impressions to express ideas.

At the target:

A mental process is excited in the hearer. The process captures the sounds as a single key and forms a PICTURE BY SUMMING THE IMPRESSIONS in it. Convention tells the identity of the sound-concept and the thing it refers to - a table, in the current example.

Words or sounds thus have the capacity to express a whole idea. Through overlapping, the sound, object and conceptualization of the idea may become one impression, such as the sound-cluster *om*.

Object and Implied Object

By convention, words point to objects. Words may or may not refer to objects, such as a single alphabet syllable. Sounds may be given discoverable objects, e.g. baby talk, Mozart talk, musical notes made up of succession of sounds.

Conception of Idea

Mental picture inherent in the sound includes the feeling and spiritual ambience of the speaker. Impression includes a past-present-future sequence in which only the present is manifest. Past and future exist in subtle form and can be realized.

Practice

By meditating on the flow of sound, conception of the passage of time by itself i.e. without an analogue device such as a clock, may be realized. By meditating on the sound-object-idea continuum a timeless transfer can takes place.

Orchestral music

It is made up of succession of sounds which do not point to specific things like literal words do, e.g. sky, water, tree etc, and have idea entities embedded in them. Nonspecific objects and complete ideas are artistically defined by the artist to create moods and paint images for the listener. Thus the receiver can realize in his mind the native impressions present in the mind of the artist at the time of composition. The feelings of the artist and the inner hieroglyphs expressed in the language of the medium, can be craved in a pin-pointed manner by the practitioner.

Baroque examples for meditative-listening
Antonio Vivaldi

Most of Violin Concertos are prayers and dialogues with Christ and God. Movements of the Rosary beads can be actually heard in some of them. Oratorical masses, a product of his priestly functions held for his congregations were all translated into his music, complete with Sermons, Psalms and confessions of his flock. Long discursive dissertations on Scriptural subjects are presented in musical dialogues. Communions, vows and ceremonies are elegantly represented in repeating patterns of ornamental sounds. Imploring and pleadings with God's angels occupy many musical compositions. "I told you so" phrases are expressed in many repetitive patterns, depicting graceful scenarios, with great elegance and charm. They are repeated thousands and thousands of times with a touch of the tragic.

He also left his supergenius behind in his ruminations on the expressiveness of nature and the architectural beauty of the church..

George Phillip Telemann

His music speaks volumes of the intensity of his feeling of freedom. Viola concertos, in particular flirt with sadness in a happy way.

George Frederic Handel

A blend of many facets. He intended his music to please everyone, the Churchmen, the Royalty and the commoners. He exploited the emotional verve for the masses. He delivered grandiose thunders for the Royalty and the Churchmen got the same as they got from Vivaldi. His deliveries, in the language of the segment of the audience he was addressing, tell us about his high spiritual status.

Johann Sebastian Bach

The grand Daddy of them all. It is aptly said: "There was Bach. Then, there was Bach and then, there is Bach". He projected musical cantilevers on which each and every composer, in his wake, built elastic swings on which they swung around the world. Then, they came home to grand Daddy. You will realize every single religious idea in his music, if you stick with it long enough.

In conclusion, a note of caution

This is all easier said than practised and realized. But stick with it with perseverance and an unwavering will. The bliss waiting for you on the other side is worth it.

Note: This section was added on October 22, 1996. The profound relevance of the date can be found in the Genesis chapter of The Three Verbs of Being, a companion book.

A practical guide to realizing Classical music by meditation.

Music can be heard. Music can be felt. It can be experienced and even realized. The map of the paths is presented in five streams. Some streams are standalone efforts. They can be practised in parallel or in tandem for continuity of effects, leading to a most enjoyable journey for self-recognition that may not be as tedious as the strict regimen of meditation alone may be for some, at times.

Stream A

a1.   Read the traditional model chapter again.

The Latitude Syndrome

a2. Fully comprehend and soak in the concepts.

a3. Perceive your mind as being everywhere. Think of this reality frequently and remind yourself of it.

a4 Build mental reference points. Levels shown are on a scale of 1 to 5 of relevance. Reference points provide signposts of progress.

a5. Concentrate on *om* consciousness to distance yourself from cerebral and intellectual overload. Be aware of the "tyranny of words". Practise silence.

Stream AA

aa1. Fully understand and study the principle of the feminine spiritual primacy in a nongender context. Do not give literal importance to the words. Soak in the essence of the principle. Can you relate to its energy for step (aa3)?

aa2. Select an external maternal symbolic object/image and get fixated on it. *Gayatri*, Mary, a Mythological figure or even Jesus as a symbol devoid of gender identity will serve the purpose. Connect with the symbol intimately. Plead with it, revealing all your secrets to her. If you select Mary, take care to avoid a feeling of sadness or tragedy.

aa3. Plead and worship your heart out till you crave a feeling of infancy. This is a reference point of weight 4.

Stream B

b1. Develop extreme admiration for and idolize the members of the Classical music trilogy, Haydn-Mozart-Beethoven. In the musical firmament their stars shine the brightest. Their place is so special that it will never be duplicated.

b2. Study and grasp facts about their accomplishments, immerse yourself in their music (or other like it).

Meditative Listening

b3. Now think of Mozart-Beethoven music as one entity. This is a reference point of weight 5.

Stream BB

bb1. Listen to the trilogy's master compositions. Listen again and again, till you are totally absorbed in them. Make a short list of four Mozart-Beethoven compositions that grab your heart and soul.

bb2. During meditation fully internalize the concept of the verbs of the three solitudes as described elsewhere in the book.

bb3. During meditation fully internalize the concept of cantilevers as described elsewhere in the book.

bb4. Work on separation of melody and rhythm in compositions. If you go to a symphonic performance watch the director's baton follow the rhythm. Do not get hooked on melody (pleasing tune) as it is favored by the ears. It is easy to fall into this trap, especially in singing and choral works because of the distraction of literal meaning of the words. Appreciate the discriminant variables, i.e. the minutest detail of the sound in the notes.

Hints and tips for Path Map

In order to develop a feel of the rhythm, slowly walk to orchestral music in the room. If you are sitting down, fold hands palm-to-palm and follow the beat by separating the forefingers and tapping them. Your head may sway from side to side. Close your eyes and plead with your heart to your merciful goddess. This form of meditation will internalize music. You will automatically memorize the sequences of musical notes and instruments and you will start assigning elements of personal relevance to them.

Singing and choral music is not suitable for this technique because of the distracting effect of the brain's responses to verbal stimuli, dubbed "the tyranny of words" in this application.

The Latitude Syndrome

The following technique works miraculously for some *savants*. If you are into gardening you may know some of the details. Select a seed to grow a plant in potted soil, possibly indoors. Meditate on the seed and associate a personal thought fragment with the seed. Plant the seed and place the pot in a sunny spot. Everyday at watering time, focus your eyes on the soil for a period, developing a feel for the grains of the sandy soil. You are developing discriminative knowledge, that is, the ability to perceive the smallest possible detail of change (mutation). This way you will be able to sense the first Tanmatra of the sprout when it is still underneath the surface and photosynthesis has not yet commenced.

As the plant grows, you will take quantum leaps in your mental development during meditation sessions. If you bring devotion to bear on *om* and bring it into the picture you will "see" each cell of the leaves, buds and flowers forming for growth. Simultaneously, you will perceive each and every note in your music stretched out and you will start to see your cantilever rolls in luminous colors. This is a very effective technique. If a feeling of sadness or tragedy is present, please consult with your *guru*.

Stream C (This area requires concentrated effort)

You will require guidance in this area. Consult with friend, family members, *guru*, psychologist, therapist etc. There is a fork in the path here. Reference point of value 3.

Under normal circumstances, a strong urge to seek forgiveness from others, will have formed by now. If the sense has not appeared, please consult with your *guru* for direction.

c1. You have to identify obstacles, barriers and derailments in your path. A thoroughly frank and honest soul-searching is required. You are doing it for yourself, that should be a powerful motivation.

c2. Interpersonal baggage, Kshama sound-clusters.

c3. Deeper antique baggage, higher level sound-constellations, pleadings with goddess.

Meditative Listening

c4. Long term karma. Structured breathing and high level sound constellations, over longer periods.

c5. Unmanageable pathological conditions. Consult psychiatrist, therapist for help etc.

Stream D

Lists of compositions are chosen to channel *shakti* along the meridians. Some may be ordered for a sequential effect similar to the working of the *Gayatri mantra*. They all point to HEAVEN. Continue to enjoy and meditate on music until you are ready to board the HEAVEN train.

Stream E

Somewhere on the way, you will board the HEAVEN train "EROICA"(Beethoven's third symphony - author's preference). Meditatively listen to Eroica. When you realize EROICA's discriminative knowledge, that is, the rush of cantilevers in the gaps between notes, the spirituality of Eroica will captivate you. You will see Mozart and Beethoven separately, then as one entity and then as nonentity. This reference point is weight 5.

The Latitude Syndrome

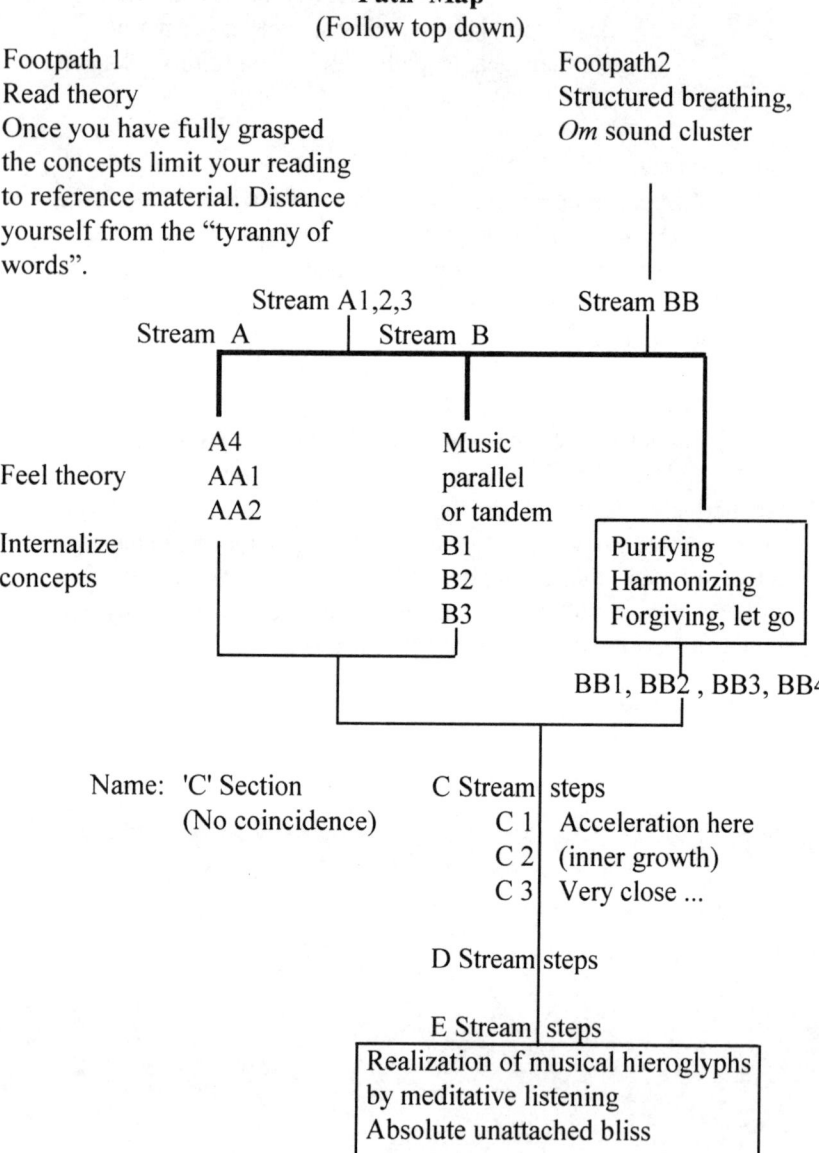

Meditative Listening

Commentary

Sameness factor: Single-culture anchors are powerful agents. They provide sheltering sanctuaries, but constrict growth. Cultures are streams that flow into the river of knowledge. So, let your soul bask in the diversity of the cultural melee, food, art, drama, dancing and music, at the noncommercial level of presentation in the unadulterated native scene. This is inexpensively gained by making incursions into the economically poorer, but otherwise richer sections of foreign lands visited. It is a powerful technique. It opens the mind for universal love, understanding and tolerance.

Telltale signs

Your meditative realization of compositions will come to a point where your heart will ache when the composition comes to an end. You will not want it to end, ever. You have internalized the hieroglyphs expressed in the musical verbs. At this stage you are on the threshold of transcending linear "time".

Inner sweet spot will strengthen (inner altar).

Sensation and pressure in head will change to music.

Feeling and pressure in eyes will change. If tears come, let them flow. These are tears of cathartic relief evoked by art and brought on by your devotion to your goddess, which can be massively joyous and overwhelming.

Bewitchingly fragrant nuances will be picked by your nose, when none are present physically.

Luminous perceptions at the inner altar can come anytime when you are completely absorbed in music. You do not have to be meditating.

You will luminously perceive cantilevers rolling and twirling in multicolours in front of your eyes for minutes. When you move your head they will move with the head. The perception may be only on the right or on the left side of either eye. You cannot block them by passing your hand in front, because they are not of optical light. This is a hauntingly beautiful experience. The clarity of your mind will leap ten-fold. A purifying fulfilment and enrapturing bliss will overwhelm your being. Joyous tears will flow and you will think of nothing but singing praises and thanks to your goddess for the blessed gift. You will luminously perceive your Emotional-Spiritual synapse in effulgent blue and dark-gray or black colors. The demarcation line will be wavy, like the profile of a face from hairline to chin. These perceptions usually illuminate the inner altar during meditation for short periods, of the order of twenty to thirty seconds. Once you recognize the synapses, the same joyous feeling will overwhelm you. Your outlook and attitude to life will dramatically change after the first perceptions appear. Then with each new experience, the *Aanand* (bliss) will heighten. You will be at peace with yourself and the world. This is only the beginning!

Pleasant sensations and chilling shudders may appear on the skin or inside the body during the perceptions. For example, on the back just below the midpoint between the shoulders, or on the back of the head. If you should see artistic forms, make a list of colors and the sequence of changes to chart your progress.

Signs to look for
When tears come they will be of boundless joy. If sadness or a tragic feeling is present, stop at once. Go back to a previous step, where joy and enjoyment were present. You probably got derailed after or near this point. You need to do more work. Usually caused by an unresolved obstacle. Search your soul and plead with your goddess.

You will start to appreciate the special effects of masterworks composed nearer to "journeys to heaven departure points" of the masters. Unfinished works like Schubert's "Unfinished" or Mozart's Requiem produce such intense displays of lingering cantilevers that transcendence persists for hours after the perceptions.

Remember, perseverance and staying power count a lot.

Choice of music for meditative listening

It is assumed that the practitioner is well-versed in the traditional meditation methods involving structured breathing and the practice of sound clustering. This has probably given you an ability to discern your three solitudes during meditation. The suitable Classical musical compositions are your most familiar ones in which you can differentiate and pinpoint the responses in your three solitudes easily and you can relate to them during repetitive listening. A musical composition capable of arousing mental processes - with verbal expressions or songs for instance, is not suitable. A composition which arouses high emotional and spiritual content in your heart, may be a suitable candidate. The selection process may tax your patience. But it constitutes a most enjoyable exploratory stage while you make mind-bogglingly beautiful discoveries during the meditation sessions.

Why Eroica?

It turned out to be a pinnacle experience for the author because the symphony was perceived as a gateway from the Classicism style or emotional projections to the Romanticism style or spiritual projections. This choice fitted in with the requirement to have a presence on both sides of the Emotional-Spiritual synapse.

When you listen to the Eroica, towards the end of the first movement, the trumpets and violins come rushing in, galloping to a crescendo and an orchestral melee leads to the end of the movement. This is one of the most brilliant moments where orchestral music perfectly expresses the sentiment in the spirit of union and forgiveness. Only music can define the harmonizing power of such events. At this time, if you are gazing at a mental picture of Beethoven in your mind, as the trumpets rush in cascading rhythms, the likeness of Beethoven's face in the picture will transform into the likeness of Mozart's face! Try it. You will not notice this phenomenon unless you have listened to it hundreds of times and fully "felt" the spiritual and sentient verbs expressed in it. As you develop towards a realization of this phenomenon, the telltale sign to watch for is when you lose your present sense of time and a new conception of the passage of time becomes distinct as your mind becomes absorbed in the flow of sounds. You may feel shivers originating at the base of your spine, travelling up to the neck in fading waves. This experiential realization is like the yogic *Kundalini agni*, progressively charging the subtle glandular centres as it moves along the spinal column. At this stage, the Eroica will intuitively pervade your being and you will experience music as Mozart and Beethoven had intended it to be!

Furthermore, because of all the reasons I have outlined so far, Eroica projects a sense of an incomplete orchestral theme in the first movement. Again and again the musical momentum is built up. It strives and fumbles but never completes the idea, reaching, aspiring, but never rounding out. It is the ultimate expression of an unequivocal mastery over displaced time achieved through wanton musical lawlessness.

Furthermore, the funeral march of the second movement symbolizes the death of Beethoven's hearing, who would have himself died on October 10, 1802 had certain events of immense spiritual significance not taken place.

The third movement takes the listener through the gateway to the other side of mourning. It is a world filled with celebration and wonderment. It starts with the gathering pace of a steam locomotive rolling on, mimicked by clarinets in short bursts, prophesying the inevitability of the era of heavenly romantic music to come. The wonder is that the Eroica is now a reality and the celebration is of the fact that the new era of music, Romanticism, has dawned. The beauty of Eroica lies in the perpetuation of the ennobling effect of its self-celebration. The extramusical inferences have a cleansing effect which leave the listener purged of the antique memory of suffering while imbuing his heart with a feeling of awe in wonderment.

Towards the end of the finale, there is a glorious dawning of affirming knowledge. Forgiveness rains down in torrents.

Painstakingly over the years, I have learnt the meaning of the spiritual verbs expressed in Eroica's hieroglyphs. As I listen to it again and again, it adds to my intuition grain by grain through subtle revelations. Answers to many questions about the relationship of the Classical style to the Romantic style of music are expressed in it. Beethoven's disproportional emphasis on his craving to be singular and individualistic and hence his inclination to compose music for the initiated and not the masses, was achieved by the resolution of the duality of the two styles. Many sounds from many instruments over a wide chromatic scale, with new constructions of even flow to please, tempered with tensions to jar and then to pacify the ear, to rejuvenate the musical curiosity - a magnificent psychological interplay between the composer and his audience - was the natural musical progression to follow. And this was to be on an orchestral scale of unimagined proportions. In Eroica the union of the two styles was consummated on an artistic plane and a new musical genius at the Emotional-Spiritual synapse was born. Musical evolution, from this point on, took off on the untrodden path to harness the dreamy romantic style. Romanticism of the unbound and the infinite spirit was launched. The realized Creativity Consciousness, fructified in a crop of gloriously sweet fruit. So'ham, Hamsah (That I am, I am That)

The artistic virtues of the Classical era

I will now describe why I selected the particular era of the golden triumvirate of musical geniuses whose August members were none other than the three great music composers, who lived in Central Europe in the eighteenth and nineteenth centuries, namely, Haydn, Mozart and Beethoven. Put concisely, my premise is that their relative positions in the development of their art precisely parallelled the focus along the Physical-mental, Emotional-astral and Spiritual solitudes of the human evolutionary experience. Haydn's work brought the orchestral music form to a peak through his masterful rendering for maximum effect in the Mental space. Mozart took his listeners to a parallel peak, but a notch higher for maximum effect in the Emotional space. By extension, Beethoven synthesized his magic at the Emotional-Spiritual synapse and took it into the Spiritual space. It has been written by an authority that Mozart wrote music for the masses and Beethoven's compositions appealed more to the connoisseurs. Clearly, it stands to reason that many more people can relate to the world of feelings and only a few can readily understand the esoteric, life-realizing works bordering

The Latitude Syndrome

on the spiritual. Haydn's genius for composing music eliciting intellectual responses among his listeners is undeniable. These points has been well documented in records of musical history by experts who studied musical development during the Classical period.

Musical feeling versus intellect

Some time ago in a class, I was watching a pupil (I will call her *chela* 2) who was sitting motionless with a frozen stare. Her mind, body and all mental processes were "locked on" to my words. She became momentarily disoriented. Periodically she would take a deep breath to dispel inner tension. While I watched her, the deep breaths became struggling puffs and the pace of her breathing quickened. She had never before in her life heard of European classical music, let alone names like Haydn and Mozart. Yet, her sentiment was drawn to the topic. The energy flow on her spinal highway ebbed. A tremor moved from the neck to the back of her head. She felt the stir of a muscular flutter on the back of her neck. She appeared shaken up. I extended my hand and called her name. She did not turn her eyes to me. Instead, she returned from wherever she had gone and regained her bearing and she assumed her original attentive posture.

At another time when I was mentioning that Mozart composed the "Die Zauberflaute", the first opera in his native German language - a shining lamp-post destined to cast light on the musical landscape forever . . . . *chela* 2 fainted. Her face, withdrawn and pale in color, exhibited the loss of spirit in her body. She lay limp with her gaze fixed upward at the ceiling. *Chela* 1 requested his teacher to stop as he was feeling a cerebral overload himself. He had been trying to understand emotion and the Emotional-Spiritual synapse by their literal meaning rather than developing a feel for the spiritual fine points. *Chela* 2 on the other hand, felt the implicit meaning of the phenomenon. The energy level in her body, ebbed and flowed with the unfolding of, what appeared to be a mystifying world to her. Automatically, she was drawn into the picture as a participant with real consequences and this showed in her condition as she lay there. *Chela* 1, with all his cerebral skills to interpret and

Meditative Listening

catalogue knowledge, could not understand the impact of emotion on *chela* 2's condition.

Later *chela* 2 explained to *chela* 1.

"In the beginning I was paying attention to the literal words as I listened to the teacher. As I went on, building links between concepts, the fullness of the picture started to take hold of my imagination. Last night I started to lose the feel for the physical environment here, the walls of this room, the houses and buildings on the outside. Their shapes and forms became insignificant and eased out of existence around me. Undefinable layers of space replaced the scene in front of my eyes and I felt that I had a home in the teacher's descriptions. The narrative became experiential for me. It went beyond the feeling state; remember, The Three Verbs of Being."

Chela 1 asked *chela* 2 if she actually heard Mozart's music.

"I did not hear any music, per se, but I felt what its effect might have been on his audiences when Mozart himself played his musical compositions. I rejoiced in its serenity. At times grave sadness filled my heart and I felt myself shrinking by its effect. Shivers drained my bodily vitality and I felt transported out of my presence."

Both *chelas* were intrigued by the mystifying revelations. They had a sound grounding in concepts relating to incarnation and embodiment of human souls. But they were not familiar with the terms I was using to describe European music and the names of Haydn, Mozart and Beethoven. They were captivated by the very practical implication of artistic creativity and how simply, I had shown that its roots can be nurtured by the humus of the native human spirituality. The two *chelas* took entirely different approaches. *Chela* 1 tried to understand the logic behind the relationships, whereas *chela* two identified with the flow of the emotion. An unknown element, buried deep inside her being, was tuning in to the intangibles of Creativity Consciousness. The energy centres in her body responded by shifting focus rapidly. Her physical condition changed in tandem but she did not say anything. *Chela* 1 knew something extraordinary was happening to *chela* 2 but he was at a loss to explain it to himself. He questioned her at times about her reactions and was puzzled by her answers.

It is clear that *chela* 1 was trying to understand the details of the musical phenomena with a high intellectual bias. *Chela* 2 on the other hand, felt the effects of the phenomena even when she had no understanding of the Classical musical structures and the rules pertaining to them.

You will not be surprised to hear that *chela* 2 has become a very successful meditator and has found Classical music to be a catalyst for her most intimate spiritual experiences.

Music as an internalizing medium

Music can be received by a listener at one, two or three spaces of his three solitudes, briefly, Physical, Emotional and Spiritual. One hears musical tones at the physical level; one feels music at the emotional level and one experiences or "realizes" music at the spiritual level. If you are initiated in the subtle phenomenon of experiencing music - and this creative ability can be acquired over a period of time through training - an unprecedented, illuminating, awakening, resembling the quality of spiritual liberation, begins to take root in the devotee-listener. One passes through a phase of total absorption, first in the sounds and tones themselves, but later in the subtle nuances placed between the musical notes. A blissful state dawns upon the intense meditator. Intuitive perception begins to unravel the hidden spiritual hieroglyphs of the original composer's work. I do not have a formal training in the Western Classical music, but by intensely concentrating during the repetitive playing, I have gained an experiential insight over a period of time. In the music of Mozart-Beethoven continuum, three distinct periods can be experienced. I am basing the observations on my perceptual insights rather than historical events, which are well-known in the music circles.

This intuitive revelation descended into my consciousness after I began to spiritually unify with the music during meditation, a stage attainable after years of listening with emotion welling up inside like a cascading gusher. A powerful emotional intensity acted

Meditative Listening

on my Emotional-Spiritual synapse and an intuitive illumination was sparked in me.

As a Hindu, born and raised in the traditional Vedic culture, my exposure to the European Classical music has been limited. When I listen to the two great masters in the manner described, I experience the unified musical continuum spanning the two lives as one period.

Their music symbolises the union of the two Creativity Consciousnesses and for the first time ever, pure emotion was uniquely expressed in musical form. When you listen to it, at first it comes to you at the sound level, then slowly you are pulled into the inner, mystical hieroglyphs, the spiritual ideas and fantasies embedded in them. That is when the composers begin to subliminally reach the serious listener in a clear, quiet language which represents the essence of the sum total of their spiritual evolution up to that point. Their expanding consciousnesses overwhelm the listener at first. But through serious practice and contemplation, the listener's Emotional-Spiritual synapse begins to harmonize with the composers' Emotional-Spiritual synapse - the original source of inspiration of the compositions in the first place. The listener then simply realizes the composers' consciousness across the chasm of time. And, with it the listener gains spiritual enlightenment across the three solitudes of his being. Meditation confers similar results on the practitioner. Both work through the awakening of *Kundalini* at the base of the spine and the flowering of the astral *chakras* along the way as progress is made. Both require a deep commitment. The rewards are worth the effort.

Now, let me pose a simple question. Does this experience touch everyone? Obviously not. The real beneficiaries of this knowledge are the people who care about self-recognition and understand the esoteric principles involved in self-realization. After years of intense study of the development of the Classical style into the Romantic style of music as an amateur and then spending countless nights listening to the sublime compositions, again and again while meditating on the inner feeling of their music, does one ultimately begin to feel the tinge of a faint shiver on the spine. At this point, modifications of the listener's mind slow down. I began to sense my inner altar - the seat of the individual "pure I-Sense".

Befittingly, the Eroica sings a monumental tribute to the golden triumvirate of Haydn, Mozart and Beethoven, the successive architects of the Classical era. Beethoven acknowledged the essence of precursory bonds residing within him through the new arrangements in the symphony. He was able to put the gilded crown on the head of musical Classicism, a refinement he so perfectly achieved in the spiritual nuances of the emotional interplay. If Haydn's work can be likened to surveying the site for a home and clearing the grounds in preparation for building, then Mozart's work can be likened to the digging of the trenches and the laying of the most elaborate foundation for the construction of a monolith. Then came Beethoven upon the scene to build an exquisite temple, except that the foundation builder was the only one who knew how to read the blueprints, and he had the good sense to hang around and direct the construction of the temple we call the European Classical music!

Darshan revisited

In the greeting of *namaste*, one acknowledges the existence of the divine in the other. An air of goodwill based on equality is set afloat in order to set the stage for one of the most profound miracles in human interaction to play its part. Implicit in *"darshan"* are subtle interactions in the three spaces - body to body, verb to verb, pure I-Sense to pure I-Sense - of the two parties.

Let me first introduce you to the subject of "how the reality manifests itself in real-time" in an interaction, specially when two microcosms meet for the first time face to face. The unfolding phenomena take place in the "ferment" of the three solitudes in both parties. In the Physical-mental space, the subjective reality is expressed through the mental processes where conceptualisation takes place serially, one thought followed by another as there can never be a recognition of multiple thoughts in the human mind at once. Thoughts can then be expressed serially, giving rise to cerebral cause and effect reasoning. Physical beauty, body language, dress code and cultural aspects play a leading role at this level. The

Meditative Listening

analytical ability to intellectually override a feeling also prevails here. Phenomenal "love-at-first-sight" is filtered out here.

In the Emotional-astral space, a component of the reality is felt through the arousal of feelings, and many feelings intertwined in complex ways can present themselves at once. Some of the superficial ones to quickly register, e.g. fondness, like or dislike, indifference, hate and anger are immediately passed on to the Physical-mental space for translation through the intellectual apparatus. The complex emotions are difficult to fathom and unravel because they may have set afloat cantilevers projecting toward the Emotional-Spiritual synapse. This is the reason why people have difficulty in thinking clearly when they are in a serious emotional predicament.

Now, in the Spiritual space, the prevalent reality of a crucial moment is not understood, until a - a - a. . how? It has to be realized experientially, that is, one has to go through the aftermath of the situation in a living mode. It materializes spontaneously at the moment of meeting at some level, but its true nature is rarely recognized right away. It can take the form of an instant flash of a "revelation", or it can be hauntingly agonizing, the meaning seeping into conscious awareness over a long period of time, if at all. It remains vague and cannot be verbalized. Most people choose to ignore it and eventually they forget about it. This happens to all of us all the time as we meet people and interact with them. Actually at the first encounter, the two consciousnesses interact with each other and undefined airs and auras of compatibilities are struck, which register as likes and dislikes superficially. If only, one could master the art of immediately understanding the true meaning of the interaction! It is this "experiential" flash of recognition that materializes in the minds of the new devotees when their true spiritual leader appears in front of them.

This is the phenomenon of *darshan*. It is capable of binding two people through a spontaneous "recognition" at the unmanifest level. In common parlance the hope is that when you seek the *darshan* of another, somehow the spiritual nuances will influence your being with a positive consequence for your evolution.

The Latitude Syndrome

Another view

When a person reads poetry or a written historical account in retrospect, the reader has the choice of either attending to the literal sense of the written word or he can step back and focus on the meaning by reading "between the lines", to borrow a popular expression. It is not easy, but it is also possible to read "behind" the lines, as it were, to harmonize with the hidden meaning in the passage. The thorniest single factor militating against this distancing exercise is summed up in what I have called "the tyranny of the words". Most people love to hear and speak "words" in endless streams in pursuit of "knowledge" because they want to quench a natural thirst. But mere "words" disable the cantilever effect. The farther you can remove yourself from the verbal ring of the "words", the more enlightened your frame of mind becomes.

For example, when one reads a passionate letter from a lover, you are at once awash in the warm glow of feelings and closeness. You are not even aware of the "words" or the physical seperation. Another case in point is when a poet invites the reader to share and relive the emotion in the picture he has painted by arranging "words" in a poem. The "words" are just the passive medium. It's the cantilevers that carry the essences and subtle nuances, frame by frame, from the poet to the reader. Granted, without words, there'll be no poems. But why limit your enjoyment to the superficial rhetoric of the words when glorious panoramas of unbridled joy are just beneath the surface, within easy reach?

Meditation on certain aspects of subject under study can make this possible. Meditative-listening becomes that much more poignant with classical music. There are no words to distract!

Basis of Surya shakti - The spiritual sun

The physical sun

It is well known that the sun is the center of the solar system in which nine planets and their many moons go around in fixed orbits. Earth is one of the nine planets. Our Earth is really blessed in many ways with countless features given to the promotion and preservation of life. For a start, it is the right distance away from the sun to capture the right amount of Solar light and heat in order to sustain life in all its myriad forms. Other planets are either too cold or too hot to sustain the many forms of life with which we are familiar on the Earth.

The earth has been given a covering atmosphere which not only provides us with breath, but also shields us from harmful radiation coming in from near and deep space. The atmosphere also protects us from large space objects like meteors, asteroids and comets, by either burning them up completely before they can do harm or in some rare cases, reducing their large sizes to as much as the forces would allow in a given situation. In addition the atmosphere serves as a gigantic storage and distribution system for heat, water, gases and other factors. It has many other life-friendly features which we may not discover until some threatening conditions come about or some other cosmic changes take place on a massive scale to trigger their role in favor of life.

Our Earth has the right amount of land surface in proportion to water surface to store and balance the distribution of atmospheric parameters like heat and water. A very special arrangement was somehow made for the lighter water molecule, made from the two elements - two atoms of hydrogen and one of oxygen - to exist in the form of a stable liquid at ordinary temperature. By contrast, the heavier carbon dioxide molecule - made up of two atoms of carbon and one of oxygen - exists as gas at ordinary temperature. The list of the life-friendly properties, such as the physical size, the tilt of the longitudinal axis, the balanced proportions of physical features of the Earth's position in the Solar system given to sustaining life, the geographical features and the riches buried in its soil, is quite long.

The grand design of the countless varieties of microbial, plant and animal species, all devoted to interdependent sustenance through complex ecological systems appears to be the work of some

The Latitude Syndrome

higher intelligence. Can these be passed off as armies that accidentally assumed their positions to blindly march forward in locked step to further the cause of evolution? Doesn't sound too convincing!

Think about the favorable mixture of gases in the atmosphere, the Ozone layer and other radiation shields in the upper stratosphere, all given to sheltering life on the Earth. Are these all coincidences? Considering these streams and streams of seeming "coincidences", it may not be too presumptuous to suspect the opposite of "foul play" at some level by some power who may have liked promoting the concept of life.

The sun is the kingpin of our Solar system. It comprises 99.85% of the total Solar system matter and supplies almost 100% of every conceivable form of energy prevailing in the system. Without its burning benevolence, no form of life could have either originated in the first place or - if somehow begun by a mutative quirk or an improbable accident to which nature was prone for a moment - could have continued to thrive profusely, the way it ceaselessly does on Earth. What is this sun and wherein lies its secret power?

Notwithstanding its physical attributes measurable only on an astronomical scale, it is endowed with mysterious spiritual powers so subtle and so profoundly benign that nothing short of a philosophical rendering will bring it within the scope of human understanding and acceptance. Regarded simply by its own devices on a physical plane, the sun embodies the antithesis of life on a grand scale. It is too hot. It generates too much poisonous radiation. Yet, on our far-off planet Earth, it is the sole provider of factors without which life would not have been possible at all!. This is the basis of *Surya shakti*, a metaphysical concept, which seems to be making the impossible suggestion that completely opposite qualities can come from something that is so vastly contrary, at least on the surface. At the risk of public ridicule, can one suggest that there is more to things than meets the eye? Can one entertain the improbable notion that the singular incidence of evolving life, as it has come into being in our Solar system, could be the result of an improbable

The Latitude Syndrome

cosmic "incident" that was meant to happen only once during the entire history of the universe?

Basis of *Surya Shatki* in man

In my companion book, The Three Verbs of Being, I have given life to the three solitudes in a human being through the persons of the characters and relationships where the verbs actually create the evolutionary experiences of the parties involved. Working concepts are living things as they physically modify neurons. It's no coincidence that the Vedic scriptures refer to the three solitudes as three bodies, namely, the physical body, the astral body and the spiritual body. The astral body is a refined volumetric outline of the physical body and is superposed over it. It has subtle internal centers, current carriers called *nadis* and other structures. All psychic phenomena and *siddhis* or miraculous feats take place in the subtle body, but are seen as taking place in the physical body and therefore appear real to the uninitiated eye. It is also stated in the scriptures that when the physical body lapses, the soul rests in the astral body for fourteen days from where it makes the final unbonding with the earthly sojourn. Out-of-body experience, the *Sushumna* canal, the *Ida* and *Pingala* currents, the flow of *Kundalini agni* and the six [3]*chakras* associated with it are all astral body phenomena. The spiritual body is even more refined and less dense.

Physical and extraphysical parallels between the spiritual man and the *spiritual sun* are drawn in the following manner. The congregation of the six *chakras* - the astral reality of the human

---

[3] Name, location, color and (number of petals) associated with the chakra are given.
1. Muldhara   Root   Red(4)
2. Svadhistan   Below Navel   Purple-red(6)
3. Manipur   Navel   Violet(10)
4. Anahata   Heart   Gold-pink(1)
5. Vishudha   Throat   Grey(16)
6. Ajna   3rd Eye   White(2)
   Sahashrar   Crown   Blue-white(1000)

being - comprises the inner universe, which communes with the *Surya shakti* or the *spiritual sun* through the *shakti* of six [4]plexus on the *Sushumna* canal. Each plexus has two polarities. These twelve centers correspond to the twelve Zodiac signs which are spaced at an interval of thirty degrees on the terrestrial longitude. They relate to the paths of the planets of the physical sun in the outer universe. The physical sun emits optical light. *Surya shakti* is realized as nonoptical light. The parallels are very real. By following a rigorous meditative path, when the *chela* succeeds in activating the thousand-petalled *Sahashrar* in the crown - the center of the inner universe - it emits nonoptical effulgence about the head. In actual practice the *chela* begins to perceive the effulgence through the journey of self-discovery long before the final plateau is attained.

Path leading to self-recognition
The scriptures lay emphases on four simple principles.
- Leading a normal, happy and satisfying life as a contributing member of the nonviolent community.
- Delivering on one's *Dharma* - duties and obligations - by following the instructions of one's conscience, with a full understanding of the working of karma.
- Integrating into one's daily schedule, a suitably chosen practice, e.g. meditation, *pranayam*, music, charitable work, communing with nature, etc to get in touch with the inner reality for enlightenment for an enriched life. The practice must run parallel to your natural grain. It must be effortless and offer joyous results to you.

---

[4] CORRESPONDING MEDICAL NAMES OF THE SPINAL CENTERS ARE GIVEN FROM TOP DOWN.
MEDULLARY   CERVICAL   DORSAL   LUMBAR
SACRAL   COCCYGEAL

The Latitude Syndrome

- Doing one's utmost to keep the sacred shell we call body in a healthy state to maximize the experiential window given to us for spiritual evolution.

Discussion of four principles

i. The fundamental consideration here is the attitude and philosophy of life that one brings to bear on one's lifestyle. The giver, one who understands, the forgiver and one who makes a point of creating happiness and goodwill for others all around, is the role-model one seeks to emulate as a shining light in the Aary community. One of the most powerful subtle forces available to bring about a change in one's attitude to life is a relaxed contemplation of the two sets of the seed-ideas before going into your chosen practice. One practical technique that works very well is founded on symbolism. At critical points in your perceived transformation, find a relaxing spot under a large tree on a sunny day. With the resolute idea of the desirable change firmly established in your mind, consciously step out from the boundary of shade into sunshine. The inherent symbolism is "from ignorance to enlightenment". Thank your goddess/god or nature for the gift of sunshine. Commune with the tree with your heart, inducing it to share its storehouse of the *Surya shakti* with you.

ii. *Dharma* is an all-encompassing action term. The nuances of commitment and the willingness to perform your end of the bargain for the "other" in a natural way are buried in it. It applies to all relationships from the most superficial to the most intimate that spring up during the course of one's life. A point most often overlooked in the act of performance is that the focus of the effort is the "other". Your reward is the joy inherent in being able to serve the "other". One can fine-tune one's attitude to *Dharma* to a point where a sense of exhilaration and liberation automatically appear in anticipation of the act. Think of reversing the roles. What would you like the "other" to do for you in the given situation. Please reread the Karma section in an earlier chapter. As a reminder, the two key negative operatives in karma are "wilfulness" for harm and "selfishness" for action.

iii. In the modern day, many different philosophies and methods of practice are available to a striving *savant*. Your choice will depend on your cultural background, your station and stage in life and an understanding of your objectives for yourself. As a general rule, during discussions for the selection of an affinity group, if you sense the presence of "politics", "inability to act on your own" or "financial commitments", it may be a good idea to explore other avenues. A general rule-of-the-thumb is based on the fundamental difference between the practice of religion as we know it and the pursuit of one's innate spirituality. In most religious practices, you are asked to follow dictates and terms of reference which are rigidly defined in such a way that a personal interpretation is not encouraged. In spiritual self-exploration, you are embarking upon a personal journey where you adjust or backtrack your course in the light of your own discoveries. You are the pilot of your course. In fact, in the quest for self-recognition, after you have discovered a plateau or two for yourself, your perceptions will become so acute and individualistic that nothing short of a personally conducted flight of fancy will further open doors for you.

I am presenting four flavors of methodologies for your consideration.

    a.   A course of structured breathing.

The Latitude Syndrome

    b.   A course of sound constellations.
    c.   A course blending the two above.
    d.   A novel course on meditative-listening based on the European Classical music of a popular era. This self-discovered and self-realized methodology is enjoyable to practice if you like the Classical music of Mozart and Beethoven. The rewards are so mind-blowing that after you have perceived the rolling cantilevers for the first time, the dawning of universal love and sheer bliss will stay with you for ever. Your life will never be the same again. You can get to this stage in a relatively short period of time!

Many philosophical viewpoints, theories and models constructed in a quasi-scientific style are presented for your study and review. Come, be my partner in furthering these to the next stage. Discovery and experimentation with a personal bias are the key here. Let us learn together and enrich our lives.

    iv.   A separate section on nutrition, with an eye to spiritual bias, including recipes and advice for an enlightened healthful culinary lifestyle is presented under the heading of The Latitude Syndrome. The special theme of *Surya shakti* is based on the traditional Ayurvedic sciences, but adapted to comply with the needs of modern living.

Nutrition and culinary lifestyle

The principle underlying a healthful culinary lifestyle is based on two pillars. First, the philosophy of *Surya shakti*, in that the underlying thinking and attitude supplant the physical attributes of food being consumed for nutrition. Ask yourself why a day without sunshine is a day without cheer and spirit. Why is one rainy day considered dull and many rainy days in a row are downright gloomy? It is impossible to capture and store sunshine as a physical entity. No form of life as we know it, can thrive without the benign effects of Solar energy.

It is in the arena of vegetation and plant life that *Surya shakti* manifests itself in a brilliant display of prolific creativity, par excellence. It turns each one of the many millions of plant species into a veritable food factory of indescribable proportions.

The Latitude Syndrome

Complicated photo-chemical processes are miniaturized within the physical sections of a leaf. Each plant is made to produce complex molecules from the basic elemental atoms, one at a time. The variability factor is so fine-tuned to the local geographic conditions that in each land area of approximately fifty square miles, the local plant species address all aspects of nutrition, healing, viral and bacterial disease-fighting for the animal life, including man's, living in the area. The most important ingredients are the concentration of the solar energy and the angle at which the photons strike the atmosphere and the land underneath, a phenomenon called The Latitude Syndrome. The countless physical manifestations brought about by sunshine under the direction of *Surya shakti* are naturally stored in the hierarchical food chain, from the single-celled spore up. This grand design of shapes, colors and grains is spiritually inspired. The philosophy of *Surya shakti* enables us to tap into the rich source of sustenance of life in a subtle way. In fact, the way is so subtle that after some self-training, you will discover that you are capable of deriving an increasing amount of healthful nutrition and spiritual rejuvenation from the same or even a decreasing amount of physical food. Your level of contentment and your feeling of well-being will increase dramatically. Most importantly, you will feel healthy and vibrant. Your sense of self-perception will augment by an order of magnitude.

Just imagine the likes and dislikes people feel for some vegetables, fruits and other members of the vegetation kingdom for no apparent reason. These feelings derive from an interaction between the subtle factors stored in the food items as a result of *Surya shakti* and the hidden factors in one's spiritual makeup. A willing person can learn the simple techniques to align these factors to gain extra benefits for the three components of his health.

Mildly contemplate the *Surya shakti* seed-idea before, during or after eating a meal or at any other convenient time when you are in a reflective mood after a session of meditation.

Surya shakti seed-idea

Food form is the manifest state of the nonmanifest Surya shakti, which is a special form of the universal Prana shakti.

The Latitude Syndrome

At this point on the road to initiating a mental stocktaking, allow me to emphasize the need for cultivating a feeling of high regard for food and a positive attitude of mind to confront and combat common afflictions. One way to achieve this: While eating the small portions of food, do direct your attention to the inherent artistic creativity in the physical features of the food; marvel at the shape, texture, color, form and location of the original vegetables, fruits and grains comprising your meal. The occasional recall of a visual picture of a sunbathed field of waving plants can be a powerful rejuvenating device for one's spirit, especially if you are feeling ragged for some reason. With your heart open to receive the subtle benefits, hypothesize a continuous, nourishing *shakti* from the source of the food item flowing through to you. For example, when you drink milk, do visualize the udders of the cow as a provenance, radiating a benign sustaining energy. The glass of milk is just the medium. In this way, the food forms not only supply the physical building blocks for a healthy body, but subliminally connect you to the real source of sustenance - *Surya shakti*. This easily realizable phenomenon is a whisker outside the sphere of one's conscious awareness. One has to make a special effort to connect with it.

In due course you will realize that this connection is well-founded. It has worked wonders for many of my students. At one time, during a serious illness, the technique saved my life!

The second pillar of good nutrition is based on the need for variability - not quantity - in what you prefer to eat. In the superabundance of the variety of fruits, vegetables, legumes, grains, nuts, seeds, beans, flowers, fungi, roots and milks, mix and match the items to your heart's content. If it tastes good and you feel that the combination is intuitively healthy for your constitution, stick with it. You can develop a variable cycle around this core and expand from it. The golden rule is that you do not consciously try to exclude a large variety of food-items from your diet. After a carefully nurtured period of self-training it is possible to acquire a sensitivity to the effects of a particular type of food on your health and constitution. From this evaluation, you can proceed to ascertain the specific benefits of a particular type of a food item to your wellbeing. My father had managed to develop a healthy relationship with hot milk! For people at the advanced stages of the rigors of self-realization, the scriptures caution about eliminating garlic, onion, chili, spices and meats from diet as these types of foods stimulate specific body metabolisms, thus creating barriers and obstructions to either attenuating or shutting down some inner physical processes.

General Notes on food items
Milk
Milks from herbivorous animals are considered vegetarian. Gandhi's breakfast consisted of goat milk, almonds and dates. Some of India's great Swamis and Yogins lived on cow milk, vegetables and fruits.

Grains and legumes
One requirement of a healthy nutritional style is based on how close to the full size of a grain of a cereal, you can include in your diet. Whole or cracked grains like wheat, barley, millet etc, unpolished brown/red rice, full-grain or half-split legumes with shells etc are preferable to finely ground up versions of the same. At the very least, settle for a coarser grind, if considerations of taste, appearance or the need for a compromise for a special occasion arises. Including the edible shell, where ever possible, can be very beneficial.

Fluid Temperature
Recent research on hydration/dehydration studies of high-powered athletes has revealed anomalous results, confirming to a large extent, what has been prescribed by the ancient *gurus* and Ayurvedic medicine practitioners in the area of fluid intake. They have consistently advised: A cold drink, such as milk, water, pop etc shuts the stomach down until the fluid temperature has risen to the body temperature. For quick hydration under extremely exhausting physical conditions, room-temperature water is considered to be the ideal hydration source. Fruit juices and pops with high sugar content

The Latitude Syndrome

actually increase dehydration because of their effect in the upper intestines. For general drinking, room-temperature water or preferably warm water should be drunk. Milk should always be drunk hot!

My own educated guess is that the prolonged practice of drinking ice-cold alcoholic mixtures, juices and pop has contributed to an increase in the incidence of hiatal hernia, an upper-stomach-sphincter disorder. It is estimated that fifty per cent of the current North American population may be suffering from a form of this disorder, commonly regarded as a stomach acid problem for which antacid tablets are consumed like handfuls of roasted popcorn.

It is also an intuitive guess of mine that the prolonged habit of drinking ice-cold milk over the last century may be implicated in the loss of the lactase enzyme in the small intestine on a epidemiological scale, thus leading to lactose intolerance in a large segment of the present western population.

The guesses are based on observations of the absence of these two conditions in the Asian populations, especially in India, where ice-cold milk and drinks invaded the industrial city masses much later, with a corresponding increase in the two conditions. In spite of high summer temperatures, rural Indians still drink hot milk. The coldest their drinking water gets to, by evaporation through a porous terra cotta sphere, is five degrees below the night temperature.

The epidemiological shifts across populations take many generations to show up. My simplistic observations are not based on hard research. But it is certainly an interesting project ripe for a thorough investigation.

Fibrous bulk

In an eating regimen where deriving the maximum from small portions is the norm, the role of fibre in diet becomes doubly important. Special attention has been given to this aspect in the combination section.

Preferences

If the opportunity of making a choice exists.

The Latitude Syndrome

Generally select:
- Brown rice over white rice.
- Raw brown sugar over white sugar.
- Whole grain over processed partial.
- Coarsely ground grains over finely ground.
- Multi grain over single grain.
- With-shell legumes over shelled legumes.
- Fibrous food-items over nonfibrous food-items.
- Hot/warm food-items over cold food-items.
- Hard wheat over soft wheat.
- Sun-ripened fruits and vegetables over shelf-ripened.

The Latitude Syndrome

The model dramatized in the book, The Three Verbs of Being, underscores the proportion of the three solitudes or bodies comprising our being at a given time. Everyone is at their own unique mix of the Physical-mental, the Emotional-astral and the Spiritual, which varies from person to person. For a person, the relative proportions of the three solitudes vary from one minute to the next, as momentary experiences in day-to-day living are subconsciously assimilated. As a general rule, whether one realizes it or not, a person naturally becomes more spiritual with age for that is the normal course of evolutionary events. This model is the basis of individuality and the unique nature and outlook of a person and the unique set of responses that a person makes to different situations. For example, everyone responds differently to the same medication with their own set of symptoms and side effects. If we were all purely physical and therefore purely chemical in composition, we would all have the same set of responses to the intake of medication or chemical compounds.

With the freedom of action given to us by the kindly judge karma, an ingrained sense of personal liberty and the Bill of Rights, we can direct our efforts to seek progress in any one of the three solitudes. And many do in their own ways. Some people are overly physical, many may be excessively emotional and yet many more may be too spiritual, all proportions considered in a relative sense

The Latitude Syndrome

as made up by the three solitudes of their being. The degree of balance among the three solitudes, either consciously sought or unconsciously accepted for peaceful coexistence in society by an individual is a matter of personal choice. The underlying natural factors militate in favor of a balance to give one the prospects of happiness and contentment, which may appear during the course of a life in personally interpreted ways. Of course, there may exist pathological exceptions and mental aberrations in some inhabitants of the world which run contrary to the intent and spirit of this natural outcome.

For those who seek to advance spiritually, either for inner calm in the short run or for the ultimate enlightenment in the long haul, and I count myself in the ranks of the latter exalted company, I want to present a case for a hybrid lifestyle with emphases on healthful eating habits based on the Ayurvedic principles tempered with modern research findings. Of course, geography and cosmology have a big say in the matter whether we decide or not, to bring this notion into the nucleus of our inner logic.

Basis of the Latitude Syndrome

Although the burning Solar mass comprises 99.85% of the matter in the Solar system and photons of light are the most abundantly flowing commodity, their effect on the surface of the Earth varies dramatically. The sun is remarkably reliable and consistent in its outward behavior. The rotation of the Earth's surface on its longitudinal axis at over one thousand miles per hour and the Earth's travel at a velocity of about 18.5 miles per second in a slightly eccentric orbit around the sun cause massive cyclic variations in the conditions on Earth's surface. The Earth's tilt of 23.45 degrees and its mostly spherical shape cause other variations which are represented on the scale of the latitudinal lines placed parallel to the Equator. It is a well-known fact that the North Pole enjoys a low-level, continuously oblique Solar energy exposure for many months in the summer (North hemisphere), while the South Pole is shrouded in darkness for as many months. The positions reverse in the winter months. These gradations are the basis of the phenomenon of the Latitude Syndrome which affects the air, water

The Latitude Syndrome

and land masses of the earth. The latitude variations directly affect all forms of animal life and plant life on which the animal life is heavily dependent for nutrition. In extreme cases, mental and physical pathologies develop in the human being when they are deprived of the *Surya shakti* by the lack of direct exposure to photons and by the lack of adequate photon-ripened plant life in their diets.

Even when copious quantities of meats, seafood and eggs - supplemented by the basic vitamins and the necessary elemental compounds are consumed in the diets, the effects of photon deprivation cannot be escaped. Nearer the Equatorial regions of the Earth these deprivations do not exist. Between the two extremes lie gradations of tolerable or manageable photon deprivation symptoms which are directly attributable to the sensory and the extrasensory benefits of the ambient sunshine. The extrasensory symptoms are related to the Emotional-astral and the Spiritual solitudes of the individual.

This roundabout brings us back to the *Surya shakti* seed-idea stated earlier. All forms of food in their manifest representation or gross matter level of *Surya shakti* provide the basic building blocks for the physical constituents of the body. The subtle aspects of food-forms, related to the hidden state of *Surya shakti*, play a role in sustaining the Emotional-astral and the Spiritual solitudes of the individual. Both aspects can be enhanced by a judicious manipulation of certain factors related to the Latitude Syndrome and the composition of one's diet. The information presented in the next section deals with techniques designed to maximize the effects for physical, mental and spiritual health. Recipes and suggestions for combinations of food-items are offered with regard to these considerations.

Balancing for the Latitude Syndrome

The difficulty with the task of simplifying a complex problem where an almost inexhaustible supply of variables seriously impinge upon human health is that some critical information may be left out of the picture. Secondary tier difficulties relate to the organization of the information itself, such that the techniques

The Latitude Syndrome

clearly define the objective related to the key parameters. After a careful examination of the outcome desirable from an exercise of this magnitude and from the standpoint of this discussion, I have settled on the latitude parameter itself as the critical marker for a small number of important parameters - by no means exhaustive, bearing on the holistic health of the individual. Simply stated, the basic premise is that a person's feeling for overall well being at a given moment responds to changes in ambient temperature, air pressure, humidity, nutrition, sunshine and subtle emotional, spiritual and other factors.

Table A

Latitude	Group A	Group B	Group C	Group D	Axial	*Shakti*
60.0 N	.99	1.33	1.66	1.82	22.5	90, 5, 10
45.0 N	1.68	1.99	2.49	2.74	14.93	75, 5, 10
30.0 N	1.99	2.66	3.32	3.65	11.22	60, 5, 9
22.5 N	2.24	3.00	3.75	4.12	9.94	30, 5, 8
10.0 N	2.67	3.56	4.45	4.88	8.39	10, 5, 7
Equator	3.00	4.00	5.00	5.50	7.46	1, 5, 6

Diminution factors

Shakti column: Sunlight, Structured Breathing, *Surya Mantra*.
Axial: Curvature, reduction in arc length
Objective: A daily score of 20 is highly desirable for the four food groups.

The Latitude Syndrome

Table A offers guidelines to achieve and maintain a balanced health style by following nutritional standards and by compensating for the variations in *Surya shakti* on the surface of the earth as a natural consequence of the Latitude Syndrome.

Foods are broken into four groups for balancing. Please refer to Table A.

Group A
Grains
Wheat, barley, oats, millet, couscous, brown rice, partially polished rices, whole-wheat bread, multi-grain breads, soybeans and textured soybean products.

Group B
Legumes, nuts and seeds
About fifteen to twenty varieties of *Dals* (legumes) available at an East-Indian food market, beans, small brown chickpeas, white chickpeas, almonds, cashews, pistachios, sunflower seeds, peanuts, sesame seeds.

Group C
Tropical fruits
Kiwi, Papaya, Mango, Oranges, Cantaloupes, Guava, Lichees, Bananas, different sorts of Melons, Arrayan (Mexican), Passion fruit.

Group D
All vegetables, but five groups in particular for which recipes are provided in the recipes section.
- Green tops of most root-vegetables like baby turnips, kohlrabi, mustard seed greens, a variety called Rapini, Swiss chard.
- Karela also called bitter squash (wrinkly oblong green objects 6 to 8 inches in length).
- Long green Squash.
- Fresh Ginger roots.

The Latitude Syndrome

- Chili, fresh green, yellow or vine-ripened red; hotter the better.

If you are not accustomed to using fresh hot chili pepper in preparing your food, experiment at first with small slivers of a mild variety like the East Indian green or the Mexican jalapeno in cooked vegetable, salad and raita. Progressively increase the quantity and the "heat" of the chili by graduating to the spicier variety. At this deliberate rate you should be able to stand the bite of a raw fresh chili by itself in about a year. This habit should be actively cultivated till hot chili, cooked or raw, becomes a part of your meal. sun-ripened fresh red chili of the hottest variety offers many benefits, which come from its role as a catalyst in the digestive processes. As a general rule, the smaller the size of the chili, the hotter its bite.

Most ancient herb cultures assign a high medicinal value to chili. Many revere it as a noble fruit and use it extensively in their diets to prevent ailments associated with the organs of the alimentary canal. In the beginning, a moderately continuous use, experimenting with the different varieties with different foods and keeping notes on the combinations will soon open the door to your personal landscape of the magical powers of the chili. It will soon become addictive because the internal processes will come to depend on the catalyses.

Caution: After working with fresh chili in food preparation, exercise extra care that you don't touch any part of your face with your hands without first giving them a thorough wash with soap and warm water.

Discussion

Table A shows the reduced effect of foods from the standpoint of *Surya shakti*, relative to the latitude variable for freshly harvested products. Minimum of one item each from groups A and B and two items each from groups C and D must be eaten twice a day with full regard to balancing the four principle components of a meal; proteins, carbohydrates, vitamins and elements and fibre.

The Latitude Syndrome

The three numbers in the compensatory *shakti* column of Table A stand for:

First: Daily direct exposure to sunlight in minutes.
Second: Daily structured breathing practice in minutes.
Third: Number of the following *Surya mantra* chants with feeling during meditation.

***Surya mantra*:**
Om tud vishno param padam sada pashyanti surya diviev chakshu raat tum

Brief form:
Om surya namah, Om surya namah.

Recipes and Food Preparation

In the preparation of food meant to enhance the subtle aspects of nutrition, the importance of a feeling of a quiet reverence and love cannot be overemphasized. Together with the concept of the embodiment of *Surya shakti* in food forms, the idea of serving the family members or guests for the spiritual aspects, the food-idea rises to a sublime height. In the demanding rigors of modern life, you may be able to save on cooking time by increasing heat or by adopting some other shortcut. But this gain is achieved at the expense of other attributes of the finished product. Cooking on low-but-adequate level of heat always produces a tastier dish. More importantly, it demands an involvement bordering on the ritualistic, in which feeling plays an important role. Time-sharing, i.e. minding other things while performing culinary steps around the stove, like stirring at five-minute intervals, maybe an alternative. Remember, cooking itself must be an uplifting experience to produce uplifting subtle effects of nourishing and nurturing! Feelings and thoughts present in your mind while cooking for others have the same creative force as Mozart's feelings when he composed some of his noblest music. This is the essence of hospitality. Some western Shivalik hills recipes are offered in the next section for their *sattvic* or mind-purifying and balancing qualities as a supplement to your own eating regimen. The recipes were developed in keeping with the Ayurvedic principles by *guru* Gopal for the kitchen at the Dhulli *gurukul* (seminary) where advanced meditators were trained.

Please note measurements are by volume.

Quantities of sugar and condiments may be varied to suit personal taste.

Suji Halva

16 oz. Durum hard wheat suji (wheat hearts)
2 oz. butter or low-fat vegetable oil
6 oz. dark, raw lump sugar (gur or pilloncio)
8 oz. raisins, washed
4 oz blanched, slivered almonds
4 split cloves cardamon; pinch of whole fennel seeds
4 large eggs (optional)

The Latitude Syndrome

1 oz wheatgerm flakes (optional)

In a 10-12" heavy skillet (preferably cast iron) mix the *suji*, wheatgerm flakes and butter over low-medium heat. Fold and stir *suji* until it turns light gold in color. No smoke should emanate. Lower heat setting, if *suji* smokes during frying.

Simultaneously, pour 35 oz of water in a pot on medium heat. Add sugar, cardamon with shell, fennel seeds. Stir until sugar is dissolved. Add raisins and cover. Don't bring to boil.

Pour the contents of the pot on the light gold *suji* in the skillet. A steaming bubbling mixture will form. Stir until the mixture thickens. Add eggs and fold halva toward the center from the rim, until eggs disappear. If a richer halva is desired, one-two oz of butter may be added as it is stirred. Sprinkle almonds and serve piping hot with hot Ovaltine or Milo milk.

A typical Sunday breakfast at a meditation ashram.

Carrot halva

4 lbs fresh carrots
1 liter 10% cream
6-8 oz dark raw sugar
1 lb ricotta cheese - drained
6 oz raisins
4 oz blanched slivered almonds
4 cloves cardamon, split and crushed in skin
2 squares pure silver varak

Wash carrots in cold water. Remove ingrained soil marks with the tip of a knife, taking care to leave skin intact. Remove ends minimally. Grate to medium-size shreds. It is best to use a heavy cast iron pot. Put grated carrots in pot over a low-medium heat. Add cream. Do not cover as the cream will boil over. Stir occasionally, from bottom to top until the cream has disappeared, about two hours. Increase heat to medium. Add sugar, raisins, cardamon and stir until firm. Add ricotta and fold from bottom to top for twenty minutes until fully blended into a very thick consistency. Sample for sweetness.

Two modes of serving may be used:

- Pour on a buttered plate and press into a two-inch thick slab. Sprinkle almonds. Spread silver *varak* on surface. Store for two hours in fridge for setting. Cut into 2" X 2" squares. Can be used for dessert or for entertaining with tea or coffee.
- Serve the hot halva in bowls, garnished with almonds and the silver *varak*, for breakfast with hot milk, tea or coffee. A boiled egg may be added to the meal.

A typical, special-occasion, festival or birthday breakfast at a meditation *aashram*.

Khir
2 oz Baasmati white rice, preferably broken pieces
1 liter homogenized milk
1 liter 10% cream
4 oz white sugar
For garnishing
Blanched, slivered almonds
Unsalted coarsely crushed pistachios
Shelled kharbooza (cantaloupe) seeds
Pinch saffron, 2 squares pure gold varak, rose-water.

This simple traditional dish for a very ceremonial occasion, no less than *Janam Ashthmi*, Lord Krishna's birthday in the monsoon month of August, is not prepared anymore because of the bother. But there is no substitute. If you want to please your *guru*, you may prepare it as a special treat or as a complete surprise.

It is cooked in a heavy, wide, cast iron wok-like pot called *Karrahi*, with two handles designed for reduction by evaporation. A non-aluminum wok may also suffice. Add rice, milk and cream into the *karrahi* over low heat. Stir occasionally while scraping the bottom until a very creamy and thick rice pudding is formed by reduction. Add sugar and stir until consistency returns. Sprinkle nuts, seeds and drops of rose-water. Serve in bowls with the saffron point in the center with the gold varak pieces spread around like the orbiting planets. Freshly harvested, firm-pulp mango slices are served on the side. While eating the *khir*, mango juice is sucked out

The Latitude Syndrome

of the stem side of a soft-pulp mango, especially grown and served for the occasion.

The symbolism inherent in eating the *khir* on Lord Krishna's birthday is *Pralaya* - dissolution of the cosmos, leading to the recreation of the universe by Brahma. *Khir* in the bowl represents the universe. The pieces of rice are the suspended celestial bodies in the *akash* of creamy *prana shakti*. The saffron point represents the *spiritual sun* around which the material planets, shrouded in the glitter of goldleaf go around. By eating the *khir* you are ensuring continuity ad infinitum for your pure I-Sense..

Having gone to the temple early in the morning for puja and meditation, the family returns home for a lunch of *khir* and mango juice. The afternoon is spent in a siesta as it usually rains in the monsoon season.

Dalia
16 oz cracked durum hard wheat (coarser the better)
2 oz butter or light vegetable oil
8 oz raw brown sugar
1 lb fresh carrots
6 oz raisins
4 oz blanched slivered almonds
4 cloves cardamon, coarsely crushed in skin

Wash carrots and remove soil stains without scraping the skin. Remove ends minimally and grate to fine or medium shreds. In a heavy cast iron pot, melt butter on medium heat. Add cracked wheat and stir-fry for five-seven minutes to seal surfaces. An agreeably appetizing aroma will fill the kitchen. Add grated carrots and stir blend for half minute. Add 16 oz boiling hot water, sugar, raisins. A steaming, bubbling mixture will form. Stir very carefully, turn heat to low and cover pot. Dalia will expand to more than double its volume, so make sure the pot has ample room. You may add hot water to maintain semifirm, wet consistency while Dalia simmers on low heat. It is ready when the expanded wheat pieces offer little resistance between teeth. It is overcooked if the skin separates on the wheat kernels. Turn heat off and do not remove lid

for the last five minutes. All juices should have been absorbed. It is a little tricky to get the finished dalia in perfect condition. The type of durum wheat and the quantity of juice in carrots are the two unknowns. You will become an expert after a couple of tries.
Wheat-germ rich dalia is laden with essential elements and the pack of quick energy. It is favored by soccer and field hockey players, usually eaten half an hour before important games. Serve in a bowl garnished with almond slivers and crushed cardamon seeds. Boiled egg may be served on the side. Hot milk is the favored drink to go along. May be served for breakfast or late afternoon snack before a demanding physical activity.

Toasted wheat-germ granules
8 oz wheat-germ flakes (hard durum wheat)
2 oz sesame seeds
6 tbsp. vegetable oil
8 tbsp. light honey

Mix honey and oil in a small pot over middle heat, stir until honey dissolves (2-3 minutes). Spread wheat-germ in a one-two inch deep metal tray. Examine for fluffiness. Add hot honey-oil mixture, mixing the contents over to spread and coat all wheat-germ with the liquid. Add sesame seeds and mix. Small granules will form.
Brown in a 275-300 degree oven, turning from bottom to top every two minutes as top will roast first. Remove when medium brown and air cool. Granules will become crunchy as they cool. Bottle and store in fridge.
Size of the granules can be made bigger by increasing the quantity of honey.
To serve, sprinkle over yogurt, morning cereal, hot Ovaltine milk. Ideal for breakfast.

Toasted grain mixture
5 eight-oz cups raw rolled oats
2 cups raw unsweetened coconut shreds
4 oz sesame seeds

The Latitude Syndrome

    4 oz raw sunflower seeds
    4 oz pecans, walnuts, slivered almonds mixture (may be increased to suit taste)
    6 oz wheat-germ flakes
    1/4 tsp. salt
    4 oz polyunsaturated vegetable oil
    6 oz honey
    2 tsp. vanilla extract

    Mix dry ingredients in a 2 inch deep tray of a size to hold mixture well below the top. Fold from bottom to top to produce a uniform mix.

    Add the three liquid ingredients in a pot and bring to a quick boil, stirring often to make a smooth mixture. Remove from heat and pour over the dry ingredients and mix well with a wooden spoon to produce an even soak. Bake in a 300 degree preheated oven, folding from bottom to top as an even golden hue covers the grain mixture (about twenty minutes). Remove and air cool. Store in three or four jars for storage in freezer for later use.

    Best eaten with fruit and ten percent cream for a quick pick-me-up. Sprinkle over yogurt for a snack.

Khichari

    4 oz brown/white rice, washed
    4 oz moong dal, split, with shell
    Onion, garlic, ginger, salt, pepper, cumin seed powder, coriander seed powder, to taste.
    Dash of turmeric, chopped tomato (optional)

    Start cooking the ingredients in 16 oz water on medium heat. When the mixture comes to a boil, turn heat low and simmer until the rice turns soft. Maintain a thick, juicy consistency by adding hot water in small quantities, if needed.

    Ideal for convalescence after common afflictions. Suitable food for a reducing diet. May be eaten with natural yogurt and/or butter milk. If Khichari diet is eaten for more than a day, it must be supplemented with Isubgol for fibre balance and vitamin supplements..

Mustard greens, Rapini etc

1 lb mustard or rapini greens with yellow flowers, washed and drained
1/2 lb spinach greens (optional), washed and drained
1 oz fresh ginger root,
2 green chili peppers
2 medium onions
1/2 teaspoon salt
2 tbsp. butter
1 tbsp. Hard durum flour

Finely chop rapini and spinach greens including the fibrous stems. Scrape skin off ginger root and chop. Slice onions longitudinally into thin arcs. Slit chili peppers and remove seeds; if desired seeds may be included. Put all prepared ingredients into a cast iron pot and cover. Cook on a medium heat until tender and mashable by a potato masher. Mash greens into a paste.

Put butter and flour in a small frying pan and fry till flour turns light brown. Add to the rapini paste on medium heat and stir until smooth and thick in consistency, adding additional butter if calories is no problem. Let cool. Store in containers in a fridge and let age for a few days. The taste reaches a peak in five days.

Serve hot with a dollop of butter in a depression in the center and a green chili for garnish. Best eaten with a piping hot high-fibre whole wheat pita bread or chappati. Natural yogurt is an ideal combination for this delectable meal for lunch or dinner.

Karela (bitter squash)

10 small karelas (the smaller the better)
4 medium onions finely chopped
2 tbsp. powdered green mango powder (amchoor)
1 tsp. powdered coriander seeds (dhania)
1/2 tsp. powdered cumin seeds (mild jeera)
1 tblspn vegetable oil

Remove karela stems and ends minimally. Scrape out any black marks on skin. Slit one side longitudinally and remove seeds. Lightly salt inside of karelas with finger and let stand for four hours.

The Latitude Syndrome

This will reduce bitterness. Drain but do not wash. Smear outer skin with a thin coating of oil with finger. Let karelas and seeds stand in an oven at 225 degree heat until dried out. Skin will become leathery. Seeds should be dried crisp (may need longer time in oven). Fry onions in a skillet in oil on low heat until smothered. Add coriander and cumin powders and lightly fry for two minutes. Remove from heat; add mango powder and stir into a pliable filling. Stuff karelas with the prepared paste. Wrap with thread to seal and fry in a skillet over medium heat with a few drops of oil, rolling frequently to get a uniform brown all around. Lightly press each karela in a paper towel to remove oil before serving with crispy seeds sprinkled on top. A delectably healthy and unusual side dish for a meal with an unforgettable taste and flavor.

Loki
2 tender long squash, 10-12 inches long
1 large tomato
2 medium onions; 1 green chili
1 oz fresh ginger root
1/2 tsp. each, salt, powdered coriander, cumin seed powder
1/2 tsp. turmeric
1 tblspn vegetable oil; 2 - 3 chopped garlic slices (optional)

Wash loki and dry. Remove ends and blemishes minimally taking care to preserve skin. Do not remove skin. Dice in half-inch thick flat pieces about two inches long and one inch wide.

Dice onions and fry in oil in a cast iron pot over medium heat until glossy. Add turmeric, coriander and cumin powders and fry lightly for two minutes. Add loki pieces and gently fold from bottom to top until yellow. Add sliced tomato, diced ginger and garlic. Add salt to taste. Fold gently and cook over medium-low heat with cover. Tender loki hydrates profusely as it cooks quickly in about ten minutes. Juice may be removed for a more consistent side dish. It is the juice that is full of phytochemicals and enzymes that work wonders in the digestive tract. Drink it with the dish or separately for a healthful repast.

Serve with brown rice, high-fibre pita bread, yogurt and legume as a side dish for a meal.
When in season, try to include it in your menu twice weekly.

Fresh Ginger root
Has a high-profile role in Ayurvedic style of eating meals. Use it extensively with many vegetables and legumes where tastes and flavors complement as shown in the generic recipes for vegetables and legumes. For additional effect, it can always be served as a condiment or a pickle with a meal.

Ginger root condiment
1 lb fresh Ginger root
2-3 fresh thin-skin firm limes
2 tbsp. coarse pickling salt
1 tsp. garam masala mixture (optional, adjust to taste)
4-6 long green chili peppers, mild or hot
1 tbsp. *ajwain* seeds (available at East Indian store)

Scrape off ginger root skin and cut into one inch long pieces about quarter inch in thickness. Cut limes into quarters. Smear ginger and lime pieces in salt, garam masala and *ajwain* seeds. Put in an appropriately sized sterilized jar. Cut in green chili peppers. Top with any leftover spices. Seal airtight using a polyethylene film under the lid. Rotate jar everyday on its side as juices ooze out. Expose to direct sunlight for hours everyday for three-four weeks until ginger turns pink and lime skin softens.

The medicinal qualities that this condiment imparts to the digestive system when eaten moderately with a meal are boundless. Use sparingly at first as taste develops. Serve as a condiment or pickle with a main meal. It will keep for months in a refrigerator.

Generic recipe for vegetables
As the taste buds for Ayurvedic style of healthful eating develop, quantities of spices may be adjusted to suit taste and eating habits. More green chili peppers may be added as they can do no

The Latitude Syndrome

harm. Quantities shown are for average tastes. Adding potatoes for taste and flavor enhancement is a personal choice, e.g. with cauliflower and green peas, it is a must. A willingness to experiment will reveal many a culinary surprise.

As a general rule, if the skin is edible, it contains a very large portion of the nutritional elements. So always try to leave it on the diced vegetable.

- 1- 1.5 lbs of diced or sliced vegetable
- 2 medium potatoes with skin (optional), washed and diced in about one inch cubes
- 1 large tomato, quartered
- 2 medium onions, finely chopped
- 1 oz fresh ginger root, slivered in one inch long, quarter inch thick pieces
- 1/2 tsp. each, salt, powdered coriander, cumin seed powder
- 1/2 tsp. turmeric powder
- 1 - 2 tbsp. vegetable oil or butter (calories permitting)
- 3 - 4 chopped garlic slices (optional)
- Small quantities of V-8 or spicy clam juice to control consistency

Always use a cast iron thick-bottomed pot if available. Thick-bottomed stainless steel cookware will work as well but the ferrous compounds will be missing from your diet.

Begin by frying the onions in oil or butter over medium heat. When they turn glossy, add turmeric, coriander, cumin and saute for two minutes, stirring constantly. Optional potato pieces may be added now with a few drops of oil and stir-fried for a few minutes making sure that spices don't burn on the bottom. Add salt and diced tomatoes and stir-fry into a thick paste, adding V-8 or clam juice as necessary. You'll become an expert at it before long. Extra doses of spices and green chili peppers may be added now. Add in the vegetable pieces and fold from bottom to top, covering them with the spicy paste. If the vegetable is of a hard variety this fold-fry step may be required a little longer. Five to seven minutes is about average.

Add a little water or V-8 or tomato juice or additional tomatoes to maintain a thick consistency, cover and simmer over low heat until tender. Sample for taste. Adjust quantities of spices and ginger for next time. This is the ideal consistency to eat with a high-fiber whole wheat pita or chappati.

Note: With vegetables like cauliflower, broccoli, *shalgum* (baby turnips) and lotus stems, skip the last addition of water or V-8 or tomato juice as the final preparation is expected to come out moist and thick.

Generic recipe for dry legumes
1/2 lb whole or split with shell
1 large tomato
2 medium onions, coarsely slivered into arcs
1/2 oz fresh ginger root, slivered in one inch long, quarter-inch thick pieces
1/2 tsp. each, salt, powdered coriander, cumin seed powder
1/2 tsp. turmeric powder
2 - 3 garlic slices whole (optional)
For garnishing
1 - 2 tbsp. butter
1 medium onion, finely slivered into arcs
1/4 tsp. whole black Jeera seeds (a pungent variety of cumin)

Inspect legume kernels by spreading a small quantity on a large plate for stones and other debris. Repeat till you have a cleansed all. The presence of a small stone in the finished dish can upset the peaceful ambience of a meal, especially when entertaining guests.

Quantity of water required varies as different legumes have different water absorption rates. The thickness of the final preparation also dictates the quantity of water required at the outset. As a general rule start out with two to three times the quantity of the dry legume used for the recipe. A heavy cast iron pot is desirable for a well-simmered preparation. Add all ingredients into the water, stir, cover and bring to a boil. Reduce heat to maintain a medium simmer for ten minutes. Stir and examine for consistency. Add another tomato or water to suit taste. If a dry dal is desired, skip these additions. But stir gently and examine often as some legumes crumble quickly. Red lentil and split moong without shell may cook in forty minutes. Other harder varieties like the Italian chickpeas, Indian *channa*, black *mahn* and French red beans may take one to three hours.

The final dish should come out as homogeneous and thickly-consistent where the cooked grains do not fall apart. It should not be pourable. Some measure of control may be gained over the consistency problem by leaving the pot uncovered in the last stages for a thicker finish.

For the garnishing of the *dals* or lentils, saute the finely slivered onion in butter until pale brown. Add a pinch of whole black jeera seed and saute for fifteen seconds. Pour the garnish on top in the serving bowl and don't stir. Sprinkle fresh coriander leaves.

Raita
16 oz natural yogurt
Salt, black pepper, dry mint, red paprika for taste and color

Beat yogurt with a fork to a Swiss cream finish. Add salt. You can add one of the following for different effect and taste.

4 oz boiled diced potatoes
1 raw peeled grated cucumber
1 oz Rice crispies
2 oz finely-chopped tomato and onion mixture

Fold the ingredients into the yogurt. Sprinkle black pepper, powdered dry mint leaves, red paprika and a pinch of salt on top in the serving bowl. Do not mix.

Combinations
Certain items complement each other to become nutritionally enriched as building blocks missing in one type are

Recipes

found in the other. Not only variety is highly desirable, but combinations where constituents dovetail each other are more beneficial, especially in the formulations of phytoproteins from available amino acids. Some well-known matches are noted for guidance and not as complete meals.

- Dry legumes like moong, and red lentils go with rice and yogurt.
- A meal consisting of vegetables only complements whole wheat with fiber bread or pita. Textured soya or peanuts must be included to supply the broad spectrum of the amino acids to dovetail for proteins.
- If you are on a vegetarian diet for weight control, a tablespoon of Isubgol stirred in eight oz. of water or fruit juice may be taken before bedtime for bulk.
- Brown rice, turnips, peanuts and yogurt.
- Mustard greens, Swiss chard, dandelion greens, kale, chives and fennel greens match with corn breads.
- Cauliflower, potato skin, ginger and multi-grain coarse pita-bread with fibre..
- Green cabbage, green peas, ginger and whole wheat bread.
- You may be able to develop the habit of starting your day with a sliver or two of fresh ginger with breakfast. May start with ginger marmalade but sugar reduces the effect by more than half. Ginger condiment may be another alternative. Follow it up with kiwi, papaya or mango, alternating to suit. So it's ginger and one of the other three.
- Unpitted fresh Halawi or Barhi dates and blanched almonds placed inside after pitting.
- Bananas, figs and cheese.

Typical meal

A well-balanced meal consists of different combinations of foods prepared according to the recipes. Fresh, wholesome and firm

The Latitude Syndrome

textured vegetables and legumes provide the best results. Thoughts of caring and goodwill at preparation time also help the final result. Vary items available in the season daily. Remember, it is not the quantity but the variability of the ingredients that work in the best interests of health.

High-fibre whole grain or multi-grain pita or chappati; other similar breads.

Whole-grain brown rice

Two vegetables

One legume or peanuts or textured soya

Raita, ginger condiment and pickled green mango or vegetables in mustard oil. (Pickled vegetables can be purchased in an East-Indian, Mexican or health food store).

One or two glasses of red wine.

Usually watered-down buttermilk with a sprinkle of black pepper and salt is drunk with a meal in the summer. A real thrust-quencher; helps restore sodium-potassium balance.

Make generous use of almonds, hazelnuts, dates and dried figs for dessert.

Given below is a bonus for the adventurous
Patzcuaro omelette mound for two
♡ My favorite mother-in-law pleaser ♡
All quantities to taste. Be creative and express yourself!

Mildly saute onion, tomato, garlic, green-yellow-red pepper.

Beat two-three large eggs and 2-3 tablespoons each of cream and piquant V-8 juice. Add salt and pepper. Lightly smear a heavy pan with butter on low-medium heat. Add the egg mixture. Let it firm up. Arrange a 4 inch mound of crushed sharp Dorito chips in the middle; evenly cover with the sauted stuff and sharp cheese, jalapeno and salsa. Fold firm omelette toward center to form a 6 inch mound, 3-4 inches high. Add butter sparingly around the mound bottom. Lower heat. Glaze top with a thin quoting of chilli salsa, arbol or habanero. Serve after three minutes on a cornbread toast. Golden and yummie!

To please mother-in-law serve her the bigger portion!

Esoterica

Unrelated spiritual connections
It is claimed by some people that certain geographical areas on the surface of the Earth are more prone to giving a "spiritual enhancement" to the health of a certain kind of beholder. The serene temples of Kyoto, the magical settings of Buddhist temples in the Orient, the setting of Hindu temples in South-East Asia are well-known examples. The settings of some European Cathedrals and middle-eastern mosques are rich with spiritual nuances. I am a meditator and a thinker of a Vedic background and training. Yet, the spiritual ambience surrounding the Cathedral at Strasbourg, France, is overwhelming for me. I am quite certain that everyone has a similar episode of a place of their own to tell. The phenomenon at work is related to the first set of seed-ideas defined elsewhere in this text. Memories of past actions performed with feelings and devotion at a "geographical area" are in the mind, which is everywhere. Having come into being, these "things" cannot be obliterated. Somehow, my local keys resonated when I was in the vicinity of the Strasbourg Cathedral, triggering a recall of the original feeling and idea from the mind. Because I may not have been a participant in the creation of the "memory" of the original event, my perceptions are vague and I am overcome by a powerful, nebulous "spiritual enhancement". Something draws me to the substance of the past events to which I may or may not have been a party.

A place of special spiritual nuances is under the grand *Bodh* tree at Foster Botanical Garden in Honolulu, Hawaii. The baby-tree has quite a history to it. Its "father" is the recorded, oldest historical tree in the world having been brought as a young plant to Anuradhapura, Sri Lanka in 288 B.C. It was sired by none other than the *Bodh* tree in Gaya, the very tree under which Gautam Buddha meditated for years and received enlightenment.

Other reported cases of unmarked "geographical areas" capable of imparting a sudden unexplainable "spiritual enhancement" to unrelated visitors, lend support to the principles inherent in the seed-ideas. Many travelers have been seized by a feeling of powerful "spiritual enhancement", in their first visit to Sedona in Arizona. First-time visitors to a location in Hawaii were seized with the prompting to suddenly fall into a chant of the *om* syllable. They have dubbed the spot, "source of *om* vibration on Earth". In both cases, it points to a high probability that significant events with feeling and devotion must have occurred at the sites in the past. Well-documented cases abound in the Himalayas where wandering *chelas* seeking specific instruction, in order to further advance from their plateaus of stalemated progress, have accidentally discovered a secluded spot where a great Swami sat in *samadhi* in the past. Somehow the connection was made and the specific instruction came to them!

In this connection, you would recall the recent quantum Physics experiment at the CERN institute in Switzerland where two photons sharing a "common past" made a "mysterious connection" with each other from a distance of ten kilometers! And photons are not imbued with the equivalent of human intelligence or perception, although they do have an unmanifest reality associated with them. Similar events occur all the time all over the world. Most people, uninitiated with the subtleties of this esoteric know-how are usually preoccupied with their immediate personal concerns. They do not have the inclination or the finely honed perception to notice such events. Because a vast majority of the people do not understand the phenomenon, it does not mean that it does not occur. Those who are really interested and are trained to recognize such events are the real beneficiaries of the rewards of the illuminating spiritual experiences.

The human skin

The role of the biggest organ of the human body, the skin, as an intermediary between the sensory and the extrasensory aspects of *Surya shakti* cannot be overlooked. While the covering on the surface manufactures many chemical compounds in response to the ambient sunlight, such as Vitamin D, pigments, numerous volatile ethers, and is involved in complex elimination processes related to the physiology of cellular metabolism, its more telling functions are hidden. In a simple way the skin may be described as a network of a million ultra-sensitive active and passive probes that acts as a go-between the three solitudes comprising the microcosm and the surrounding environment. Sensory and extrasensory feeds and signals travel in both directions responding to physical, emotional and spiritual factors ceaselessly at play in the microcosm. The outward appearance of the skin is an accurate indicator of the overall health of the person to a trained eye. The invisible fluxes and fields emanating from it are a continuous source of the evolutionary wherewithall of the person in which the physical and spiritual solar aspects play principal roles. A great deal can be learnt by the person about the status of his progress on the path to self-recognition by concentrating on the skin fluxes and auras during meditation.

While an elaborate treatment of the subject is beyond the scope of this text, a few simple exercises are suggested to introduce the advanced *savant* to this interesting area.

- Periodically massage the skin with naturally extracted Almond oil, especially during the prolonged winter months. Don't soap the body for the next three showers. Most of the water will bead off the skin; use gentle dabbing if towelling is necessary, taking extra care to avoid rubbing action. If circumstances permit, give the skin a thorough solar soak from head to foot for ten minutes, turning often for a uniform application. (Tanning machines are not suitable for this).
- If you are practising meditation using the structured breathing and sound clustering techniques given in the *ten-session* chapter, prolong the session by two minutes. While still sitting in your comfortable *aasan*, mentally trace a diffusion of light starting from the focal point on the inside of your forehead following the outside contours of your body embracing the skin down to your toes. Concentrate on the tip of your toes while you visualize a stream of light escaping from them. Softly reverse mental focus and visualize the light stream entering your toes and retrace the ring back to the inside of your forehead, following the same course in reverse. A state of immense happiness

will result from this relaxing exercise, which will eventually lead to a feeling of the flow of *shakti* through the skin .
- While sitting in a relaxed posture, extend your hands in front of your chest, palms facing each other in the manner of the *namaste* greeting. Fingers on each hand should not touch adjacent fingers. Gently stretch out fingers to protrude pads and mounts on each hand facing each other, paying special attention to the minuscule distance between them. Develop a feel for the umbra-penumbra zone in the gap as you move your hands barely touching each other in tapping motion. The surface tension will increase as the counterparts of the two palms pull each other in pranic concentration while a discernible resistance is felt between them. If you progress thus far, you are feeling your *prana shakti*, the most constructive and creative energy in the universe. You can put it to many uses for yourself and others who may be strangers or in special relationships with you.
- While holding one hand in position, you may move the other to a millimeter above an area of skin for effects related to the supersensory *Surya shakti*.
- May be used for self-healing and relieving pain in others.

The success of this and other similar meditative techniques is directly related to the degree of earnestness and depth of feeling you can develop in yourself. A few Sound Clusters or *mantras* help develop the feeling and can be learnt easily.

Gonadic health and ambience

Introduction

The topic may seem somewhat unconventional and even farfetched in the current climate of medical advances in molecular miracle-making. Although the word "gonad" straddles the physical gender divide of ovaries in women and testes in men, the underlying phenomena must be understood in the context of what lies behind the quality of the sequence of reproductive functions and processes. However, other broad splits exist where specialized knowledge of the physical functions may be required. First, the special needs of the couples who want to have children versus the rest. Second, time periods in a woman's life when reproduction is naturally feasible because this does not apply to men. Third, healthy and fully functional people versus those who may face nonmedical difficulties. Fourth, gender-differentiated menopausal imbalances in women versus the very specific prostate problems in men. Fifth, the complex and medically undefinable factors dividing the five to eight per cent of the population into the preferred homosexual way of life. Sixth, underlying the health of the physical organs and processes, Gonadic well-being includes subtle factors bearing on one's emotional and spiritual makeup. Social, cultural and lifestyle preferences and various other factors create "invisible conditions" that may bear heavily on the subject's mental health. Here the emphases is on "invisible conditions" that arise out of the psychological responses of the person. Upon reflection it becomes increasingly clear that the subtle Gonadic "ambience" is complex and its consequences reach deep into the person's very foundation, engulfing his libido, self-preservation and nurturing instincts. In keeping with the thrust of the underlying philosophy of this work, it may be noted that the flow of *prana shakti* in the physical body and the awakening of *Kundalini* in the meditator are affected by this "ambience".

These notes are offered in the spirit of the very desirable preventative approach to staying healthy and fully functional versus the more common approach of seeking advice after problems manifest themselves. It is well known that the staying-fit approach does not guarantee absolute results but it does add a layer of favorable factors, just in case. It is a question of personal philosophy and attitude to life. Concepts, procedures and practices offered in the following pages are uniform in their application to benefit everyone, including those with the exceptions noted in the preceding paragraph. In addition, they bestow remarkable qualities on those engaged in meditative practices to improve the flow of *shakti* along the longitudinal axis of their bodies for an enlightened lifestyle.

Background facts to keep in mind.

Please note that the term "feminine" in this discussion has no gender bias. Equating it to "life-giving and nurturing" may be more comfortable for some readers.

- A woman's ovaries come equipped with a very large number of preconceived nascent master cells wrapped in individual sacs at birth. In later life these eggs mature one at a time on commands from glands in the physical brain. The maturing process is strictly regulated and has a well-defined lifespan in which it may occur. This complicated staged chain of events may be originally initiated and progressively refined by the higher extraphysical forces overseeing human evolution on earth as the scheme suggests a continuation or the result of some processes from the 'past'.

- In vivid contrast, a man's testes come empty at birth. After puberty they start making master cells or sperm in very large numbers in a continuous stream that has no preset lifespan to it. It can be reasonably argued that millions of sperm are quickly cast on the assembly line and lovingly presented to the "knowing" ovum because it has directly descended from processes imbued with the higher plan reaching back to when the ova were conceived. Note the many to one ratio!

- At preconception, the mature ovum "invites" the sperm to penetrate its covering for fertilization, thus making it the command master cell. The feminine ovum absorbs the masculine sperm within the confines of its physical attributes under the guidance of feminine spirituality, the mother spirit. Because of the feminine nature of this spiritual transaction, the instinct of "respect for life" pervades all levels of animal life.
- Individual *Kundalinis* of two spiritually matched soulmates can be conjugated by giving the pledge of irrevocable commitment. Symbolically they re-enact the ovum-sperm ritual at conception, in that, the masculine aspect dissolves in the feminine (e.g. Shona and Ram Dave in The Three Verbs of Being).
- Even after the pairing of the XX or XY sex chromosomes has been made inside the ovum during the conception stage, the gonadic development in the fetus remains neutral for many months for either set of physical organs to form. Again, this period of "waiting" or "coasting" suggests a higher level "control" or decision-making "authority" at play. This interval has immense implications for the pure I-sense, the spiritual nucleus around which the physical body is taking shape in the *jivatma*.
- Of the three possible combinations of intersex relationships, namely, male to male, male to female and female to female, the last is founded on most compatible dovetailing because of the feminine aspects of spirituality. The first may be an expression of machismo or a mistake; the second supportive of the propagation of the human race - a dire necessity, but it is very difficult for the uninitiated male mind to fathom the subtle nuances of the intrinsic harmony in the third (exceptions

do prevail at all levels in nature). Perhaps the bonding between the mother and her infant is the only thing that may exceed its profundity.

Keeping the above points in mind, if you close your eyes and objectively think about the most critical elements of the scenario in which the new life is about to be launched within the mother, under the light of her capacity to form and sustain life - the surrogate Mother Spirit, you cannot escape the fact that an immensely vital interplay between the biological and extrabiological roots of the new life takes place before and during conception. Extrabiological roots are an expression of the series of lives or sets of organic experiences a singular soul has passed through to reach its present status. It is the propagation of one line, albeit a complicated one. The biological lineage, on the other hand, is far more complex as it is derived from a succession of dual or binary sets of antecedents where one member of the given set has mated with one member of another set, each following his own extrabiological roots. What evolutionary forces cause any two independent extrabiological lines to intersect at a given point of the evolutionary continuum? The outcome of the complex interplay between the two roots is resolved at preconception before the pure I-sense is localized in the mother. For evolution to succeed, the essential property of the roots must be to accumulate the "abiding essences" across organic experiences. Are "abiding essences" somehow carried forward in the mind from where the stock of nascent ova is allocated to a pair of ovaries before a female child is conceived? If "abiding essences" are the "one particle" of the entangled pair of quantum physics, what forms its counterpart? Whatever the answer might be, it is obvious that gonadic wellbeing is of prime importance in the evolutionary aspect of life .

Simple procedures and practices

During any fitness program of regular exercise such as walking , jogging or playing sport, it is important to be consciously aware of the flow of air through the nasal passages and the blood flow through an area of concentration or interest in the body for rejuvenation or enhanced effects.

Structured breathing

There is an intimate connection between respiration and the state of the mind. Because the passage of air during respiration produces subtle *Ida* and *Pingla* currents travelling along the spine towards the extremity where the gonadic region lies, the practice of structured breathing is a natural starting point to initiate positive influences for gonadic ambience within the physical body. Structured breathing courses are described in detail in an earlier ten-session chapter. I strongly suggest that the serious pupil follow the simple exercises with a strong will and perseverance for at least a year or until such time that the pupil gains a measure of control over the contraction and expansion of the diaphragm muscle. This is easily achieved by breaking the in and out breaths into three draws and thrusts, with brief holds, to suit personal comfort.

Blood circulation

Blood is the carrier of all assimilated nutrients to sites in the body. Its rate of flow responds to the varying needs of the sites and the diameter of the arteries. As arteries divide, subdivide and propagate along the networks in their territories, their diameters become progressively narrower. At their farthest extremities, arteries become capillaries through which the flow of blood becomes very lazy when a person has been inactive for long periods. Sometimes blood cells get stuck at the end of a capillary in the skin and eventually die, thus starting the formation of a wrinkle as the choked skin cells accumulate with age. For maintenance purposes it is important to form a habit where you can flush out the smaller arteries regularly through a brisk walk, run or playing of a sport. These habits yield the best results when qualities of comfort and enjoyment are present in the routines.

It is particularly important to ensure that a normal circulation of blood is maintained in the front and back pelvic regions. It is not customary to think of these areas of the body in these terms and they do become neglected. Body weight and sitting for long periods with dangling legs cause a concentration of pressure on a very small base area around the rectum. A "damming effect" may develop in the tissue mass and impede the blood flow

The Latitude Syndrome

to inner gonadic regions. Being passive, normal flags of pain or discomfort usually don't appear and the condition goes unnoticed until common viral infections draw attention to the region.

Periodic strolling, skipping, tapping and kneading help in restoring normal internal circulation. Often limbs do fall asleep from lack of circulation. Being aware of such possibilities is a good starting point.

Massaging

To add to the many methods and techniques to augment circulation and regulate specific flows at specific sites in the body available these days, the author has researched one technique of outstanding benefit based on traditional Vedic knowledge. Warm almond oil is rubbed into the skin along the longitudinal axis in a prescribed manner after the *prana* wave has been initiated from the region of the coccyx bone by the pupil. Certain aspects of this technique are particularly suited to generating a favorable gonadic ambience, the key prerequisite to well-being and functioning.

Prana shakti

We wouldn't be alive but for the *shakti* flow in our body, vitalizing each and every cell in it. But being aware of it and then getting a feel for its presence in the body requires some training. Detailed procedures and sequential steps are given in the ten-session chapter. Advanced techniques are noted in the preceding section on Skin.

Physiological arousal versus sexual arousal

Every serious pupil comes to a stage in their work where an understanding of this distinction presents a framework for a window of opportunity in which they can move on to advanced stages of training to achieve an objective or address a specific problem.

Advanced techniques

The author has researched a series of procedures based on a combination of simple sphincter exercises, warm water and manipulation of *shakti* on the subtle spine in conjunction with controlled rhythmic breathing. Within a short training period of a few weeks, these techniques enabled his serious pupils to direct the *shakti* wave at will to the gonadic and other regions in the upper body. Internal blood flow and vitality were enhanced which resulted in discernible volumetric movements and sensations in both men and women students. Being strictly in the experiential domain and because of the synchronization requirements of some movements, it is not possible to adequately describe them in a brief text format. However, the techniques and methods will be made available in a one-on-one counseling format in practical sessions. Further information on schedules and booking will be made available after author lectures in different locations.

Genesis of evolution - food for thought

The trilogy of *akash* or pure space, *shakti* or pure energy and *Brahma* or pure emotion, the genius loci - the *unattached emotion* realizable by the human mind, implicated in pregenesis may be stated as follows:

For easier assimilation, the sequence of events is described in the language of taking a snapshot of a process in progress, as having commenced at a point called "start" and then progressing on to another point called "end" to comprise the subject of study and stocktaking in a given attention span. Otherwise the points of reference are lost to the mind. How truthfully this approach represents "spontaneity" is open to debate. It can be argued that a series of definable quick events fill the interval of "spontaneity", but this is tantamount to an oxymoron. A similar problem exists if you apply the logic of cause and effect to it. Being a slave of "time", how else will the human mind acquire this knowledge if he is not prepared to meditate upon it and take it in one fell swoop! Always lurking in the shadow is the question: "is this truth knowable?"

The discussion presupposes that the power to evolve preceded conceptual evolution which preceded genesis. If you take away all matter, all forms of energy and the physical space itself that's been created and put into what we consider the universe, what's left is *akash* or pure space; it's not the same as ether or void but is more along the line of "extreme emptiness or nothingness."

The Latitude Syndrome

Human mind, consciousness and will do not take up physical space but they do take up or occupy *akash*. Other formless things - and therefore without the attributes of mass - like thoughts, ideas and concepts like "time" and "space" occupy *akash*. Karma and its influences or karmic forces exist in *akash*. Everything is moving and mutating from "future" to "present" to "past". The "present" occupies space and is therefore amenable to the human senses. The "future" and the "past" of a thing do not take up space, but they do take up *akash*. By definition, the "memory" of a thing or event exists in *akash* side by side with all knowledge. No new knowledge is being made or will ever be made in the future. It is all here. That which didn't have a presence before cannot come into being. That which has come into a real being of any fineness - subtle or material - cannot be completely eliminated from the universe. Everything has existed, exists and will exist. Things move from *akash* into space and then back into *akash*.

Shakti is so powerful and pervasive that only a microspeck of it - a *tanmatra* - was fructified when she took part in the original genesis of the conceptual universe and the potential for everything that followed in what science calls the "big bang", which marked the beginning of the appearance of matter in the space of the universe. In the very first frame of genesis there was no "big bang". From *akash*, first came the elastic universal space. Maybe the "big bang" happened in the physical space when pure *shakti* encountered it and was itself transformed into its many subtle and physical forms and forces - the physical birth of the first impression of the ever changing spatial universe impregnated with matter and energy. Cosmologists put the duration of this phase at about ten nanoseconds. One has to keep in mind that science's "big bang" applied only to physical forces. The transformations preceding the "big bang" being spontaneous were silent and had no physical attributes.

How and what caused the *akash* to give birth to the universal space and make itself manifest? This is where the third component of the supernatural reality, the pure emotion or the super genius, came into play. It has been conceptualized in many ways and names like God, Superconscious Will, Brahma, Allah, *Gayatri mata* and other constructs that may lie in the realm of ideation preceding and therefore mothering the notion of evolution itself, have been used throughout the world since the dawn of civilization. Closer to home the perennial riddle is how man came upon the earth. An intuitive guess may be that whatever caused the *akash* to express itself in the form of universal space may be no different from the very genius that may lie at the root of placing intelligence or what we call "life" on the earth. Are the two events connected in some way?

In my humble opinion, yes, they are. Every human being is capable of realizing "things" from the *akash*. In fact we do it every day during our wakeful and sleeping hours without being aware of it. That's why the two events may be inexplicably entangled.

Is pure emotion the most powerful subtle motive force?

What subtle forces guide the processes behind the "survival of the fittest" in the Darwinian model of evolution? As it is, it sounds like an unquestionable given.

As to entertaining the notion of *why* the pure emotion prompted *akash* to express itself in the form of physical space, the answer may lie beyond the human intellect.

Theoretically it is inconceivable that intelligence exists on only one site - mother earth - in the universe. Based on the duality principle a sustainable case can be made that the miracle of life is no less brilliant than the intrigue of the mystical universe and the two events may be an integral part of this once-ever cosmic happening. Moment of pre-conception of new life may be no more than a mere reenactment of the moment in which the first iota of universal space (the body) came into being in the all-pervasive *shakti* (pure I-Sense). The miracle of life, simply, is that at every conception the equivalent of the whole universe comes into being!

Bibliography

A sampling of pertinent references.

A Lifetime in Preparation, Sri Prabhupada-lilamrta.
International Society for Krishna Consciousness.
Bhaktivedanta Book Trust. Los Angeles, USA 1972

Autobiography of a Yogi, Paramahansa Yogananda
Self-Realization Fellowship, Los Angeles, USA 1993

Gayatri, The daily Religious Practice of the Hindus, I.K. Taimni
Ananda Publishing House, Allahabad, India 1967

An Introduction to Hindu Symbolism, I.K. Taimni
The Theosophical Publishing House, Adyar, India 1965

The Science of Pranayama, Swami Sivananda
Divine Life Society, Yoga-Vedanta Forest Academy Press.
Garwhal, Himalayas. 1975

Upanishad, Guru Gopal, Published by Service Mandal
15, Hanuman Road , New Delhi, India 1950

Sanjeevanee, Havan and prayer Mantras. O.P. Verma
Dayanand Colony, New Delhi, India 1975

Yoga Philosophy of Patanjali, Swami Hariharananda Aaranya.
University Of Calcutta Press, Calcutta, India 1977

Mozart, His Character, His Work, Alfred Einstein
Oxford University Press, London UK 1977

Mozart, Marcia Davenport
Avon Books, New York 1979

Mozart, Hugh Ottaway, Wayne State University Press
Detroit, USA 1980

Wolfgang Amadeus Mozart, Enzo Orlandi
Engel Verlag, Mondadori Press, Verona, Italy 1988

Ludwig van Beethoven, Enzo Orlandi
Engel Verlag, Mondadori Press, Verona, Italy 1988

Beethoven, Romain Rolland
Verlag Rolf Kugler Oberwil b. Zug, Augsburg, Germany 1930

Beethoven, Biography of a genius, George R. Marek
Funk and Wagnalls, New York, June, 1969

Medieval Art, James Snyder
Prentice-Hall Inc., Engelwood Cliffs, NJ, USA 1989

Psychoanalysis: The Impossible Profession, Janet Malcolm
Alfred A. Knopf, New York 1981

Psyclosis, The Circularity of Experience, Ralph Berger
W.H. Freeman and Company, San Francisco, 1977

The Seven Mysteries of Life, Guy Murchie
Houghton Mifflin Company, Boston 1978

Ideas and Opinions, Albert Einstein
Crown Publishers, Inc., New York 1982

The Silk Road, Jan Myrdal
Translated from Swedish by Ann Henning, Pantheon Books, 1979

INDIA, Roloff Beny, Essay by Aubrey Menen
McClelland and Stewart Ltd., Toronto, Canada 1969

Documenta Geigy, Scientific Tables, Seventh Edition
Edited by K. Diem and C. Lentner, J.R. Geigy S.A., Basle, Switzerland

The Human Body The Brain: Mystery of Matter and Mind
Torstar Books, New York 1984

INDEX
AARY (13, 20-22, 27, 30, 68, 87, 147)
ARTISTIC CREATIVITY (34, 37, 59, 71, 76, 78, 115, 116, 137, 151)
BIBLIOGRAPHY (188)
BIOLOGICAL ROOTS (III, 8, 12, 16, 27)
BODH TREE (18, 175)
BUDDHA (17-19, 67, 79, 80, 175)
CANTILEVERS (35-40, 45, 55, 60, 63, 66, 78, 103, 117-119, 125, 127, 129, 131, 132, 141, 142, 149)
CHAKRA (107, 145)
CLAIRAUDIENCE (36, 37, 109)
CLASSICAL MUSIC (40, 78, 125, 126, 136, 138-140, 142, 149)
CREATIVITY CONSCIOUSNESS (33, 34, 37, 71-73, 75, 76, 114, 115, 120, 135, 137)
DARSHAN (30, 70, 140, 141)
DHARMA (13, 17, 22, 146-148)
DUALITY (15, 43, 85, 90, 105, 108, 135, 187)
EXTRABIOLOGICAL ROOTS (III, 12, 16, 27, 182)
HIEROGLYPHS (36, 39, 116, 124, 130, 131, 134, 138, 139)
KARMA (IV, 13, 14, 16, 17, 22-28, 38, 58, 69, 112, 129, 146, 148, 154, 186)
KUNDALINI (6, 93, 100, 105-107, 109, 111, 112, 121, 134, 139, 145, 179)
LATITUDE SYNDROME (2, 7, 11, 12, 149, 150, 154-156, 158)
MEDITATIVE LISTENING (114, 115, 117, 120, 121, 130, 133)
MEMORY (3-5, 38, 42, 57, 65, 78-83, 96, 106, 118, 122, 134)
MEMORY-JOGGERS (IV, 38, 81, 122)
MUTATION (15, 27, 33, 34, 54, 128)
NAMASTE (31, 140, 178)
NUTRITION (112, 149-151, 156, 157, 161)
OM (20, 22, 31, 32, 37, 40, 87, 89-91, 94, 97, 98, 101, 102, 123, 126, 128, 130, 160, 175, 176)
PATZCUARO (174)
PRANA (5, 6, 40, 41, 87, 89, 90, 92, 99-107, 111, 150, 164, 178, 179, 184)
SEED-IDEA (96, 150)
SELF-RECOGNITION (25, 32, 35, 116, 125, 139, 146, 148, 177)
SPIRITUAL HEALTH (1, 6-8, 10, 25, 156)
SURYA SHAKTI (143, 144, 146, 147, 149-151, 156, 158, 159, 161, 176, 178)
SWASTICA (43-45, 47, 48)
TAJ MAHAL (74, 117)
VERBS (2, 27, 47, 55, 58, 66, 71, 101, 112, 114, 115, 125, 127, 131, 133, 134, 137, 145, 154, 181)